1

Nora looked around the odd little back-street restaurant where they'd arranged to meet. It was like all the people she had ever swiped to the right were in one room.

'Deliveroo collections, that side,' said one of the waiting staff, scanning Nora briefly. Harsh. Nora whipped off her turquoise waterproof jacket. It was mid-May and there had been a 70 per cent chance of rain when she'd left the house and statistics were rarely wrong. Thankfully another member of staff appeared and showed her to her table.

Despite the data to the contrary, here she was giving dating another go. The odds of Nora finding someone she wanted to spend her forever with were already slim at best; she knew because she'd crunched the numbers. Perhaps Nora's standards were set too high. However, there was still a chance and Nora had always loved a challenge, which was good, given that her date had just arrived wearing a trilby, cravat, shiny waistcoat and red trousers. She'd seen salads better dressed than him.

'Gareth?' she asked. Nora needed to be certain; there was always a possibility that this was the wrong person and she remained hopeful.

'That is I. You must be the delightful Nora.'

'I don't know about delightful,' she said as every fibre of her being cringed.

He held up a palm. 'Let me be the judge of that.'

This was not a good start. But she'd tasked herself with waiting until after the date to analyse their suitability.

Men had come and gone and then a couple had popped up again like whack-a-moles and Nora had accepted that love was fleeting, messy and frequently deceased long before she'd realized it. As a statistician she had a logical approach to love and relationships. The odds of finding someone she wanted to spend eternity with were, according to her reckoning, about one per cent. The odds of her making it to a year in a relationship weren't much better but she had accepted that that was how things were. Or at least she had, until her birthday came along.

On her twenty-ninth birthday her mother had tried to pay her a compliment by saying, 'My Nora, you are our greatest blessing. We are so proud of you and the kind, hard-working person you have become. You have a well-paid job, lovely home, it's just a shame you're still single.' The last few words felt like a piano had crushed her, the odds of which were about one in 250 million, which thankfully was something even less likely than finding a perfect love match.

'Full of quirky humour – great fun!'
KATIE FFORDE

'Sweet, funny and so relatable . . . Charming, fabulous cast of
characters, chuckle-inducing – another winner from Bella.'
MILLY JOHNSON

'A gloriously quirky, laugh-out-loud romantic comedy
that shows there's a soulmate out there for everyone.'
PHILLIPA ASHLEY

'Many-layered characters bring this lovely story to
life. Bella Osborne has a wonderful touch.'
SUE MOORCROFT

'Follow the spreadsheet . . . or follow your heart? I
loved Bella's funny, sparky tale of finding love amidst
a sea of hideous dates and heartwarming friendships.
A novel to put a huge smile on your face!'
FIONA GIBSON

'Warm, witty and full of fun; the quirky characters
spring to life immediately and leave the reader
wondering what they'll get up to next!'
CELIA ANDERSON

'A deliciously warm and funny romcom. I loved the
beautifully-drawn Nora and her circle of friends. Renee had
me laughing out loud. How nice to see an older character
brimming with mischief and wisdom. I adore the uplifting
mixture of comedy, sparkling wit and magnetic romance,
with a few hilarious bad dates thrown in. And what a
wonderful ending. Bella has become a new favourite.'
JUDY LEIGH

'So funny and warm, *(Not Quite) Done with Dating*
has the most brilliant cast of characters, witty repartee,
and such sparkling romance . . . I sped through it!'
LAURA JANE WILLIAMS

Also by Bella Osborne

(Not quite) DONE WITH DATING

Bella Osborne

PENGUIN BOOKS

TRANSWORLD PUBLISHERS

UK | USA | Canada | Ireland | Australia
India | New Zealand | South Africa

Transworld is part of the Penguin Random House group of companies
whose addresses can be found at global.penguinrandomhouse.com.

Penguin Random House UK, One Embassy Gardens,
8 Viaduct Gardens, London SW11 7BW

penguin.co.uk

Penguin
Random House
UK

First published in Great Britain in 2026 by Penguin Books
an imprint of Transworld Publishers

001

Typeset in 11.75/15.25 pt Sabon MT Pro by Falcon Oast Graphic Art Ltd.
Printed and bound in Great Britain by Clays Ltd, Elcograf S.p.A.

The authorized representative in the EEA is Penguin Random House
Ireland, Morrison Chambers, 32 Nassau Street, Dublin D02 YH68

A CIP catalogue record for this book is available from the British Library

ISBN: 9781804995235

MIX
Paper | Supporting
responsible forestry
FSC® C018179

To Kate Nash – Thank you for being in my corner
from the very start!

(Not quite) DONE WITH DATING

It wasn't that she needed a man in her life, far from it. She was completely self-sufficient and happy in her own skin. But thanks to her parents who, unlike most couples, had enjoyed a long and happy marriage, Nora knew it was possible to be even happier and if she wanted a family one day she wasn't keen on doing it on her own.

The question was this: was she the happiest version of herself when she was single? It was certainly better than being in a bad relationship, but the truth was that she wanted the sort of loving, supportive marriage her parents enjoyed. The more she thought about it, the more long-term relationships appeared to be flukes. She wasn't going to accept just anybody. Mainly because she'd tried that and it had been disastrous. Her little experiment of just stick with the next man she fancied had landed her in a Spanish police cell for the night and a tattoo of SpongeBob on her left buttock. At least José still wrote to her every Christmas, even if the Spanish prison service were censoring the letters.

Nora's latest approach was to give dating apps one last try. They promised a 70 per cent success rate although, on her calculations, from the data available, she felt it was nearer 15. But it did mean she could narrow the target audience by going for those with a similar career path to her own. She'd reasoned that someone else with a mathematical brain would hopefully see things as she did, giving them common ground.

She had vowed to make it to the end of the date before she began any sort of assessment. First impressions weren't always right. She repeated that in her head as she watched Gareth remove his trilby and try for a trick throw on to the back of his chair. The hat plopped into a man's sticky toffee pudding on the next table.

'I am so sorry,' said Gareth. 'I don't know what happened there.'

After an extensive search she'd found Gareth online and initial exchanges had been hopeful. He was a book-keeper from Leicester with his own home and car. He didn't have his own hair though, she now realized, the restaurant lights bouncing off his bald head, giving it an ethereal halo effect. The photograph he'd shared had clearly been old. There was no way he was thirty-three. He was forty if he was a day. Gareth was now explaining in a nasal voice about the trials he'd experienced on his journey, and it was taking Nora all her time not to run.

'To avoid any embarrassment at the end of the meal, shall we agree now that we'll have separate bills?' he suggested.

'That's good with me,' said Nora.

'I did have a little looksie online at the menu and their small plates seem the best value for money,' said Gareth.

Looksie? Who said that? She gave herself a mental shake. The analysing needed to stop. She stared at the cravat. Gareth needed a fair chance, even though the voice inside her head said 'Run, run, run!'

Gareth unfolded his serviette very precisely and tucked it in his shirt, which was quite a tricky task given the bulky cravat already in residence. 'I must say, Nora, I am pleasantly surprised.'

'About the prices?'

'Not just those. I've had some very poor experiences with internet dating but—' He was interrupted by his phone ringing on full volume. Nora felt the scorn of the other diners. 'I'd better take this, it's my mother,' he said with a dramatic roll of his eyes. 'Howdy, Ma. Yes . . . No . . . Actually that's spooky because not ten seconds ago I said *I* was pleasantly surprised.' He didn't disguise the fact he was openly appraising Nora. 'Definitely has potential.' What was she: a doer-upper? 'Yes, I'll ask her. OK, byesie. Love you too.' He ended the call. 'Mums – what are they like, eh?'

The waiter appeared at their table to take their order and Nora was grateful for the interruption. 'I think I'll go for a Diet Coke and the scallops.'

Gareth snatched up the menu. 'Don't do that, there's a supplement,' he announced.

'But if I'm paying I can have what I like,' said Nora.

'Ooo-ooh, an independent woman. I'll have to get used to that.'

'And for you, sir?' asked the waiter.

'Standard burger, no extras. And iced water for the table, thanks.'

The waiter left and Nora hoped they'd be quick with the food so that she could eat and leave. 'What was it you were going to ask me?'

Gareth clicked his fingers. 'It was Mother. She wanted to know if you have any hereditary illnesses.'

'None that I know of.' Although she could feel a rash

appearing on her neck. Was it possible to be allergic to another human being? 'How about you? Any diseases in your family?'

He pulled in his chin, seemingly irritated at the suggestion. 'Not unless you count the bedwetting, though I suppose that's more of a habit than an illness. But enough about me, I don't like to dominate, I'm not that sort of man. Unless that's something you're into?' he said with a tilt of his head.

Nora gripped the chair. It was the only way to force herself to stay seated. She was still processing what he'd said when he leaned forward.

'Which of the following would you like to choose as a topic for discussion?' he asked. 'Finances, political views or past relationships?'

An unhelpful statistic flashed into her mind – 50 per cent of first dates ended with a first kiss. She would have to discard her no-analysis-until-after-the-date rule because she couldn't risk being in a situation where Gareth wanted to kiss her. Her body cringed at the thought and she found her shoulders making for her ears.

'Actually, I'm just going to pop to the ladies, if that's OK,' said Nora, getting rapidly to her feet.

'Don't go climbing out of the window!' He guffawed at his own joke. Little did he know he'd foiled plan A. She'd have to come up with something else, and fast.

2

Nora had returned home after her disastrous date with Gareth, poured herself a large glass of Merlot and updated her dating spreadsheet. Nora loved a spreadsheet. She liked to be objective, and scoring her dates was a consistent and logical approach. Numbers were reliable, and reliability made her happy. She felt a little bad when she hit the total button on Gareth's score but there was no point in continuing with the date when there was nothing they had in common and his ick level was off the scale. Maybe she needed to accept that the odds were very much against her and give up.

She didn't need a random man, she needed the right one, and if they were too hard to track down, perhaps it was better that she remained single. If all failed, at least she still had Oliver. He was easy to live with, a great listener and had almost 360-degree vision. Oliver was the silent type whose favourite hobby was sitting on Nora's head. He was a veiled chameleon who most of the time was a lovely green colour, who liked to watch David Attenborough programmes with one eye and observe what Nora was doing with the other.

Nora loved her life. A daughter of immigrants who had arrived in England from war-torn Bosnia with very little other than the clothes they were wearing, each other and a baby. She had been brought up to embrace new opportunities, work hard and be thankful. Nora had done all of this and had the photographs of her parents, crying with pride at her graduation, house-warming and every school play she'd ever been in, to prove it. She could picture her parents dancing at parties, kissing under the mistletoe at Christmas and holding hands in the park. Her parents were devoted to each other and had been through a lot together – escaping Bosnia was just the start. Negotiating the challenges of a new country, strange language and low-paid jobs had made them an unbreakable team. By comparison, Nora had had things easy, and being in her parents' protective bubble filled with love had got her through any trials life had thrown her way.

Perhaps she was simply trying to find what her parents had, or sometimes she wondered if she was trying to prove what a rare thing it was that they shared. At this stage she was no longer sure. What she did know was that she was twenty-nine and single and thanks to Gareth that's how things were going to stay for now.

Instead of an evening out with Gareth, Nora's best friend Dixie came round for a debrief. Dixie unlaced her Doc Martens and they took their usual seats on the sofa while Nora provided a detailed update.

'You told Gareth you had diarrhoea?' asked Dixie with a splutter.

'No, I got the waiter to tell him I had diarrhoea while I paid and got my scallops to go.'

'I take it you've not heard from him?'

'Only to ask if I wanted to pay half towards his car park fee. I declined and then blocked his number.' Nora noisily puffed out a breath. 'There must be a better way?'

'Stay single?' suggested Dixie. 'It has its benefits.'

'I know. I can choose what I want on Netflix without judgement, I get both sides of the bed and the toilet seat will be forever down. And there's always the single council tax reduction.'

'I was thinking more that you can put yourself first for a change and there's nobody to let you down.' Dixie was still getting over a nasty break-up. Not that she was admitting that she was still recovering. It had been quite a few months but she still twitched when her ex was mentioned and could no longer walk past the squirty cream in the supermarket without blushing.

'How was your week?' asked Nora, feeling better for unburdening herself.

'Yeah, bit mixed.' Dixie sipped her wine. 'Monday I made my first successful batch of tiger loaves. Wednesday a customer said I had a lovely smile. But yesterday Glenda sacked me.'

'No way. What happened?'

'You know I was on my final warning because I told her it was a bad idea to have pre-wrapped alphabet cupcakes out on display that people could rearrange, so when we went viral on TikTok along with the hashtag "pooey bum cakes", Glenda thought it was me?'

'Yes,' said Nora.

'So, Glenda asked me to finish off a cake for a local youth cricket team and deliver it to them.'

'That's good,' said Nora.

'I thought so but' – Dixie pulled a face – 'it wasn't until all the teenage boys were laughing and filming the cake that I realized there must be something wrong with it. I had looked at that cake so much that morning and had read and reread the inscription – Congratulations County Youth Cup Winners. However, it was only when it was sitting in the middle of a buffet table that I noticed I'd missed the letter O out of County. Unfortunately, Glenda didn't see the funny side and sacked me.'

Nora stifled her laughter. 'Sorry, I know I'm not meant to laugh but it is quite funny.'

'Even I can see the comic value and the lads all thought it was hilarious and had their photograph taken with the cake. Unfortunately Glenda is blind to seeing the humorous side of anything.'

'Still quite harsh to sack you over that,' said Nora.

Dixie winced. 'Actually I think what tipped her over the edge was that while I was at the cricket club there was a bit of an accident. I'd forgotten to put the handbrake on in the van and it rolled down a slope into a tree. But nobody was hurt,' she added hastily.

'Blimey, and I thought I'd had a bad week.'

'I know, right? I did try to explain that I'm not used to a handbrake. I mean, I know she calls the van vintage but that's just code for old and clapped out.'

'It would seem that we're both back at square one,' said Nora. 'You still haven't found your ideal job and I'm no closer to proving or disproving whether my love match is out there.'

'I'm sure we'll both find what we're looking for. As long as we live long enough to hunt them down, that is.'

'Cheering thought,' said Nora, taking a swig of her wine.

Nora had slung a pizza and dough balls in the oven, so while they munched their way through them and the scallops, they mulled over their dilemmas.

'Everything is just a bit harder when you're on your own,' said Dixie, looking downbeat. 'Not that I want you-know-who back because I definitely don't. But sometimes I think it would be nice to come home to someone who has run you a bath and cooked tea.'

'You don't need a partner, you need staff,' said Nora.

Dixie gave her friend a withering look. 'Is it so bad to want a bit of romance in my life?'

'Knights on white chargers are hard to come by these days.'

Dixie, unlike Nora, was a romantic. 'I don't need the white charger. I'm actually allergic to horses. But someone who cared would be nice.'

'You have lots of people who care about you,' said Nora.

'You're right. I need to sort myself out first before I do anything else.' She puffed out a breath. 'But finding a career that's right for me is almost as hard as finding the right man.'

'I think your problem is easier to solve than mine.' Nora grabbed a notepad and pen. 'Jot down jobs you'd like to do.'

'I quite liked working in the bakery,' said Dixie, sounding a bit glum.

'You can still put that on the list. Maybe there's another bakery you could work in.'

'I'm pretty sure Glenda won't be giving me a reference.' Dixie took the pad and twizzled the pen around her fingers while she pondered. At last, she began to write. Nora ate her pizza and didn't say anything so as not to interrupt her friend's flow of ideas.

After a few minutes of writing, Dixie was staring into space. 'I think that's all I can come up with for now.'

'OK,' said Nora, getting comfy on the sofa. 'How many have you got on your list?'

Dixie counted them up. 'Eleven.'

'Great. Read them out,' said Nora.

'Number one is bus driver because I've always fancied that. Next is professional sleeper. You know where you get to test mattresses and stuff because I am dead good at sleeping. Olympic level, Ma always says.'

Nora doubted this was a paid role but Dixie didn't seem to notice her frowning and carried on with her list.

'For number three I thought being a living statue

might be fun. I have the perfect bag to be Mary Poppins, but I don't think it pays very well. Next is I thought a job with animals like in Jurassic Park or maybe the Sea Life Centre would be fun but there isn't one near here.'

'There's no Jurassic Park anywhere,' pointed out Nora. 'Only in the film.'

'I didn't mean Jurassic, I meant Exotic, sorry.' She grinned and went back to her list. 'Number five is a social media influencer and—'

'Stop there,' said Nora. 'That's the one.'

Dixie seemed surprised. 'Why? How do you know?'

'Because I applied the 37 per cent rule.'

'The what?' Dixie was doing the squinty-eye thing she did when something puzzled her.

'The 37 per cent rule is a business tool to solve something mathematicians call an "optimal stopping problem". That's when we are presented with a number of options and don't know which to go with. You'll have the highest chance of choosing the best option if you look at and reject the first 37 per cent of the total options available to you. And 37 per cent of eleven is four, so the fifth idea on your list is the one you should go for.' Nora knocked back her wine as a little reward for solving Dixie's problem. It was a bit of a simplified version of the rule but Nora was happy this was the best way to apply it to Dixie's dilemma.

'But there might be something better on the list.'

'And if social media influencer doesn't work out you move on to the next on the list and so on until you find something that does.'

'Oh good,' said Dixie. 'Because I've got housekeeper down for number eight. Like in *Downton Abbey*.'

'Until someone perfects time travel you're going to struggle with that one.'

Dixie gave her a look. 'I meant a modern-day version of it. The Wilson-Browns have a lady who keeps their whole house running like clockwork and she gets to live in their annexe.'

Dixie had a distinctly different background to Nora. Dixie's parents were a mix of old and new money and the two had combined to make a winning combination. They had businesses across three continents and were out of the country more than they were at home, but that was mainly for tax purposes. They gave their only child an allowance but had been keen for her to work and eventually run one of their businesses, but Dixie wanted to make it on her own. It was an admirable goal, but her disastrous CV was evidence that she hadn't as yet found her professional calling.

'But that's the beauty of the rule. It stops you from procrastinating and encourages you to focus on one thing at a time,' said Nora.

'Hmm.' Dixie pulled her feet up underneath herself and circled social media influencer on her list. 'You really think this is what I should do?'

'Yep.'

'Even though I only have two hundred and thirty-three followers on Insta?'

'Yep. Growing your brand and followers would all be part of the job,' said Nora.

14

'I like the idea of having a brand,' said Dixie sitting up. 'And this rule works on anything?'

'I've seen it in action in business and it definitely works there, so why not with any big decision?'

'OK, I'm going to do it.'

'Excellent,' said Nora, feeling helpful. But the cogs in her mind were whirring. 'I've an idea,' she added. 'How about I apply the same rule to my love life?'

Dixie had a vexed expression. 'I don't think that would work because you can't know how many people you'd date in a lifetime.'

After a quick Google, numbers were already buzzing around Nora's head. 'If the average relationship lasts two years nine months, or thirty-three months for ease of calculation, and—'

'Which yours don't,' said Dixie.

'True, but for maths' sake let's say they do. If you date between the ages of sixteen and fifty-five, that's 468 months (or thirty-nine years) divided by the average relationship duration we calculated of thirty-three months, that's 14.18 suitors, which sounds plausible for me, I think. And 37 per cent of that is 5.24.'

'And what does that tell you?' asked Dixie, looking excited.

'That I probably should have stopped dating about four years ago.' Nora felt like she'd been hit in the face with her mum's biggest casserole dish. If she was to apply the 37 per cent rule to her love life in the same way she had done with Dixie's career choices, then she needed to ditch the first five people she dated and then go with the next best option, which statistically should deliver the optimal partner. However, she'd gone through quite a few relationships and was now wondering if maybe she'd been a bit hasty when she'd instigated break-ups. 'When I ditched Tyler a year ago, I think he was my ninth relationship, so I'm way past number six, which means I've most likely missed my opportunity.' The possibility that she had had a potential match and let them go hit her harder than she thought it would.

'That's a shame,' said Dixie. 'It would have been cool if we could have solved both problems with the same thing. Never mind.'

'Hang on. Slow down. I still think I might be on to something.' Nora sat up straight. She wasn't going to dismiss it that quickly. Numbers were her comfort blanket and here was a way to apply them to the one thing that was eluding her in life. 'Maybe I should go back and double-check just in case one of the men after my 37 per cent cut-off is the one. What harm can it do, looking up a few old boyfriends?'

'Because you must have broken up with them for a reason.'

'True. Maybe it needs a bit more thought.' She wasn't one to rush into things.

'Maybe,' agreed Dixie. 'For a start, you don't want to dig up the past. Remember that guy who wanted to be called Hashtag.'

'Hashtag was a fun bloke though. What number was

he? I wonder if he makes the 37 per-cent cut-off,' she said more to herself than Dixie as she began counting.

'This is completely brilliant,' said Dixie picking up her wine. 'Here's to the 37 per cent rule solving our problems.' And they both clinked glasses, even if Nora thought Dixie's celebrations were a little bit premature.

3

Nora and Dixie were good friends even though they hadn't known each other that long. About eighteen months ago Nora had picked up a flyer for a new local club, having found it on a table in her usual coffee shop. With nothing else planned, she'd decided she might as well check it out. It had been wintertime and, if she was being honest, she went along purely out of intrigue at the title of the proposed new club rather than anything else, as the flyer promised rafting and cocktails – a combination even she struggled to calculate the odds of danger and death for. But it turned out to be a printing error that Dixie hadn't spotted. The first few had come out correctly and read 'Crafting & Cocktails'.

Only three people had turned up. They were Nora, a man called Jay and an elderly lady called Renee. Renee was the most disappointed of all to discover that they were tackling crochet squares rather than white-water rafting as she had been looking for an adrenaline rush that the sheltered housing was not providing and thought rafting and cocktails was right up her street. She'd been a young woman during the swinging sixties and was not how Nora pictured the average eighty-year-old. With short, stylish, light blonde hair, bright red lipstick and a sheepskin flying jacket, she had more than an air of a rebel Helen Mirren about her. Despite Renee's initial disappointment, after a couple of Porn-star Martinis she had knocked out a number of granny squares that evening, even if some of them had been a little less than perfect.

Jay had also been disappointed, but to his credit he had joined in and with some help from Dixie and Renee became quite the dab hand with a pair of knitting needles. And so the odd bunch had become firm friends and met every Tuesday in the little side room at their local community centre on the outskirts of Melton Mowbray. Renee liked to call it the 'bloody broom cupboard' because it pleased her to add a mild swear word to most of her sentences. But the bigger rooms were used by the local Brownie pack and a wellness class, so it all worked out.

'They're buggering about with the heating again.' Renee patted the radiator. 'What idiot puts the heating on this time of year?'

'I think the caretaker is doing a check,' said Dixie.

'He's not on the last few rows of a double-bed-sized blanket, now is he?' Renee lifted one end of the impressive piece she had crocheted. A carnival of reds, pinks and purples with a distinct tulip border. 'I'm hotter than a Scotch bonnet's bum crack under here.'

'Do chillies have bum cracks?' asked Dixie, looking confused.

'I love the colours in that,' said Jay, picking up one end of Renee's blanket. He was still doing granny squares, although they were getting more intricate.

'Thanks,' said Renee. 'If you could keep wafting the blanket that's sending a lovely breeze to my—'

'Anyway this week's cocktail is . . .' Dixie left a dramatic pause to no effect. 'A Painkiller.'

'I'm on enough of those buggers,' said Renee. 'Bloody arthritis in my knee is playing up again. Go on then, what's in the cocktail?' she asked.

'Rum, pineapple juice, orange juice (from a carton, not fresh), with creamed coconut. It's meant to have freshly grated nutmeg on top too, but I've brought this.' She dusted the already poured drinks with some ground nutmeg from a little jar.

Renee was first to taste hers. 'Lovely, but could do with more rum.'

'You always say that,' pointed out Nora, and she took a sip of hers before cracking on with her knitting.

'Three things to update you all on,' said Dixie, and Jay and Renee froze. Nora carried on knitting her project as she figured she knew what was coming. She was working on a jumper for her dad's birthday and she needed to get on with it.

Dixie took a deep breath. 'I've got a discount code for the online wool place we all like. I've lost my job and—'

'Oh bad luck,' said Renee.

21

'Dixie, that's awful,' said Jay. 'I'm so sorry. Are you OK?'

Dixie grinned. 'I am great. Thanks to Nora it's the best thing that could have happened. I drew up a list and now I am absolutely focused on my next venture.'

'That's a splendid attitude,' said Renee. 'What's your new job?'

'I'm going to be a social media influencer,' she said proudly, pausing her crochet to watch for their responses. 'Instagram-focused mainly.'

Nora gave what she hoped was an encouraging nod.

'Sounds blinking brilliant to me,' said Jay. 'All the big brands are reaching out to influencers to spread campaigns. It's absolutely the future of marketing. Well done you.'

Renee was squinting at Dixie. 'Sounds like gibberish to me. Who do you work for?'

'Myself,' said Dixie, pulling back her shoulders.

'Hmm. Good luck with that.' Renee went back to speed crocheting.

'I need to get established first,' said Dixie, looking less certain.

'You really only need your mobile phone and an angle,' said Jay.

'What do you mean by an angle?' asked Renee.

Jay put down his knitting and gave her his full attention. 'There are lots of people on social media. Big-name celebs the brands are always going to want to work with, the reality TV lot who do pretty well . . . There's all sorts really but it's a lot easier if you are already famous.' Dixie's smile slid from her face. Jay noticed and hastily continued. 'But,' he said, waving his hands in circles as if winding himself up, 'among the millions of wannabes there are the canny ones who have carved out a niche for themselves. They've done something a little different so they appeal to the masses but also stand out from the crowd. You could easily be one of those.'

'Nope, all bloody gibberish to me,' said Renee. 'Times like this I wish I hadn't given up smoking pot.'

Jay ignored Renee and carried on. 'There are too many people doing it for you to follow everyone but you can find people who interest you. There are parents dealing with kids of all ages, the "mumfluencer" if you will.' He left a pause for laughter but there wasn't any. 'Gamers are very popular. Fitness is a biggie – there's everything from puppy yoga to unicycling.' Dixie wasn't looking any happier. 'If you enjoy knitting, you can follow people who do the same. They post videos with tips and hacks and share their latest projects. Is that what you're going to do?' asked Jay.

Dixie swallowed hard. 'I don't know yet. I'm just building my following.'

'Cool. How many have you got?' he asked.

'Two hundred and thirty-four now.'

'That's a lot of people,' said Renee, finally looking impressed. Nora was shaking her head for Renee's benefit. 'You can have a damn good party with two hundred people.' Renee seemed to focus on a spot on the wall. 'We

23

had one hell of a night in sixty-five, until Cilla started singing. Luckily the Monty Python lot drowned her out until one of them got punched on the hooter. Someone chucked up in my bath and I don't know what Norman Wisdom did to my potted orchid but it never flowered again after that night.' Renee chuckled. 'Happy times.'

Jay pulled out his phone. 'I'll follow you on Instagram.' He tapped away until he found Dixie's profile. 'There you go. Now you have two hundred and thirty-five followers.'

'Thanks,' said Dixie. She was also now checking her phone. 'Jay, you've got three thousand, seven hundred and something followers!'

'He is an actor,' said Nora.

'It's not many really. Ryan Reynolds has over fifty million,' said Jay. 'But we all have to start somewhere.'

'I guess,' said Dixie. 'I'm going to need loads before companies will pay me, aren't I?'

'According to the internet,' said Nora, 'not a reliable source, but still – it says you need a minimum of five thousand followers, and with good engagement and affiliate product links you could make a thousand pounds a year.'

'That's not much, is it?' said Dixie.

'That would barely keep me in gin,' said Renee, more to herself than the group.

'Maybe I would have been better being a living statue.' Dixie stared at her yarn. 'And now I've lost count of my stitches.'

'Don't give up at the first hurdle,' said Nora. 'You simply

need to think about what your angle is.' She looked at Jay and he nodded vigorously. 'Once you know that, then you can start to target followers and build your brand. You've got this.' Nora did her best to sound positive.

'I guess.' Dixie didn't sound convinced.

'Can you *see* yourself being an influencer?' asked Nora. 'Is it something you think you'd enjoy?'

'Visualization is a great technique. Fake it till you make it. Imagine yourself doing the thing you want to do and then you'll do it,' said Jay, losing conviction the more he went on.

'How does that work exactly?' asked Dixie.

'It's not bleeding magic, is it?' Renee knocked back the rest of her Painkiller cocktail. 'If you can see it happening in your mind then you're tricking your brain into believing it's possible.'

'I couldn't have put it better,' said Nora.

'I have to believe first and then it'll happen?' said Dixie, brightening up.

Nora nodded. 'You need to believe but then you need to take action. That's the only way anything ever happens.'

'Then I have to come up with an angle pretty quickly.' Dixie became animated. 'Like knitting for prisoners or cocktails for pets or making friends with wild animals . . .'

'Maybe have a bit of a think about that,' said Nora, topping up Dixie's glass.

'Yeah, good idea.' The others both agreed.

4

Nora was getting ready to leave the house on Friday evening when a key went into her front door. For a second she wondered what was going on. Her imagination conjured up a number of scenarios where she died horribly in every single one. But the images disappeared as soon as her parents walked in chatting happily to each other.

'Mum, you gave me a fright,' said Nora, giving her a hug.

'Why? Who else has a key?' asked Una.

'Nobody, although my neighbour has one in a box locked with a combination for emergencies. Anyway, your key is just for when I'm away.' This was not the first time she'd had this conversation with her parents.

'Put the chain on if you're worried,' said her dad, kissing her cheek and walking through to the living room carrying a shopping bag.

'Actually, guys, I'm just going out. I'm climbing tonight.' Nora indicated the front door but no one was paying attention.

'I thought you would be out, which is why I used my key,' said Una, lifting her chin.

'It's always lovely to see you both, but why have you come round if you thought I was going to be out?' Nora checked her watch. There was only about five minutes before she needed to leave. She hated being late for anything.

Nora waited for her mum to reply but she just stared at her and smiled. It was the exact same thing she did when people used words she didn't understand. 'Dad? Why are you here?'

'Your mother thinks you're hiding—'

'Ali!' shouted her mum.

'What do you think I'm hiding?' asked Nora, amused by the horror on her mother's face at being ratted out by her husband. 'Treasure? A man? An illness?' It was only fleeting but her mother's expression changed. 'You think I'm sick?'

'Nooo,' said her mother. 'Because you would tell me, wouldn't you? You would say if something was wrong? Anything not right with you. Yes?'

'She thinks you're too skinny,' called her dad from the other room.

'Ali, I swear, one day your mouth—'

'Mum, I'm fine. I'm not too skinny. I'm in the green zone on the BMI chart along with 29 per cent of the population. I'm perfectly fine.'

'You have no fat on you. Only muscle. It is not healthy. Women are meant to have curves.'

'Actually, Mum, it is healthy.'

'I disagree. You need stuffing up.' Una gestured with her hands.

'Mum, I'm stuffed up enough, thanks. What were you going to do? Load my cupboards with doughnuts?'

'I made a goulash . . . Ali! Bring the goulash.'

Nora knew they meant well but they did drive her slightly potty. 'Thank you. I think. Can you pop it in the fridge please? And now I really do need to leave.'

Nora's other hobby was indoor climbing. She loved to climb, and as the indoor version was approximately 35 per cent safer than the outdoor version, was lots of fun and had safety at its core, it ticked all her boxes. She went to a smallish club on the way to Loughborough where the walls were regularly updated and the people were friendly. Climbing wasn't exactly a team sport but to do it safely Nora did need a partner who could belay and for that she had Jay. Handily he had been looking for something exciting when it became clear Dixie's club did not involve rafting of any description.

Nora and Jay had discovered a mutual interest in climbing and a partnership had been formed. Jay made her laugh and they had an easy friendship. As they lived near each other, they travelled together and took it in turns to drive. Jay parked and they walked inside. Coming out of the sports centre was a group of boys at the younger end of the teenage spectrum.

'Hey!' shouted one of them, and he began pointing frantically at Jay. 'You're that guy.' His friends looked both alarmed and embarrassed by his actions. 'He's that man on the advert.' They all stared at Jay as he and Nora walked up the steps. As the penny dropped, the lads all started burping loudly. This happened quite a lot.

'Thanks, boys,' said Jay, giving them a wave and ushering Nora inside as the youngsters fell about laughing.

'You OK?' asked Nora.

'Yeah. It's the price of fame,' he joked. 'One day I would like to be famous for something other than burping a lot in an indigestion advert,' he added wistfully.

'One day,' said Nora, and she gave him a reassuring pat on the shoulder.

They got changed and met on the mats by the climbing wall where other climbers were putting on shoes and harnesses. Another regular was Trent. He liked to climb in a tight-fitting racer vest and even tighter shorts that left little to the imagination about how excited he was about climbing. In contrast, Jay favoured a long-sleeved top and baggy joggers. Trent and Jay were like the yin and yang of men. Trent was tall and blond with muscles like the Hulk whereas Jay was not much taller than Nora, classically handsome with a slender build and the ability to wiggle his ears. Trent did a few one-armed press-ups for no apparent reason. That level of warm-up wasn't necessary for climbing but there were a couple of women watching from the reception desk so that was most likely why he was putting on a display.

'Hey, check this out,' said Jay, wiggling his bum as he showed off his new chalk bag.

'Very nice,' said Nora. 'How's things with work?' she asked as they roped up.

'I had four auditions this week,' he said, looking quite pleased.

'That's brilliant. I hope one of them hires you.'

'Thanks. Because I also had three rejections so it all hangs on the truck company health and safety video.' He grimaced and crossed his fingers and Nora mimicked him. She felt for Jay. He was a jobbing actor, and as someone who cherished her steady nine-to-five job, she struggled to understand how he coped with the constant auditions and frequent rejections. Somehow he managed to make a living from it, thanks mainly to voiceover and audiobook work.

'Sorry about that. Otherwise you're good, are you?' she asked.

Jay's expression became serious. 'Actually, I had a bit of a shock in the shower this morning.'

'If this is a gross body thing, then I'm out,' said Nora.

'It's not. I thought I was losing my sight. Everything went all foggy and blurry,' explained Jay.

'Are you OK now?' asked Nora.

'Yeah, I'd left my glasses on,' Jay gave his frames a wiggle. 'What a doughnut I am! It took me a moment to realize but for a second I really thought there was something wrong with my eyes.'

Nora chuckled. 'I'm glad you're OK, Jay.'

'Me too,' he said, with feeling. 'How did your date with the bookkeeper go?' he asked, handing Nora a cup of water from the cooler.

'About as badly as it could have done.'

'Not what you ordered?' he asked, beginning to do some warm-up stretches side by side with Trent, making him look like an Ewok next to Chewbacca.

'Funnily enough, I did not order a bald forty-year-old who chats to his mother when he's on a date.'

Jay was making a face. 'So what now? You could take Miley Cyrus's advice.'

Nora began to sing 'I Can Buy Myself Flowers'.

'Exactly.'

'Nope. I've done that. Turns out flowers are really expensive and the florist had no idea what I was on about when I sang that line. Uber embarrassing. She just felt sorry for me and added in a few extra blooms and packaged it all up in cellophane. I left with a hole in my bank account, a pink-bowed arrangement and feeling like a right loser.'

'You're not a loser,' said Jay, trying to copy Trent's exaggerated leg stretches.

'Cheers. But I think I might take myself out of the equation. Stop dating altogether.'

'Ooh, now don't be too hasty,' said Jay, lunging forward and yelping. 'I think I've pulled something.' His voice was higher-pitched than normal.

'You OK?' asked Nora as Jay held his groin.

'Fine,' he squeaked. 'I'll just get some ice on it. On this. On the muscle. The one I pulled.' Nora and Trent stared at him. Jay pointed to the refreshments area and walked away as best he could with his thighs clamped tightly together.

'Ouch,' said Trent, doing some impressive tuck jumps. 'You know, Nora, we would make an exquisite couple.' He gave her a toothpaste smile as he walked to the wall and got his first foothold stable before stepping up. His arms flexed as he climbed higher. 'Would you like to go on a date with me, Nora?'

She couldn't help thinking that she was very much not Trent's type and he was only being kind. And while on the face of it Trent was definitely *her* type with his beefy physique, he was too vain and arrogant for her, plus she wasn't sure they had anything other than climbing in common. 'Thanks, I'll think about it.'

'What did I miss?' asked Jay, walking back with a large icepack clutched to the inside of his thigh like he was trying to ride it.

'Nora has turned down my offer of a date.' Trent pulled an overly sad face.

'You asked her out?' Jay's head swivelled unnaturally between the two of them. 'He asked . . . but you declined. You're not going out then. Right. Good. Or shame. You know. Whatever.'

'Actually, I think I'm going to retrospectively apply the 37 per cent rule to my love life.'

She wasn't sure why that popped into her head at that precise moment but it felt like a plan.

5

'What's this?' asked Jay, turning his head so fast she feared he might need a chiropractor. He re-adjusted the ice pack on his groin, gasped and returned it to where it was.

'Are you familiar with the 37 per cent rule?'

'I've never heard of it,' said Jay, fine-tuning his stance but still looking uncomfortable.

'It's a recognized business rule but in theory it can be applied to anything that requires a decision, including relationships. To have the highest chance of picking the best partner, you should date and reject the first 37 per cent of your total group of lifetime suitors. The next best option after you've ditched the first 37 per cent is your most likely chance of success. And I thought I would give it a try.' She'd been mulling it over since her evening with Dixie and as far as she could see there was little risk, with potentially everything to gain.

'Love and life aren't really like that, though. You can't just apply a theory that was created for businesses to something like this. Can you?'

'It's been statistically proven that the rule works, although I don't think it's been applied to relationships before. If it works with other decisions then it has to be a viable option. Who am I to argue with numbers?' The more she thought about it, the more Nora liked it. It was logical and it would prove things one way or the other. Either she had overlooked The One or it wasn't meant to be and she needed to draw a line under her searching and simply enjoy life as she was. And it was a great life, so she was fine with that. In fact, it would be quite a relief to stop searching, so whatever the outcome she was on to a winner.

'Sounds hellishly complicated to me,' said Trent, jumping the last few feet to the ground. It gave Nora a bit of a start as she'd forgotten he was climbing only a few feet above them and must have been listening to every word.

'It's not,' said Nora.

'What would be simpler would be a date with me?' There was that toothpaste smile again.

'Um . . . thanks,' she said. 'I'm sure you are simpler but I'll stick with the numbers for now, if that's OK with you?'

He gave her a wink and tipped his head at the women who had been at reception and were now walking past. 'Ladies,' he said. Once they were out of sight he wriggled out of his harness. 'I'll be back. See you later.' He jogged to catch up with the women.

'See, Trent doesn't use a business rule to find a partner,' said Jay.

'I don't think Trent is looking for a partner,' said Nora. 'Sex alone does not a relationship make.'

'So wise,' said Jay with a wince.

Nora decided to belay for the person Trent had abandoned as Jay looked like he was out of action for a while. When she took a break, Jay was on his mobile, clearly looking up the validity of the rule.

'This can't be right,' he said. 'The internet says that the average man – i.e. me – has six serious relationships in his lifetime. And 37 per cent of six is two point something. That means my third serious relationship was the one I should be with. Right?'

'Using averages might lessen the accuracy. Maybe think about how many partners you think you could have in a lifetime,' said Nora. 'Trent's probably looking at one every six months so his total number will be well over a hundred.'

Jay blinked a few times. 'OK, I think my number will be somewhat lower. So far I've been out with . . . And potentially there could be . . .' He looked to the ceiling and mouthed out numbers as he tried to do the maths. 'Actually I don't think I've cleared 37 per cent yet,' he said brightly.

'According to the numbers,' said Nora, 'for me, it's serious boyfriend number six I need to focus on but I'm going to check out everyone I've dated from boyfriend number four onwards to ensure I've covered all bases. Are you going to be OK to belay for me?' She nodded at Jay's ice pack.

'Sure. No problem,' he said, waddling from the bench to put the ice pack in the bin before kitting up.

When he was ready, Nora chose a starting hold and climbed on to the wall. 'I need to do a bit more research on my ex-partners first. That's code for stalking on social media. Mainly to check they're still single, and then I'll call them up.'

'Out of the blue?'

'Yeah. What's wrong with that?' she asked.

'Let's pretend I'm boyfriend number four.' Nora gave him a look. 'I know I'm way out of your league but pretend,' he said with a grin and she stuck her tongue out at him.

'Hiya, Salvador, it's Nora—'

'Salvador?' Jay chuckled. Nora glared at him. 'Sorry, unusual name. I didn't mean to judge. Carry on.'

'Hiya, Salvador, it's Nora. I was wondering how you were and thought I'd give you a call.'

'Oh crap, have I got a kid I don't know about? Or a rare sexually transmitted disease? Brrrr. That's Salvador hanging up,' he said, keeping tight hold on the rope but moving back slightly to be out of swiping distance.

'He won't think that. Will he?' she asked, but Jay was already nodding furiously at her. Maybe this needed a tad more thinking through.

Nora got in from climbing to find her parents were no longer there, the goulash was in the fridge and there was a bag of doughnuts on the counter with a note in her mother's handwriting that just said 'Eat' followed by a row of kisses. She heated up some of the goulash and sat down with a fork and her laptop.

Once she'd cleared away she retreated to the living room and took Oliver out of his glass terrarium and he slowly made his way up her arm to her shoulder. Nora flipped open her laptop. She created a new spreadsheet and filled in basic details for the first three ex-boyfriends she was going to track down. She had taken on board what Jay had said, and as she didn't want to freak anyone out, she decided a more sensitive approach was in order.

As she was a logical person, falling in love fascinated her. There was simply no logic to it and yet it was happening all the time. Like most people she didn't believe love at first sight existed, which meant love was something that took a little time to develop, and herein lay the real issue. How long should she stay with someone to see if it was going to become love? And while she was waiting, was she missing an opportunity for another that could have been The One? Looking back, she had been quick to call time on some of her relationships. Basically it was all a gamble and mostly people didn't even realize the odds they were dealing with. Nora loved odds and probability. As a statistician it was basically what she did all day and she was immensely grateful that someone paid her for it.

Nora sipped her caffeine-free Diet Coke. She'd already had two coffees and while the odds of dying from too much caffeine were lower than even she could be bothered to work out, the chances of her struggling to go to sleep if she consumed more caffeine were much higher at 30 per cent.

She decided to have a bit more of a scroll on social media for ex-boyfriend number four, then she'd head off to bed. Her phone buzzed to let her know she had a message and she half glanced at it. It was from Jay.

> Thought I should let you know that the swelling is going down in my groin so fingers crossed I'll be able to climb next week.

Ugh. Jay's groin was not something she'd been thinking about.

> Thanks for letting me know. Take good care of the injury.
>
> Thanks Nora that means a lot ☺

Jay was a bit accident-prone and Nora wasn't sure climbing was the safest sport for him, but he persevered and she admired that about him. She returned her attention to her screen. Ex-boyfriend Salvador. It appeared that she may have been part of his discarded 37 per cent because there on the screen was Salvador beaming back at her along with a stunningly beautiful woman and a super-cute baby. Maybe she'd check the others out tomorrow, she thought, as she updated her spreadsheet.

*

On Saturday morning Dixie called Nora and asked her to be out the front of her house at eleven o'clock precisely. Dixie liked to add a little drama to proceedings, otherwise life could be quite dull and she felt it was her mission to zhuzh it up. Unfortunately she had vastly miscalculated her arrival time, so was disappointed to see that Nora wasn't outside when she pulled on to the driveway at half past two. Nora lived in a nice little side street full of robust semi-detached houses with family cars on the drive. Nora always put hers in the garage because she said it was less likely to get stolen.

Dixie jumped out of the driver's side and knocked rapidly on Nora's front door. The door opened and Nora waved her inside.

'No, you need to come out. Ta-dah!' said Dixie, unable to contain her excitement any longer.

Nora peered past her and spotted the vehicle on her driveway. 'Is this yours?'

'Yes. I traded in my Mercedes and got this. It's a genuine vintage VW campervan in Niagara blue and white. Well, it was white once and it will be again.'

'Vintage. You said that was code for old and clapped out when it was Glenda's van,' pointed out Nora.

'Ahh, but this is a campervan. That's different. They're a real classic. The garage even gave me some money too.'

'I would hope they did,' said Nora, coming outside to inspect it. 'It must be at least fifty years old.'

'It's fifty-three and that means it doesn't need road

tax or an MOT!' Dixie had been thrilled to discover her new pride and joy was exempt.

'I doubt it would *pass* an MOT,' said Nora, poking at a rusty patch on the wheel arch.

'It's completely roadworthy. The man assured me it was safe to drive. And I have three months' warranty on it. It's just a bit slower than I'm used to. But at least I'll have to learn to use a handbrake now, which will be a good skill to add to my CV. Although it sticks out of the dashboard rather than the floor but maybe if it's there I might remember to use it.' Dixie got back in the driver's seat and attempted to start it again. The poor old van did a lot of chugging but wouldn't start. Nora came to the driver's window and scrunched up her face, the way she did when she was worrying about something. With some effort Dixie cranked down the window. 'How quaint is that?'

'There's a reason why things advance. Not only do they improve, it also makes them safer. Although if it won't start, I guess that makes it very safe,' said Nora, with a wry smile.

'It's OK. The man said it does this sometimes when it's choked or something.' It was possible Dixie hadn't taken in all the details because the man had spoken fast and Dixie struggled to listen when she was excited.

'It might need the choke. Is there a knob to pull out?' asked Nora.

Dixie had a scan of the black plastic cab. 'I don't think so.' She tried to start it again. After a bit of chugging there was a loud bang, followed by a plume of black smoke out of the exhaust. It was working and Dixie was thrilled. 'See, it's fine. Look inside,' she added, switching off the engine and almost sending Nora flying as she got out. Dixie proudly pulled open the door on the side of the van to reveal the interior. It was currently wall-to-wall beige vinyl with faded daisy-patterned curtains and a grubby orange carpet, but Dixie had plans. She'd seen renovated interiors on the internet and they looked amazing. She had no doubt she could do the same with this. 'I'm going to redo the inside so it's all swish, like that George Clarke programme where they have everything doubling up and surprise extra space everywhere.'

Nora rolled her lips together. 'I think it needs a lot of work but you have an eye for colour so I'm sure when it's finished it will look great. I'm just wondering why you've swapped your car for this?'

Sometimes Dixie got ahead of herself and this was one of those times. 'Sorry. I forgot the most important part.' She waved her hands in lieu of a drumroll. 'This is my angle!' Dixie had spent a lot of time researching her options and the ones that appealed required an upfront investment and there was no way she was going to ask her parents for a handout. When she'd found she could trade her current car for the van, it had seemed like the perfect solution. She pointed at the vehicle. 'I'm going to video myself doing up the campervan because people love renovation projects. There's a Victorian house one that's had thousands of views.'

'Good idea. I think there's months of work in this project so that's a lot of Instagram content,' said Nora.

Dixie looked inside the van. 'I wasn't thinking it would take that long but whatever.'

'And then are you going to sell it for a profit?' asked Nora.

'The plan is to go travelling in it.' She threw up her arms but Nora's expression said she wasn't feeling as enthusiastic.

'When you say travelling . . .'

'I mean anywhere and everywhere. To be honest, I haven't got an itinerary, but how cool would it be to take it to Val d'Isère for the ski season? I could catch up with Ma and Pa there too. And then on to Paris for spring, where I could film all the gardens and cafés and then do the Greek islands in summer and—'

'I hate to be a downer but you might want to do a course in mechanics before you go. A car of this age is 80 per cent more likely to need towing off the motorway than a newer one.'

'But the salesman said vans like this were made to last. Actual people put them together, not robots,' said Dixie, remembering how impressed she'd been with that fact. 'She's solid,' she added, tapping on the front wing and sending rust flakes floating into the air.

'She?' questioned Nora.

'Yes. I'm ignoring the fact that she's blue because I hate the gender stereotype of blue for boys and pink for girls. Yuck. Down with the patriarchy. But I can't ignore that her numberplate ends with the letters LC.'

Nora was doing that thing where she squinted like she was properly concentrating on something. 'And what do the initials LC stand for? Lily Collins? Lewis Carroll?'

'He was a man. But Lily Collins was a good call because I'm kind of doing an Emily in Paris but with a campervan and without the unfriendly people. But neither of those. It's LC.' Nora was still looking vexed. 'Like the old-fashioned name Elsie.'

'Oh OK. Now I get it. I think,' said Nora, still looking a bit confused.

'Nora, meet Elsie. Elsie, this is my good friend Nora.' Nora smiled politely as Elsie's exhaust emitted a delayed rumble and another cloud of smoke burst out.

'Elsie says hello.' That was what Dixie hoped it meant, and not a death rattle.

6

Nora didn't have many close friends. Primary school had been a bit patchy in terms of friendships. Quite a few in her class seemed to be mates with others because their mums chatted at school pick-up time. Nobody spoke to Una at school pick-up. At that stage her English had been improving but her accent was obvious. Discussions in class about simple things like what everyone had had for tea were baffling to a child who had no idea what a spaghetti hoop was, let alone eaten one. The few friends Nora had made went on to a different secondary school. When the popular girls at her school found out she was a maths geek, that was the final straw and she was singled out for seven years of misery.

So it was a revelation to Nora that she'd found people she called friends at Crafting and Cocktails and she was always pleased when it came around. Nora was focusing on her knitting because with her dad's birthday fast approaching she really needed to get the jumper finished. Renee's expert eyes would definitely help with the couple of issues she'd encountered. She'd somehow ended up with the wrong number of stitches at the end of a row so daren't go any further until it was resolved.

Dixie had set up the cocktails and after a brief welcome hug Nora was already taking a sip. 'It's like a slushy but for grown-ups. Very nice,' said Nora, taking it to her seat.

'It's a Fuzzy Navel,' said Dixie. 'I had to freeze it for four hours.'

Jay and Renee arrived together and after a quick run-through of the cocktail ingredients they all sat down.

'How's the van?' asked Nora. 'I didn't see it outside.' Dixie usually drove as she had the cocktail ingredients and didn't like walking along the road, clinking.

'It's not good for the environment to drive everywhere,' said Dixie, avoiding eye contact.

'Is this your vintage campervan?' asked Jay. 'Nora told me all about it and I think it's a wonderful idea.'

'Thank you,' said Dixie. 'It's not running at the moment and fixing things under the bonnet wasn't the sort of work I was planning to do on it. Mainly because I don't know anything about vans or cars. Or bikes, to be honest.' She looked thoroughly dejected.

'The engine's not under the bonnet,' muttered Renee, but she received no response.

'It'll still be in warranty so you need to get the garage to sort it out,' said Jay.

'That's the darnedest thing,' said Dixie. 'I called them but nobody is answering and I can't take Elsie to them because she's too poorly. I guess they'll pick up eventually.'

'I'd go down there and make a fuss,' said Renee. 'Which garage was it?'

'It wasn't local. It was a big one in Yorkshire, but the salesman came all the way here to deliver it, which was kind.'

The others shared knowing looks. 'What?' asked Dixie.

Nora felt for Dixie. She was a lovely trusting person but having lived her life in an upper-class bubble she wasn't the most streetwise. Nora needed to break the bad news. 'I'm a bit worried that maybe—'

'It's a scam!' butted in Renee. 'There are some rotters about. Don't worry. I'll have a look at it for you. I know my way around VW campers. I spent most of the Flower Child Festival in one. I'll soon have it back on the road.' All heads spun in Renee's direction. 'What? You don't think I shared one of those with half the members of The Alan Price Set in sixty-seven?'

'I do believe you but sleeping in one is quite different to fixing one,' said Jay.

'True, but Robin Gibb would tell you I'm a dab hand with a spanner. If he was still alive, of course. Anyway, do you want me to have a look at it?' Renee tilted her head at Dixie.

'Er . . . yes please,' said Dixie. 'When's good for you?'

'Well, weekends are at leisure, which means we do sod-all. On Mondays we have armchair Zumba, Tuesday is Singalong Sally (who can't actually sing a sodding note but that doesn't stop her), Wednesday's Mindful Meditation, which is when everyone falls asleep and I

49

play who will fart first, bloody Brain Training Bingo is on Thursday, and Friday is Ninja Jigsaw night.'

'Really?' asked Dixie.

'OK, I added the Ninja part, it's just chuffing jigsaws. And I can't stand any of it so there's naff-all in my diary – take your pick.'

'Great. I'll pop around tomorrow,' said Dixie.

'Not too early,' said Renee. 'The chiropodist comes on a Friday morning. I don't have an appointment this week but he's nice to look at. It brightens up an otherwise piss-poor day.'

Nora shared her knitting with Renee and she did a lot of tutting before declaring it 'thoroughly ballsed up'. Nora sipped her cocktail while Renee tried to fix it. Nora was a bit down about her dad's jumper but it was nice to catch up with friends and have a chat.

When their time was up, they packed away, and Nora and Jay said their goodbyes to Dixie and Renee and left them to fine-tune arrangements for Renee to look at the van. 'Any news on that audition?' asked Nora.

'I didn't get it. I've got a couple of auditions coming up, to destroy my already fragile ego again. So, yay. And the film I did last year where they ran out of money – *Undercover Bullets* – found some cash from somewhere so it's in editing. Mainly because the American actor Tasha Blake was in it and she's just had a break-out hit.'

'Oh, the sexy spy thing with the bloke from that film we watched and the woman that did that series I binged?' said Nora.

'I believe that's exactly how they will describe it in the trailer.'

Nora stuck her tongue out at him, then said, 'Oh wow! Jay, this is immense. Tell me everything.'

'But then I'd have to kill you.' He gave her his Roger Moore eyebrow. And in return she gave him the chilling stare her mother had taught her.

'Fine,' he said. 'It's an action thriller with a touch of comedy and a sprinkle of romance. Chances are it won't be a huge smash hit, but my agent is positive about it, which is a weird thing because she rarely is about anything.'

'Sounds great,' said Nora as they left the building and began walking back to hers.

'It also means I'll be doing some schmoozing and publicity stuff with Tasha and she's basically a goddess.'

'Strong words. Does someone have a crush?' Nora teased.

'Totally. I'll not even bother to hide it. She's a talented actor, utterly gorgeous and supports a donkey sanctuary. Which ticks all my boxes.'

'Does that make her your number-one celebrity crush then?' she asked, quite interested in this revelation as Jay never talked about dating or who he fancied.

'Definitely. My top three would be Margot Robbie, Sophie Turner and Tasha Blake.'

'Got a bit of a thing for blondes then?' she asked, given all the women he'd named shared that obvious characteristic as well as being stunningly beautiful.

'I suppose I do,' he said thoughtfully.

They walked on a bit. 'Any news on your, um . . .' Jay was tipping his head and raising his eyebrows as he clearly tried to convey something he wasn't happy to speak about.

'What?' asked Nora.

'The ex-boyfriend project. Or have you decided against tracking them down?'

'I found Salvador. There are pictures of him with a woman and a baby so I don't want to contact him if he's in a relationship. That would be weird.'

'It's all quite weird,' said Jay. Nora shot him a look and he held up his palms. 'If these guys weren't what you were looking for the first time around I can't see how they would be now.'

'There's a chance I was a little hasty in the past. I'm not known for my patience.' Nora knew she could sometimes be quick to judge.

'What are you looking for in a man? Other than someone who looks like Timothée Chalamet.'

'I actually lean more towards the Viking look, if I'm honest. Jason Momoa, Chris Hemsworth in his Thor phase, The Rock or—'

'Yep, got the picture,' said Jay. 'Apart from looking like a marauding Scandinavian, what qualities are important to you?'

'Good question.' Nora gave it some thought as they walked in step along Dalby Road. 'I like a man who knows his mind and will stand up to me. I can be a bit belligerent sometimes and I need someone who will call me on it but at the same time not piss me off.'

'So an alpha male then.'

'Not necessarily, although I guess a beta isn't going to confront me. But I also want someone who is kind, funny and an animal-lover.'

'Those things are more important than being solvent?'

'Definitely. As long as he's not sponging off me I don't care what he earns but I do think someone who cares about animals has a good honest soul. And they'd need to love Oliver obviously.'

'Obviously.'

'On that note, I'm going on a course with work in a couple of weeks. I'll feed Oliver before I go but do you think you could pop in and check on him please? I'd ask Dixie but she gets freaked out that his eyes look in different directions at the same time.'

Jay laughed. 'As long as I've not had the phone call and been whisked off to Hollywood in a private jet to star in a multi-million-pound blockbuster alongside Margot Robbie, or absolutely anyone really, I'm not fussy.'

'I love that you have standards,' she said, giving him a nudge.

*

Dixie had only ever gone past Brinkley Place Retirement Village on her way to the village hall so it was a new experience to press the buzzer for Renee's flat. Known locally as Wrinkly Place, it had a reputation as being at the luxury end of retirement living.

'Welcome to Mozzarella Fellas Pizza. Can I take your order?'

Dixie faltered for a second. 'Renee, is that you?'

'Of course it's me, you silly beggar! Come on in. Lifts or stairs on your right, I'm on the second floor, number twenty-two.'

'Right, and do you buzz me—'

A click from the intercom and a buzzing sound from the door answered her question. Dixie wasn't sure what she'd been expecting inside but having visited her great-nanna in a nursing home some years previously she had prepared herself for the lingering smell of bleach with a hint of urine. But what she was met by was something more akin to a Jo Malone candle. She had a quick look in a room to her left where the door was wide open and was impressed by the comfy-looking sofas and rows of filled bookshelves. She took the stairs to find Renee in her doorway wearing denim dungarees and waving at her. Dixie waved back and noted the thick carpet underfoot as she made her way to number twenty-two.

'Drink first and then work? Or the other way around?' asked Renee, ushering Dixie into a small, bright pink hallway.

'By drink, do you mean alcohol?' asked Dixie, walking through to a good-sized living room painted entirely in lime green.

'Nooo, don't be daft. I was thinking a small G&T

would set us up. What do you say?' Renee picked up a bottle from the top of a 1930s sideboard.

'If we get Elsie going, I'll need to drive her to get petrol.' Dixie dangled the keys. 'And there's a taxi waiting outside. Although there's no rush,' she added hastily.

Renee looked disappointed for a moment. 'Oh well, I'll pop a few in a flask in case of emergency.'

Dixie had a little browse while Renee sloshed alcohol into a Thermos. 'Your home is really nice,' she said. 'I love the colours.'

'I can't stand sodding magnolia, and it's a bonus to think that after I've pegged it it'll take someone quite a few coats to cover it up.'

'Well, I think it's lovely,' said Dixie. 'Shall we head off?'

'Let me grab my tools and I'll be right there.' Renee went to a tall cupboard in the hallway and started rummaging. 'Here, take this,' she said, passing a large toolbox to Dixie before reversing out carrying an industrial-looking piece of equipment and wearing a full-face shield.

'What on earth is that?' asked Dixie.

'MIG welder,' said Renee. She really was full of surprises.

Dixie had explained to Renee what it entailed to be an influencer and that she would be recording Renee working on Elsie for content.

'OK, hello viewers, I'm Renee and I'm the oldest mechanic in the west.'

'I'm not recording yet,' said Dixie. 'And I was thinking more fly on the wall, not directly to camera.'

Renee looked disappointed as she went to the rear of the van and popped the engine bay open. For a moment Dixie thought she was going to dive inside as she leaned so far over and stuck her face close to the engine. After a lot of tutting Renee declared, 'It's not pretty.'

'But it's fixable, right?' Dixie had everything crossed, possibly including a part of her gut, because that was feeling particularly strange.

'She's a rhapsody in rust but there's nothing I can't weld. It's the engine I'm most worried about. I'll do my best but I think it might be, well . . . buggered.'

'I had a nasty feeling you might say that, but I'd be grateful if you had a go at repairing her. I really don't want to have to tell my folks I've been scammed . . . They'll be so disappointed.'

Renee put an arm around Dixie. 'I'm sure that's not the case. Your parents obviously love you. I bet they're quietly very proud of you.'

'Hmm, I've not done much for them to be proud of. Well, not since being voted Most Adorable at university. That's why I was hoping this time would be different.'

'And it will be.' Renee rolled up her sleeves. 'Get recording again. I'll fix Shitty Shitty Bang Bang if it's the last thing I do.'

Dixie very much hoped it wouldn't come to that.

7

After a number of phone calls, Jay had decided to adopt a pet and Nora had agreed she would look after it if he was suddenly whisked off to Hollywood. Nora was meeting Jay at the local animal rescue centre. As she pulled up she could hear a cacophony of barking even before she'd got out of the car. Jay was already there and waved as she parked next to him.

'Hiya, thanks for coming. I thought it was best to have you with me when I'm choosing a forever pet as it's potentially going to be spending some time with you,' he said, his tone quite serious.

'You know I love animals so this is my idea of a perfect trip out.'

'And you're a star for committing to being my back-up and pet-sitter.' Jay had explained that he really wanted a pet but was worried about what would happen if he had to work away. 'I can't think of a better auntie than you.'

'Thanks, but this all feels a bit sudden.'

Jay forced out a chuckle. 'Nooo, I've been thinking

about getting a furry companion for like yonks. Literally ages. Eons. There's just so many options. And I'm a big believer in "adopt, don't shop", so here I am, ready to find out what sort of things they have.'

The barking inched up in volume. 'I think one option is definitely a dog.'

'You could be right,' said Jay. 'Or I was wondering about a ferret?' he added as they walked towards the entrance. 'When the magazines do those At Home With features, I think a ferret would make people think.'

'They'd think, why's he got a ferret?'

He stuck his tongue out at her.

'It is an unusual choice,' said Nora. 'They can give you one hell of a bite.'

'So can a dog,' said Jay.

'True. You might find, like me with Oliver, that finding a pet-sitter for a ferret is trickier than popping them in a kennel or a cattery. You know, just in case I'm away at the same time as you.'

The reception area was also the gift shop, where a jolly lady in an orange-logoed fleece and sensible shoes was overly keen to help them. She introduced herself as Elaine and took down some basic information before giving them a look Nora had frequently seen on her mother's face – playful curiosity. 'Is this your first pet as a couple, by any chance?'

'Oh, actually no. She's not mine,' said Jay quickly.

Nora raised an eyebrow at Jay.

'Not that she would be mine if we *were* dating.

Because women are not possessions or chattels. That's a very old word.' He cleared his throat.

'We're not a couple,' said Nora. 'I'll be its auntie.' Why did she say that? 'Not that he's my brother, because he's not that either.'

'We're friends,' said Jay and they both nodded along, relieved they'd finally managed to end the confusion.

Elaine didn't look convinced. 'OK. Let's give you the tour and then you can see if you're drawn to any species in particular. A big deciding factor might be your lifestyle.'

'I don't smoke. I do drink but I'm not a drinker,' said Jay hastily. 'I like a night out but I am totally ready for this commitment and—'

'I meant your home arrangements,' said Elaine.

'Of course, sorry,' said Jay. 'My style is comfortable Scandinavian with a minimalist twist.' He seemed pleased with his answer.

'I was thinking more about whether there was someone at home during the day,' said Elaine. 'It's important that dogs aren't left alone for hours on end.'

'Ahhh, right, I get you,' said Jay. 'I'm at home most of the time. My work is sporadic but Auntie Nora is my back-up plan for when I'm working away.'

'I work from home mostly so . . .' added Nora.

'I'm glad you've thought this through.' Elaine led the way through a couple of mesh doors to a courtyard. They had the tour of the guinea pigs and rabbits first, followed by reptiles and rodents. Jay liked all the guinea pigs with their wacky hairstyles and was rather taken with a hamster called Fluff but given he was two years into a likely maximum three-year lifespan, Jay felt he was setting himself up for heartbreak. Elaine led them through another door into an inside section where a multitude of cats snoozed behind glass windows. Elaine began pointing out various residents she thought would be a good match for Jay.

Jay hung back and whispered to Nora, 'I'm not sure I'm a cat person.'

'Why not?'

'They don't like me.' The one nearest to him hissed as if on cue.

'This is Jemima,' said Elaine. 'She likes the quiet life and a lap to sit on.'

'Don't we all,' said Nora. Elaine gave her a look. 'The quiet life was the bit I meant. Anyway, Jemima seems sweet.' The cat was watching them closely. When Jay approached, Jemima turned her back on him.

'See,' said Jay. 'I'm not being paranoid. Cats don't like me.' He pointed at Jemima's bum.

'Cats aren't for everyone,' said Elaine. 'Shall we look at the dogs?'

Jay was pulling a face. 'I quite like the hamst—'

'Oh yes, let's look at the dogs,' said Nora excitedly.

'Yay, dogs,' said Jay, mustering some enthusiasm from somewhere. They followed Elaine outside to the kennels. The sound of the entry door closing was enough to set the dogs off. 'Do you have any small, quiet dogs?'

he asked as the barking hit new heights, but his words were drowned out.

'Hush!' bellowed Elaine, making Nora's ears ring a little. But it did seem to silence a few of the worst offenders. 'That's better. Now let's have a look at who might be right for you two,' said Elaine more to herself. She pursed her lips as if in deep thought as she slowly walked past the kennels. She paused at one where a slobbery, stocky white dog was licking the bars.

'I don't think so.' Jay recoiled a little as they went by.

The next pen had a tiny dog. 'Oh, you're cute,' said Jay, crouching down. The dog began a high-pitched yap.

'Chihuahua,' said Elaine. 'He's high maintenance and probably won't cope well with the shared approach.'

Jay quickly followed after Elaine. 'Now, maybe this fella is for you.' She pointed into a kennel and Jay and Nora both looked inside. There was a large dog bed, and overflowing it was an even larger black, furry mass. Elaine tapped the mesh. The mass moved a little and two eyes appeared at the opposite end to where Nora was expecting them. 'He's a black German Shepherd. One previous owner. Relinquished due to a house move. Rentals rarely accept big dogs. He's partially trained. Quite laidback so would hopefully be happy with your arrangement.'

'His name's Bruce,' said Nora, looking at the info sheet on the door. At the sound of his name the large dog got up, stretched and came to investigate. 'Like Bruce Wayne. That's so cool. Hello, gorgeous boy.' Nora put her fingers to the mesh and Bruce tried to lick them.

'Careful,' yelped Jay.

'He's not going to bite,' said Nora with a chuckle. She'd thought about getting a dog but it had felt like a big commitment. Now, seeing Bruce, she knew this was a good decision. A dog share was the perfect solution. Maybe love at first sight *did* exist. 'He's the one, Jay. Don't you agree?'

'Er, well, he's quite a big fella. But if you think he's the one. And we've rejected at least 37 per cent, so . . .'

Nora gave him her best Paddington Bear stare.

'Let's let you two in and see what he thinks of you,' said Elaine.

'Great,' said Nora. Jay swallowed hard.

Elaine went in first and received a warm welcome from Bruce. His big fluffy tail swished from side to side. Bruce then made straight for Nora. She rubbed his head and he pawed at her jeans.

'You like that, don't you, boy?' Bruce walked around Nora, sniffing as he went. He approached Jay, who froze. But then Bruce had wedged his nose firmly in Jay's groin.

'Here, give him this,' said Elaine, handing Jay a small dog treat.

Bruce's bum hit the ground and he stared at Jay. Jay looked at the tiny treat in his hand and at the large dog. 'He's got a lot of teeth,' he said.

'They're in good condition. He's used to them being cleaned, so that's something it would be wise to continue,' said Elaine.

'Putting my hand in there?' Jay gestured with the treat. The motion had Bruce's attention and in a flash he had swiped the snack from Jay's grip. 'Argh!' shrieked Jay, rapidly checking his hand was intact and counting his fingers.

Nora giggled. 'Are you OK?'

'Me? Yes, absolutely fine. I was just taken by surprise. Only for a moment. Split-second thing.' He double-checked his fingers.

'I'll leave you to it. Take as long as you like. I'll be at reception when you've made a decision.' Elaine reversed out of the cage.

'You're leaving us alone with him?' said Jay, pointing at Bruce but quickly pulling back his fingers when the dog showed renewed interest in them.

'I trust you,' said Elaine with a smile. 'Make sure the bolt is properly in place when you exit.'

Nora realized this was predominantly Jay's pet and therefore it had to be his decision. She'd be disappointed if he didn't choose Bruce but it wasn't up to her. 'Is he too big for you, Jay?'

'Nooo,' said Jay, stepping back as Bruce bounded over with a large toy dumbbell. 'Good dog,' said Jay, and Bruce promptly dropped the dumbbell on Jay's foot. 'Ow!'

'Aww, he wants you to play with him,' said Nora. 'He likes you.' Bruce stared at Jay and licked his lips.

'Or he liked how I tasted and now he wants the rest.'

'He's fine, he's a pussy cat,' said Nora, rubbing

around Bruce's pointed ears. He had such a thick coat.

'That's not a positive thing in my book. Remember, cats don't like me, and he only does because he thinks I'm edible.'

*

Dixie felt a bit redundant. She'd tried passing Renee the tools she'd asked for but she wasn't mechanically minded so generally had to hold up three things for Renee to choose from, in the hope that one of them was what she was after. Sadly, she wasn't entirely sure that she excelled at anything much.

University had been fun but a 2:2 in Fashion, Patterns and Textiles wasn't exactly going to set the world on fire. Looking at her friends she could see what their strengths were, but when she studied herself they were less obvious. She had friends who were able to sew and paint, some with their own businesses and others climbing their way up the corporate ladder. Then there was Nora who could do anything with numbers, and Jay who was a talented actor, he just needed a break. And here was the incredible Renee, who seemed to be able to excel at pretty much anything she set her mind to.

Dixie decided that comparing herself to others wasn't healthy. Renee's huffing and puffing had increased, which was cause for concern.

'Renee, are you OK? Shall we take a break?'

Renee pulled her head out of the engine bay, rubbed

her cheek and instantly left a grubby smear on her face. 'I won't be beaten,' she said.

'I'm not saying give up. Just maybe have a rest for a bit. How about a cup of tea?'

Renee appeared mildly repulsed at the suggestion. 'Perhaps a cheeky G&T might give me inspiration.' She put down her wrench. 'I hate to say it, but this fella has sold you a pup.'

'A pup sounds like a nice thing but I'm guessing it's not.'

Renee shook her head and Dixie found herself copying. 'I'm afraid it means they sold you a pile of crap.'

'It's probably not good for me but I think I'll join you in a G&T and I'll get petrol tomorrow,' said Dixie, as Renee put her arm around her shoulders.

'My aunt swore by having a bar of Cadburys Dairy Milk and a large gin every day and she lived to be a hundred and two.'

'That's a good recommendation for a long and happy life.'

'And she *was* happy, right until the end,' said Renee. 'Of course, she didn't have a tooth in her head and she believed there were fairies living in her commode but, apart from that, she was grand.'

8

Nora wasn't entirely lying about being away for a work thing, but she had omitted to tell Jay that she was also using it as an opportunity to catch up with one of her exes. She had sent a friend request to ex number five, which had been immediately accepted and they had exchanged a couple of messages. Nora had asked what was going on in Hugh's life but he'd gone with a very general response that everything was great and how about her. Nora decided that if she wanted to find out if she'd been too hasty in dumping him because of his nail fungus, then she needed to meet him and find out what his relationship status was and whether there was any potential. Hugh had been keen to meet up, which was a positive start.

Nora's course was in Leicester and thankfully that day's session had finished on time, so she was already at the café where she had arranged to meet Hugh. Her drink had just arrived when she saw him outside on his mobile. It was a great opportunity to do a brief assessment. While Nora hoped she wasn't shallow, it didn't do any harm to see if the previous attraction was still there. He was rather broad at the shoulders and slim at the waist and he'd used to keep fit by training for and competing in Ironman triathlons. Hugh turned, spotted her inside and beamed a smile at her. It made her smile back and give him a little wave. He'd always had a lovely smile and good teeth.

Hugh ended his call and came inside to greet her with a kiss on the cheek. 'Nora, you look amazing.'

She was pleased because she had made quite an effort, reasoning with herself that it was worth it when she had a potential relationship to rekindle. On an average day Nora let her hair dry naturally and put on lip balm but today her hair was styled and she'd done her make-up. 'Thanks, Hugh, you're looking good too.' His hair was shorter and his arms looked toned. She so wanted to glance downwards to his feet as he stepped forward to pull out a chair and sit down. She closed her eyes briefly in a bid to keep her mind away from thoughts of his fungal nail infection. That was a very long time ago. Nora didn't like that she'd been so fickle as to dump an otherwise nice person for something so trivial and short term. But if he didn't spend the small amount of effort it took to look after his feet, then in her mind that didn't bode well for other things in life, including her.

He ordered a drink and they soon slipped back into easy conversation as if they'd seen each other recently, not years ago. He was working as a computer analyst, something he'd always wanted to do, and was looking at potential flats to buy. This was hopefully a subtle way in to finding out some key information. 'Working out your maximum mortgage is always a downer unless you're buying on a joint income, in which case a lot more possibilities and properties open up.' She watched for his response but then worried that she was staring at him so she studied the foam on her coffee instead.

'You're right. It's a bit of a wake-up call to realize you can only afford a one-bed flat when you'd been looking at three-bed semis,' he said with a laugh. Nora wasn't laughing because now she didn't know if that meant he was buying solo or just had a partner on a low wage.

'And then once you've found somewhere, the bills start coming in and you go out less. But that might just be me and my single income.'

'Nah, it's not just you,' he said, letting out a little sigh. 'It's so nice to see you again, Nora. Did I already say that? Don't think I'm a dweeb.' He rolled his eyes. 'And now I've put the word dweeb in your head so you'll definitely think I'm one now.'

'No I won't. It's good to see you too.'

He leaned on the table and fixed her with interested eyes. 'I'm dying to know why you've got in touch after all this time. I did have a mild panic that you were going to tell me I was a dad and then I remembered that my brother bumped into you a couple of times after we split up and you definitely weren't pregnant so it can't be that. Can it?' He looked a little uneasy.

Thanks to Jay's male insight Nora had already figured

that she would be asked this question and she had a response prepared. 'There's no long-lost family reunion. I just thought that—'

'Oh crap. Are you ill?' Worry flashed across his face.

'No, I'm fine. It's just that if two people liked each other enough to date, why move on and never interact again? We have a shared history so why not stay connected in some way?'

'But why now?'

Ah, that was an element she hadn't prepared for. 'Why not?' She went back to staring at her coffee. She wasn't about to share any details of the mission she was on. If she was to find out she had mistakenly ditched her perfect match, then she had to discover that for herself and not be swayed by anyone else's emotions.

'I wondered if you'd had an epiphany and realized I was a great guy and wanted me back.' He looked her straight in the eye.

'But you might be in a relationship.'

'You're in luck. I'm single.' He grinned at her. At last she could mentally tick off the key question. 'I dated this girl for nearly a year,' he said, 'and then she changed jobs and dumped me for some bloke she'd just started working with. I was gutted.'

'I'm sorry. Did you think she was the one?' asked Nora. She was also mentally totting up what she knew about Hugh, his love life before her and an estimate of how many partners he would likely have had since, in a bid to work out where he was on his own 37 per cent journey.

'Nah, I don't believe in that and nor do you.' He was giving her an odd look and she stopped the calculations she was doing in her head. 'Come on, Nora. It's great to see you and all that, but there's something going on.'

Nora wondered if there was a way to tell him part of her plan. She needed a few minutes to conjure up something plausible that wouldn't have him running for the hills.

'I'm going to pop to the restroom,' she said, standing up. But as she did so she bumped the table, sending a teaspoon to the floor. Nora bent down and stuck her head under the table in search of the cutlery. She was immediately confronted with Hugh's feet. He was wearing flip-flops so it was impossible not to be drawn to his toenails. And there it was. Horror of all horrors, Hugh still had fungus and it was spreading. Nora retched.

'You OK?' he asked.

Nora hastily retreated from his manky toes. But she misjudged things and whacked her head on the table again, which violently jolted everything on top. 'Sorry,' she said, coming out from under the table to see the mess of overturned cups and spilled coffee.

Hugh was mopping things up with an already dripping serviette. 'It's OK. Are you all right?'

'Yeah.' She rubbed her head. Images of his fungus-ridden toenails swam into her mind and she retched again.

'I don't think you are.' He looked concerned. 'Shall I call you a cab or something?'

'Honestly. I'm good. But that's really kind of you.'

'Shall I get more drinks?' He looked around for a waiter.

'Actually no, maybe I will head off. But it's been lovely to catch up. I'm really pleased that you followed your dream of working in computers,' said Nora, inching her way around the table.

'It's been great to see you again too. We mustn't leave it so long,' he said, giving her a hug. 'How about next week? There's a band on at the Red Lion pub.' He looked keen.

'I'll need to check a couple of things on my calendar,' said Nora, stepping back and forcing herself not to look down at his feet.

'Oh yeah, sure thing.' Hugh tried to act nonchalant.

'It's been lovely to see you again,' said Nora, adding 'apart from your feet' in her head. 'Take care.' And with that she made for the exit. As she reached the door, something stopped her. She didn't usually shy away from things. Hugh was a decent person. Perhaps his single status was purely down to the toenail fungus. She felt she needed to step up and tell him. Nora turned around and started walking back to the table. But within a couple of steps she could see that he had sat down, taken off his flip-flop and was now picking at his toes. He looked up and they made eye contact.

'It's this, isn't it,' he said with a grimace. Nora nodded and tried to keep down the coffee that was threatening to reappear. 'I'll get it sorted.'

'Your feet will thank you and all your future girl-friends will too,' she said with a smile.

'When it's all cleared up, can I give you a call?'

'OK,' said Nora, but even without the nausea she still felt that she and Hugh weren't meant to be.

*

Jay had known that Bruce was a big dog but since he'd moved into Jay's two-bedroomed new-build he appeared to be at least three times bigger than Jay remembered. They were strangers forced to share the same space and it was going to take them both time to get used to each other. Bruce also had to adjust to a whole new living environment. He barked when the microwave pinged, he howled at the washing machine and he'd buried the robovac in the garden.

Bruce was standing in the hallway barking at Jay – something else he didn't seem keen on. The sound reverberated off the walls and the dog virtually filled the space. There was no way around him. Jay was tempted to leave him there and pop to Nora's on his own to feed Oliver but the rescue centre had been very clear that Bruce needed two good walks a day or he would become bored and destructive. At the sight of those teeth, Jay was in constant fear that the thing Bruce would destroy was him. He'd already woken up screaming thanks to a nightmare where Bruce was a werewolf ripping him to pieces.

'Shhh,' said Jay. Bruce continued to bark. Jay was starting to get one of his heads. 'Shut uuup!' he yelled.

Bruce was momentarily shocked into silence. He tilted his head and eyed Jay afresh. Jay held up the lead and the dog watched him intently as he inched closer, moving like he was on the narrow ledge of a tall building. He leaned towards Bruce. Jay had the clip on the lead open ready. He was almost there. Bruce sneezed. Jay jumped. The dog walked off. 'Shit!' Jay's heart was thumping. 'Calm down,' he said to himself. 'It was a sneeze.' He was so on edge with this giant beast in the house. With hindsight he really should have gone for the guinea pig. It would have been better to start off his pet ownership small and work his way up to werewolf.

Jay took a deep breath. Women wanted alpha males: strong, confident and fearless. That wasn't completely out of reach. He strode into the kitchen just as Bruce was bounding out. 'Bugger it!' said Jay and he ran back up the hallway to the front door with the hound right behind him. Cowering at the door with his arms over his face, he waited to be savaged.

Nothing happened. Jay peeped under his arm at the dog. Bruce was sitting next to him with his tongue lolling out. Jay slowly leaned in and attached the lead, feeling instantly better. 'There, you're not a monster, are you?'

Bruce barked, making Jay jolt and almost drop the lead. He wondered if he'd ever stop doing that.

9

Jay's plan to kill two birds with one stone by walking Bruce to Nora's didn't quite go as he'd hoped. Bruce was keen to go for a walk, which was good, but despite being new to the area, he seemed to think he knew the best route to take. Try as Jay might, he was no match for Bruce's muscle and sheer determination, so he had little choice but to go on a magical mystery tour. An hour later, an exhausted Jay finally put the key in Nora's front door. Jay walked in, expecting the dog to come with him, but Bruce was rooted to the path. Bruce looked warily inside.

'Come on. You were the one who wanted to explore everywhere,' said Jay. Bruce huffed and lay down. 'Oh no! Please don't do that. If you fancy a rest you can do that inside.' Jay waved an arm up Nora's hallway in what he hoped was an inviting manner. 'You could have a nice lie-down inside and I'll get you a drink,' he added.

'Ooh, now I'm tempted, that sounds lovely,' said a woman coming out of next door. 'I could do with being waited on by a gorgeous chap like you.'

Jay spun around. 'Er, sorry. I was talking to the dog.'

'I figured you were, love.' She turned her attention to Bruce, who still had his forlorn face resting on his outstretched paws, but his big eyes were watching the exchange closely. 'Who's this lovely girl?' she asked.

'He's called Bruce,' said Jay, wondering how she could think for a moment that this macho beast could be anything other than male. At the sound of his name, Bruce got up and came to the fence to greet the new person. He put his great paws on the flimsy structure and Jay feared he was going to push it over. The fence panel bowed but Jay wasn't keen to intervene as he was still unsure of Bruce and his many teeth. It would be easier to pay for a new fence panel than lose an arm trying to save it. At least he had taken out a robust insurance policy. 'Oh, careful, he's a rescue and I'm not sure how he'll be with strangers . . .'

Jay watched as the woman buried her hands in the dog's coat and roughly rubbed his head, oblivious to any danger. Even after living with the dog for two days he wouldn't manhandle him like that for fear of losing fingers or worse.

The woman carried on fussing Bruce and he seemed to like it. 'You're a softie, yes you are. But I have to go to work. Yes, I do. Bye, Bruce,' she said, and Jay and Bruce both watched her leave.

Bruce looked at Jay with sad eyes. 'You liked her, didn't you? Maybe you'll grow to like me. Come on.' Jay gave an encouraging tug on the lead and thankfully Bruce followed him inside Nora's house.

Jay was even more pleased when Bruce went straight to lie on Nora's faux-fur rug. He was likely worn out after his mammoth expedition. Jay had covered almost every inch of the park, been round the bandstand multiple times as well as down two side roads and an alleyway he barely knew existed, and all at Bruce's pace, which was one notch down from a gallop. No wonder the dog was tired, he was too.

'Hey, Oliver Queen,' said Jay. He liked to use the chameleon's full name, mainly because as a DC Comics fan it made him smile. Jay opened up Oliver's enclosure, as Nora always did, because she said that way he got a blast of new air. The chameleon was a brilliant green with yellow highlights. Nora said she could tell how he was feeling by what shade of green he was. Contrary to popular belief, chameleons don't drastically change their colour to match their environment, as their world is mainly different shades of green – although Nora had joked that she would have liked to see him try to match her mum's tartan throw. Oliver didn't move fast, apart from his eyes, which were permanently swivelling in different directions. In contrast, Bruce had heavy eyelids like he was nodding off. At least he was calm, that was something.

Jay went into the kitchen to change Oliver's water. Nora had a very white, modern kitchen, which was spotlessly clean. This was his last trip to Nora's as she was due back from her course the next day. A sticky note on the counter detailed instructions that Jay remembered but he glanced at it again anyway. Nora had finished her note with: *and if you have time to have a chat to Oliver I know he'd appreciate an update on your thoughts on breaking into Hollywood*. At the bottom was her initial and a smiley face. Jay grinned back at the note. Nora knew very well that this was a subject he could talk about for hours on end, given the chance. Jay refreshed the water and, still smiling, walked back into the living room. He'd only made a couple of paces across the room before he froze. Something was wrong. Bruce had his back to Jay but the sound of loud chewing was definitely coming from him. Jay's eyes shot to Oliver's enclosure – it was empty.

'Bruce?' asked Jay. The dog glanced over his shoulder and licked his lips. 'Oh, what have you done?' Bruce trotted over to Jay, sat down and stared at him. Jay swallowed hard and so did Bruce. 'Did you eat Oliver?' Jay clutched the water container. Bruce's mouth lolled open and Jay caught sight of something green inside. He recoiled.

This was a real-life horror film.

He'd been left in charge of a simple task and now Nora would never forgive him. He put the water in the vivarium and began searching the room, although he knew it was pointless. Poor little Oliver didn't stand a chance against a brute like Bruce. Jay checked under the sofa, on all the shelves and even behind the radiators – there was no sign of the chameleon. Bruce was quite interested in the game of search and followed Jay closely, double-checking after he had examined each possible hiding place. Eventually Jay had to give up and accept the reality of the situation. He'd basically sentenced Oliver to death at the jaws of Bruce and Nora would never speak to him again.

*

Dixie had never felt like such a loser. Over the past week Renee had worked for hours on the van and despite it making a vaguely promising sound once or twice, she couldn't get the engine to turn over. She'd pledged to come back and have another go after she'd made a few phone calls to friends who had once owned similar vans, but Dixie could see that they were reaching the end of the straw-clutching phase.

She'd bought a wreck, a disaster on wheels. It was time to face the fact that the van was dead and, with it, her hopes of becoming a social media influencer. It made her feel rather melancholy, which may have been enhanced by the number of G&Ts Renee had poured for her. Dixie sat in the back of the van and surveyed her seventies-themed nightmare. It looked awful and it smelt bad too. She'd had such plans for the interior and for her travels but everything had come to an abrupt halt. She lit a candle and the happy little flame danced but didn't manage to lift her mood.

Dixie switched on her phone and began an Instagram Live. It was an opportunity to pour out all her hopes and dreams for the little clapped-out van Elsie, and how she felt such a fool for being duped by a con man, and to deliver the crushing blow that this would be her last post because Elsie was dead. Dixie found herself silently crying as she watched two of her six viewers log off. She let out a sniffly sob, gave a sad little wave and ended the post and her fledgling career. That was it; she'd have to go back to the drawing board or perhaps the list she'd drawn up with Nora and see if there was anything else feasible on there. She was rapidly losing faith in the 37 per cent rule.

Right now she didn't feel like starting again. She needed a bit of time to wallow in her disappointment. Grabbing one of the slightly damp cushions that she'd planned to crochet a new cover for, she curled up in the foetal position and had another little cry.

Dixie wasn't sure how long she'd been asleep but when she awoke her eyes felt crusty from dried tears and someone was tapping on the side of the van. Renee stuck her head inside and recoiled. 'Bloody hell, what's that smell?'

Dixie wrinkled her nose. 'I lit a candle. It's eucalyptus and bay.'

'Smells more like eau de cat litter tray to me,' said Renee. 'But an unattended candle might be exactly what you need to solve your problem, if you know what I mean,' she added, with a tap on the side of her nose.

'The candle is trying to mask the odour,' explained Dixie, although she had to admit it was probably making things worse. 'I think it's damp.' She sniffed the air, detecting a more caustic undercurrent.

'It's about as pleasant as a wet football sock,' said Renee. 'Funny story. There was me, George Best and . . . never mind, that's one for another time.'

Dixie sniffed again. 'I thought it was just damp but now I'm thinking it's the smell of a dead campervan. Doesn't matter what it is. The dream is over.'

'Hells bells, someone is feeling sorry for themselves!' said Renee. 'You're not seriously giving up because of a tiny thing like this, are you?'

'It's key to everything,' said Dixie, wishing Renee would let her have a little wallow in peace. 'Perhaps I need to get an ordinary job in an ordinary shop. Perhaps Waitrose are hiring.'

'Because that's where all the ordinary people shop,' said Renee. 'If you've checked out you won't mind me having another tinker with it.' She wasn't really asking Dixie because she was already heading for the engine.

Dixie sighed. She didn't want to give up but she also didn't want to throw more money at a lost cause. Cutting her losses was the smart thing to do. She would have to have a serious think about her future because she was starting to believe she was completely useless. She got out her mobile and pulled up Instagram, expecting to see the usual twenty or so likes for her post. Dixie blinked. She had just four likes and a comment from an anonymous troll who called her a snowflake.

There was more muttering and Renee appeared with

a new mucky smudge on her cheek. 'Right. You need to make a decision. Are we quitting or are we fixing? Because personally I don't like to be beaten by things.' She arched an eyebrow at Dixie and waited.

Dixie bit her lip. This felt like one of those crossroads in life. She could cut her losses and move on or try a bit harder.

'I've not got time to waste so perhaps you'll let me know,' said Renee as she headed back to the engine.

'Hang on, Renee. I'll not be beaten either,' she said clambering out of the van. 'Let's fix this thing together. Just let me set up my ring light.'

'As long as that's not something you've bought from Anne Summers, then OK,' she replied.

10

Despite the setback that Hugh's foot fungus was still a deal-breaker, Nora remained determined to complete her mission to double-check a number of key ex-boyfriends. If anything, it was a good exercise in confirming her intuition was correct and that she and foot fungus would never be compatible. She stayed up quite late tracking down the next ex, who proved particularly difficult to locate.

There had been many wild times with Benicio but he frequently didn't have time for her and had let her down once too often. Not turning up on her birthday had signalled his demise. He'd not been easy to find online because he used a nickname. His social media had been a flurry of nights out and holidays up until Christmas, after which point he seemed to disappear. Now it became more than just ticking him off her list. She had grown quite concerned for his whereabouts and was determined to follow up the only lead she had.

A persistent knocking on her front door pulled her from her sleep just before seven on Saturday morning. She dozily headed downstairs trying to work out what she'd ordered because it could only be an overly eager delivery guy at this hour of the morning. She tied the cord on her dressing gown tight and with a large yawn she opened the front door to find an agitated Jay standing there.

'Oh great, you're up. Can we come in?' he asked.

'We?' Nora rubbed her eyes.

At the sound of her voice Bruce barked, charged past Jay and almost knocked Nora over in his excitement to greet her.

'Hiya, Bruce. You've got him already?' said Nora, waving them both inside and shutting the door.

'They seemed keen to get him out of the rescue centre,' said Jay. 'Which is probably a red flag.'

'How's it going?' she asked as she gave Bruce a fuss and he lapped it up.

'Not great,' said Jay. 'I'm sorry about the cryptic note I left you. I thought I should explain everything face to face. But then I figured you'd probably worked it all out anyway. Obviously you have. So all I can really say is—'

Nora wasn't sure what Jay was going on about. Her brain never kicked into gear until she'd had caffeine. 'You're a good boy, yes you are,' said Nora to Bruce. The dog wandered off into the living room and Nora followed him. 'You just need to get used to each other, Jay. I think you're worrying unnecessarily.' She opened the blinds and the room flooded with light. Bruce went up to Oliver's cage and barked at it, which drew everyone's attention to the open door.

'I'm so sorry,' said Jay, rubbing his hand over his face.

'Right,' said Nora, glancing around the room.

'You see, I couldn't leave Bruce at home alone because I've not left him yet and the rescue said not to for the first few days and then build up the time that he's alone because he might get stressed. Although I'm not sure he does get stressed but he's definitely a carrier because he's done nothing but cause me stress since he moved in. Anyway I brought him with me and he—'

'Oh, I see what he did,' said Nora as she rummaged in the foliage of her large paradise palm. 'He's eaten some of the leaves,' she added, turning around with Oliver on her forearm. 'Don't worry, they're not poisonous and they'll soon grow back. Look at it sprouting in all directions, even I can't kill it.'

Jay was staring at her.

'Oliver,' he said at last.

'Thanks for looking after him. And for letting him have a mooch about. Did you want a coffee?' asked Nora. Jay looked like he needed something stronger, perhaps being a pet owner was more taxing for some people.

'Have you checked Oliver over? No missing limbs?'

'He's fine. The plant is fine. Stop worrying.'

Nora put Oliver back in his enclosure and made the drinks. When she came back into the living room, Jay was sitting on the floor next to Bruce and they were both watching Oliver intensely. Oliver had an eye on each of them.

'Are you OK?' asked Nora, handing Jay a mug and taking a seat on the sofa.

'Thanks. I'm really sorry. I've been a terrible pet-sitter. Maybe I'm just not cut out for looking after animals.'

Bruce gave a huff and, as if understanding Jay's words and wanting to offer reassurance, he lay down with his head resting on Jay's thigh.

'It's OK. He's fine. It will take you both a while to settle. Don't be too hasty. I think what you're doing is amazing.' Nora feared Jay was thinking about giving up on his new charge.

Jay spun around to look at her. 'You do?'

'Yeah. Straight up. A dog is a huge commitment and I said I'd share some of that responsibility and I've not been here. I'll make sure I do more, I promise.'

'That's definitely made me feel better. It's all a bit daunting. I've not been responsible for someone else before. I guess it'll take a bit of getting used to.' Jay tentatively patted Bruce. 'Anyway, how did your work thing go?'

Nora fessed up to tracking down Hugh and Jay listened intently while sipping his drink and pulling suitably grossed-out expressions in the right places. 'I'm not overreacting, am I?' she asked at the end.

'Not at all. Some types of toenail fungus are highly contagious so you did right to avoid that. What now? Are you done with tracking down the exes?'

'Goodness no. I've got quite a few to find as yet.'

For a moment Jay seemed a little surprised but he recovered quickly.

'Actually I have a bit of a mystery and I was going

to do some more detailed investigating this afternoon. Benicio has kind of disappeared,' she said.

'Gosh. As in kidnapped or some sort of permanent demise?'

'More temporarily dropped off the radar because he's not on social media any more.'

Jay looked a little disappointed.

'But it's still weird for someone who posted fairly regularly,' she added.

'Maybe he was kicked out of his account or got hacked. That happened to James Corden.'

Nora pondered this. 'I don't know, maybe. But I've found where he was last a gym member. They're not likely to give me any info over the phone so I'm off to Peterborough this afternoon.'

'On your own?' asked Jay, spluttering into his coffee.

'Yeah. It would look a bit weird if I rocked up with a few mates. And far less likely that he'd be up for a chat. No, it's best I go on my own.' She watched Jay blow on the surface of his drink. 'Are you OK?'

'Sorry, could I have a tad more milk? It's a bit warm.'

'Sure.' Nora returned from the kitchen. She gave Bruce a carrot, which he chomped on happily while she sloshed some milk into Jay's drink.

'Thanks.' He took a sip. 'Much better.' There was a brief pause. 'Benicio is an unusual name.'

'It's from the Latin, meaning blessed. And he was, if you know what I mean.' She felt her cheeks heat up at the memories.

Jay was staring intently at his mug. 'And is it likely that Benicio is the one? I mean, statistically speaking?'

Nora moved the cushion and got herself comfortable. 'Statistically he's number six, which is definitely in the sweet spot if my projected calculations are correct.'

Bruce jumped up and ran barking to the front door, dragging Jay halfway with him. Thankfully Jay had just returned his mug to the coaster. 'Right,' called Jay from the hallway, 'I think I'll be off now. Take care. Again sorry about Oliver, and the plant. Mainly the plant.' The front door opened and Nora thought she heard him call 'Bye' but it was hard to tell over the sound of Bruce.

Nora hadn't been to Peterborough for a while and it was nice to reacquaint herself with the place as she headed for the gym. Though the people at the desk told her they couldn't share any details with her, she was pleased to find a couple of members who were happy to tell her what they knew. Women always liked to chat about pretty men and, when it came to looks, Benicio was right up there. According to one lady he'd gone travelling, which didn't ring true to Nora. For one thing, he would have been likely to share that on his social media, and secondly he was thirty and didn't like slumming it, so it was unlikely he'd have gone backpacking.

The second woman had a completely different take on things. 'He's homeless,' she said.

'What? Are you sure?'

'We were meant to meet up. Not a date as such,' she

said, although the twist in her features said different. 'He was a no-show. His mobile has been switched off ever since. I went to his place and it turns out he was only renting it. Then I was over in Corby visiting friends and he was on a park bench chatting to someone and I did a double-take. He was in these dark clothes and his hair had grown long and he looked like he hadn't showered in a while.' She folded her arms.

'And did you speak to him?' asked Nora.

'I tried. I called his name and waved but he put his hood up and jogged away. Which I personally think was very rude.'

'Yeah,' said Nora, while she pondered the vast amount of information. 'Do you not think it might have been someone who looked a bit like him?'

'Definitely not. Despite the clothes, I'd recognize that jawline anywhere.'

The woman had a point. 'Thanks, you've been really helpful,' said Nora, wondering what to do next.

*

Dixie and Renee hadn't managed to fix the campervan but Renee said she still had a few tricks up her kaftan. Thankfully Dixie was filming when the little van finally spluttered into life.

'Thank buggery for that,' said Renee, looking relieved. 'Definitely time for a gin and tonic.'

They sat in the campervan and sipped their drinks

while Dixie uploaded her latest video and watched hope-fully for any signs of engagement.

'What's the plan now?' asked Renee, leaning her elbows on the ancient table and making the hinges creak.

'I was going to do it up bit by bit. Rip out the old stuff and make it all modern.'

Renee gasped. 'This is a classic. I thought you kids were into vintage these days?'

'It's not that so much, it's more that it's falling apart,' said Dixie, pointing at where the curtains were sagging on a makeshift wire track.

'What do all your people on the Interweb say about it?'

'Ooh, good idea. I could do a poll and see what every-one thinks I should do. Excellent idea, Renee.'

'I'm frigging well full of 'em, honey,' said Renee rais-ing her glass.

11

Nora didn't entirely understand why Dixie needed her to bring all the bunting she owned over on a Sunday afternoon, but like all good friends she didn't question it and did as she was asked. When she got there, the van was looking quite shiny, apart from the rust spots, and people were bustling around it.

'Nora, you're a star,' said Dixie, skipping over and giving her a brief hug before inspecting the bunting. 'This is perfect.'

'For what exactly?' Looking around Nora wondered if they were having the smallest-ever summer fete in the car park of Dixie's apartment building.

'Did I not say?'

Nora shook her head.

'Silly me. I did a poll on Insta and the overwhelming vote was I should just go for it and start travelling.' Dixie clapped her hands together. 'Isn't that exciting?'

'Sorry, still not following,' said Nora, but Dixie was already skipping off with the bunting.

Renee appeared next to her. 'She's going off on her

adventures with Elsie. Says she'll do the makeover as she goes. Shelter in Sheffield, roof in Runcorn and curtains in Croydon, that sort of thing. Weirdest thing is apparently it was my idea.'

'Shelter?' questioned Nora.

'It's the awning but the only place she could find that started with Aw was in Devon. So she's starting in the north and then making her way down the country to Croydon.'

'Will it get as far as Croydon?'

'That's the million-dollar question,' said Renee. 'I've done my best but that engine is on borrowed time. Quite frankly, it's buggered.'

'I guess there's still time to talk her out of anything rash.'

'You'd better be quick. She's planning on having a big live send-off at four o'clock.'

'Today?!' Nora almost shouted the word in her surprise. Renee shrugged her shoulder pads.

Nora really didn't want to be the harbinger of doom but she couldn't let Dixie embark on a long journey in a clapped-out banger. Over the next hour she tried to get Dixie to see sense, but when Dixie had her mind set on something she was harder to shift than Renee off a beanbag – there had once been an incident in John Lewis. Nora realized it was pointless when Dixie came over and wrapped her in a bear hug.

'You're really going to do this?' asked Nora.

'I have to. I can't be the girl that always fails at things.

And I have a good feeling about Elsie.' Dixie looked fondly at the van surrounded by strings of bunting, balloons and happy people.

'At least you've always got this place to come back to,' said Nora, nodding at the block behind them, where Dixie lived in an apartment paid for by her parents.

'Nope, I'm going cold turkey. Tenant moves in this afternoon. I have all my essentials in Elsie, including a scooter for getting about and a port-a-loo.' She whispered the last part. 'And everything else has gone off to storage. This way I can't chicken out and there's no going back.'

Nora tried hard to hide how she felt about that. 'OK, but there's always a place for you at mine. Keep in touch. And please take extra care of yourself.' Nora didn't share the statistics regarding women on their own being attacked but it didn't mean they weren't at the forefront of her mind.

'I will message you every day but you can follow me on Instagram. Love you,' said Dixie, giving her another tight hug. 'I'm going before you make me smudge my mascara.' With a forced smile Dixie went to say goodbye to some of the others.

The sound of panting made Nora turn around. Bruce arrived, pulling Jay behind him. The dog tried to greet everyone at once. Jay was making a sort of wheezing sound. He pulled an inhaler from his pocket and took a puff. He bent over and held a hand in the air, which seem to indicate he needed a moment to catch his breath.

'Are you OK?' asked Nora.

'Did I miss it?' he asked.

Elsie chugged into life as if on cue. 'Oh, thank heavens for that. I set off with plenty of time but Bruce is like a guided missile with the wrong co-ordinates. But I did go past a lovely little café I didn't know existed.'

Dixie tooted Elsie's horn and everyone cheered. Renee was talking to Dixie through the driver's window and appeared to be passing on words of wisdom. The little crowd parted and Dixie drove the spluttering van out of the car park. With a puff of black smoke it disappeared into the traffic.

Nora was absentmindedly rubbing Bruce's head as he looked up at her adoringly. 'That's that then,' she said, feeling more bereft than she had expected to at the sight of her best friend setting off on a new adventure.

'Try not to worry about Dixie. I'm sure she'll be fine. Come on,' said Jay, giving her arm a squeeze. 'Shall we check out this little café, if I can get Bruce to find it again?'

'Thanks but there's something I need to do,' said Nora.

Nora had spent some time thinking things through about Benicio. It felt like the situation had moved on a bit from her quest. She could always come back to that but for now it felt like finding Benicio was the more pressing goal. Over a hundred people a week went missing in the UK and many were never seen again. She had briefly considered that he was no longer any of her business and she could just forget about it, but something kept niggling at her brain. From what the women at the gym had told her, it sounded like he had fallen on hard times. One in 182 people were homeless in the UK; was he now one of them? Just another statistic. He wasn't the sort of person to ask for help. He was the classic strong, silent type.

Nora put on her seatbelt. It wouldn't do any harm to drive over to Corby and see if she could find him. Right now she needed something to take her mind off Dixie travelling to goodness-knew-where in a mobile death-trap. Trying to track Benicio down, or at least find out what had happened to him, would be a distraction. She still had an old photo of her and Benicio together on her phone. He'd never liked his picture being taken but she'd managed to take this one on the sly and thankfully hadn't deleted it after the split. Her thoughts were interrupted by large paws thudding on to the side of the car and Bruce's furry face appearing at her window.

'Sorry!' said Jay. 'Are you sure you're OK?'

Nora twisted her lips. 'I'm just off to Corby to check on ex number six, Benicio.'

'Ooh, any chance you could give me and my furry *fiend* a lift? There's an excellent pet shop there apparently.'

She'd not been expecting that but she couldn't really say no. 'Sure. Get in.'

That was easier said than done. Bruce was very unsure about getting in the back of the car. They tried coaxing him but he just looked the other way. However, when Nora got out to give Jay a hand, the dog happily jumped in the driving seat.

'I'm guessing he doesn't have a licence,' said Nora.

'Only to drive a forklift,' said Jay. 'Now what do we do?'

Nora squeezed on to the seat next to Bruce and he conceded a little. 'Right, go on, over you go,' she said, pointing at the passenger seat, and happily he did as she asked. 'That was easier than I was expecting. Looks like you're in the back, Jay.'

Jay looked up the legal requirements for a dog travelling in the front seat. They secured Bruce, as he was already wearing a harness, switched off the airbag on his side and set off with the dog enjoying the view and Jay feeling slightly queasy in the back.

Their route took them through Rockingham and past the castle, and soon open countryside gave way to modern urban sprawl as they drove through Corby. Nora parked up.

'Shall I call you when I'm done and then we can meet back here?' she suggested.

'Or we could do it all together. Go to the pet shop and then do whatever it is you need to do?' Jay looked hopeful.

'Er, actually I'm hoping to track down Benicio but I don't know how long that will take. So if you wanted to get the train back rather than waiting for me, I'd understand.'

Jay pulled a number of faces. 'You saw what he was like with your car,' he said, nodding at Bruce. 'I don't think I'd get him on a train. Unless they'll let him drive it.'

'Then I'll message when I'm done. OK?'

'Of course. Good luck,' said Jay. He gave a little tug on Bruce's lead and the dog walked off in the opposite direction, taking a reluctant Jay with him. Nora decided to head for the park as that was the last place the woman said she had seen Benicio, and if there were other people sleeping rough then that might be a place to find someone who knew him. It was a sunny day and the walk was a pleasant one. It wasn't far to West Glebe park and it was nice to wander through the trees and watch the squirrels busying themselves. She did wonder what Bruce would make of them. There were a few folks about but mainly dog-walkers and people striding through on their way to somewhere else. Nora had a stroll around the perimeter while she considered her next move.

'Spare any change?' came a voice to her left. A man was sitting under the shade of a tree.

'Yes!' said Nora, making the poor man jump a little with her enthusiasm. She pulled a five-pound note from her purse and his eyes widened as he reached for it. 'Do you know this man? He might be sleeping rough.' Nora showed him the picture on her phone but his eyes were darting back to the five-pound note.

'I dunno. Are you police?' He was scanning her Wonder Woman T-shirt and black jeans.

'No, nothing like that.'

He took the note. 'Nope. Don't know him.'

'Please have another look. He's a friend of mine and I really want to help him.'

The man shoved the note in his pocket, licked his lips and then gave the phone screen his full attention. He squinted at it. 'Looks a bit like Benny but—'

'Yes! Benny! That would be him. Brilliant. Where can I find him?'

'And what would you want with him?' He eyed her suspiciously.

'I want to help him. We used to be close and I heard he was down on his luck and thought maybe I could do something. So if you have any idea where I might find him that would be hugely helpful.'

The man scratched his head. 'I'd have to have a think about that.'

'I kind of need to know now . . .'

He nodded at her purse. 'Oh right.' Nora didn't have a lot of cash on her. She wasn't used to having to bribe people for information. She tipped out all her change, which thankfully included a few pound coins, and handed it to him. He became busy counting his haul. Nora cleared her throat.

'All right,' he said without looking up. 'I've seen Benny going into a place off Saxilby Close behind the Lincoln.'

'A place? Can you be more specific?'

'There's a row of about five houses but the others are boarded up. This one is a squat.'

'Thank you, that's been really helpful.' Nora got out her phone and pulled up a map of the area. This time she was going on a proper Miss Marple mission.

12

Dixie was elated. This was her living the dream. Finally she was going places, unlike all those false starts. Countless times she had started a project only for it to fail or for her to discover that it had all been done before, like the time she thought she'd invented a new utensil. She still maintained that a foon was a much better name than a spork because that sounded like a sci-fi character.

She liked the whole vibe Elsie had, laidback and unhurried. And that was going to be her approach from now on. She was going to see all there was to see in the United Kingdom and do it at a leisurely pace. Partly because of Elsie's top speed, but also because people lived their lives at a million miles an hour so when they stopped for a coffee and a browse at her latest posts on Instagram they wanted to escape all that. Or at least that was what she was hoping.

Dixie knew she was going to miss people. That was the only niggle she had about her new venture. She'd made some good friends and she cherished them, but thanks to technology it didn't matter how far she roamed, they would still be just a phone screen away. Dixie sighed to herself. Everything was just about perfect.

Elsie began coughing and spluttering – even more than she had been. 'Come on, old girl,' said Dixie. She really couldn't have her conking out. Renee had given Dixie a whistlestop tour of the engine and other vital organs of the van but it had been a lot to take in, plus Dixie had been distracted by bunting – well, who wasn't?

When white puffs appeared in her rear-view mirror she told herself they weren't coming from Elsie. But when the smoke started billowing so much so that she couldn't see anything on the road behind her, she knew she had to accept there might be a teensy-weensy problem. She looked for somewhere to pull over but it was quite a busy road and there were no laybys or turnings. The van was losing speed and Dixie was starting to panic. She didn't want to be marooned on the A607. Thunking great lorries used this route and she had visions of one idly ploughing over little Elsie with her inside, which was possibly a little extreme but she did have a tendency to imagine the worst. At last she saw a small side road up ahead. She indicated and, as if onboard with the plan, Elsie slowed down for the turning.

Dixie was hugely relieved to be out of the traffic as the van rattled along the narrow country lane. She noticed the high hedgerows and lack of passing places and sent up a silent prayer to the gods of motoring that she didn't meet a tractor coming the other way. It felt like she had swapped one problem for another. There was still nowhere for her to pull over safely. The white smoke continued to billow out from the back of the van. Dixie's anxiety returned in a whoosh. She gripped the steering wheel. Why had she thought she could do this alone? What had she been thinking? When the rattling turned to limping, Dixie frantically scanned the lane for somewhere, anywhere she could stop. If it was someone's driveway then so be it.

As she came to some trees and bushes, a track was just visible and Dixie turned off. This was little used and the poor campervan bumped unhappily over the uneven terrain until a fateful bang erupted from the back and it stopped. 'Shit!' said Dixie, although there was a certain relief in being at a standstill. She got out and watched smoke pour from the back of the van. 'Gosh. Please don't be on fire.' All she had was half a cup of coffee and a bottle of mineral water to put it out with. Opening the van she grabbed the oven glove and used it to open the engine bay in case it was hot. She leapt out of the way as more smoke puffed out but thankfully there were no flames.

Panic started to subside. Elsie wasn't going to spontaneously combust and take Dixie with her. She'd had visions of dog-walkers finding four melted tyres and a pair of trainers. Crisis had been averted and she needed to be thankful for that. She was also pleased that she hadn't been streaming live when things had taken a turn for the worse. Looking around she could see better now the smoke from Elsie's back end had disappeared. She was on the edge of some woodland. There were a few trees and bushes on her right and then fields beyond but when she walked around the other side of the van it was a different story. It was thick woodland for as far as she could see. She looked up at the leaves and closing her eyes she heard all manner of birdlife chorusing. It was quite special. Perhaps this was where she was meant to be. A splat on her shoulder jolted her back to reality.

*

It took Nora far longer than she had expected to track down the squat, and now she was here she wasn't entirely sure what her plan was. The unloved building was down a dodgy-looking alleyway that was mainly garages and where industrial-sized bins went to die. There was a front door in various shades of old, peeling paint and windows too grimy to see through. Nora wasn't easily spooked but every fibre of her being was telling her this was not a good idea. Two per cent of the population were victims of violent crime annually. Was she about to become part of that statistic?

She didn't want to wimp out but she also had to apply caution. Her mother's voice was playing in her head. 'Nora, you have a head not a turnip. Use it.' If she knocked on the door, would anyone answer? Probably not. And apart from Benicio, who were the people who lived somewhere like this? There could be a wonderful group of people pleased to see her on the other side of the door, or she could be about to walk into a potentially dangerous situation. Even if it wasn't dangerous, why would they let her in? It was too much to hope that Benicio would answer the door. And it was hardly likely they were expecting a Deliveroo so the chances were they'd just ignore it anyway. For a moment she wished she'd been wearing her turquoise jacket.

She figured the only way she was getting in was if there was a window or door already open. The windows were boarded up. She put a hand on the door and gave it a shove. Much to her surprise the door clicked open. The time for thinking had passed. She pushed the door a little more and peered into the dark hallway before slinking inside.

Her heart was thumping, which made it hard to hear anything else other than her blood pulsing through her ears. Inside, her eyes took a moment to adjust as it was only lit by fading sunlight from the dingy alleyway. The hallway was full of cardboard boxes and she negotiated her way carefully around them across a carpet so sticky it seemed to want to come with her at every step. With all her senses on high alert she inched towards an open door at the end of the hallway.

She was shocked by what she saw on the other side of the door. To say the kitchen was dirty would be an understatement, but then she'd not been expecting Nigella's. Every surface was piled with rubbish. Bin bags of varying degrees of overflowing littered the floor and the smell of something rotting filled the air. Surely nobody lived here. That was when it dawned on her. Of course nobody lived here.

Nora's shoulders slumped. She'd been duped by the guy in the park. He might have recognized Benicio but he was hardly likely to give his address to a complete stranger. She could have been anyone. The revelation made her relax a little. She wasn't snooping around someone's home; this was clearly abandoned. The best thing she could do was leave. She inched back down the hall, but then she heard something upstairs. Footsteps perhaps? As she reached the bottom of the stairs her curiosity got the better of her. Either the house was empty, in which case it wouldn't matter if she looked upstairs, or was there still a tiny chance that Benicio was there?

Before she could overanalyse her thoughts, she crept upstairs. She'd just have a quick look around to double-check he wasn't there injured or ill, and then she'd go. That way she could leave safe in the knowledge that she'd tried to find him. At the top of the stairs she sensed there was something different. For one thing, it smelled better. There were a number of doors to choose from. Turning left she was careful to watch where she put her feet but up here were stripped boards and no smelly carpet. She pushed open a door and it creaked so loudly she almost shushed it. Her pulse picked up again. The room was dark so Nora put on the torch on her phone and shone it into the room. A bathroom. She was about to leave when she scanned the room with the torch a second time. It was a white suite and it was completely spotless. Something didn't add up.

'Stop!' shouted someone downstairs.

Shit! thought Nora, dashing into the bathroom and locking the door. The window was boarded up and she realized she was now trapped.

'Filth!' shouted someone.

On the landing there was banging, more shouting, and the sound of lots of feet on the floorboards.

'Help!' yelled a familiar voice.

Her heart thumping, she opened the door a crack but the door was shoved wide open and Nora was thrown backwards as Bruce barged in and covered her in doggy kisses.

'What the hell?' She scrambled to her feet and grabbed Bruce's lead, which was trailing behind him.

She peered out of the bathroom on to the landing to see the back of a large figure all in black who had pinned a scared-looking Jay to the wall.

What could she do? Thankfully Bruce didn't give her a chance to think. He sprang at the black-clad figure, barking wildly. Nora held on tight to his lead.

'Leave him alone or I'll let my dog rip you to pieces.' She hoped she sounded menacing enough.

'Nora, thank goodness!' said Jay as his assailant was distracted by the dog.

The black-clad figure spun around. 'Nora?'

'Benicio! Oh, thank goodness. Are you OK?'

'What the hell are you doing here?' he snapped.

Not quite the welcome she had been hoping for. 'I wanted to check you were all right.' It was good to see him, although her heart was still racing and she was a bit bewildered by the situation.

Benicio frowned hard at Nora, and at Bruce, who was straining on his lead.

'Er, sorry. Excuse me,' croaked Jay. Benicio still had his forearm across his throat. 'Would you mind . . .' Jay pointed at his neck.

'Who the hell are you?' he asked without loosening his hold.

'I'm Jay. I'm a friend of Nora's and that's my dog.'

'Oh crap,' said Benicio, releasing Jay and pulling the hood off his head. Jay slunk around to stand next to Nora and took hold of Bruce's lead. 'So there's no police?' asked Benicio, scanning their faces.

Nora and Jay shook their heads.

Benicio took a couple of paces one way then strode back, agitation radiating from him. The look he was giving both of them was making Nora increasingly uneasy.

'Deano!' shouted Benicio, which made Bruce bark. There was no reply.

'Who's Deano?' asked Nora.

'He's . . .' Benicio stopped talking. His jaw was rigid. 'It doesn't matter. He'll have run for it because, like me, he thought it was a police raid.'

'There was someone who went through that door,'

said Jay, pointing up the hall. 'I think he assumed that Bruce was a police dog and—'

Benicio strode to the door and ripped it open. Bright light flooded the landing, closely followed by an earthy smell. 'Deano!' he called again. 'Nope, he's long gone.' He slammed the door shut and spun around to stare at Nora.

Benicio always had a brooding look about him but right now he just looked cross. 'Why are you here?' he asked.

'Like I said,' she began. 'I heard you were sleeping rough and I thought maybe I could help you so I asked around and that brought me here.'

'Shit!' said Benicio sharply, making Jay jump. 'You have no idea what you've done, do you? This was a hugely delicate job. Some really serious criminals at the top of this food chain. And now arghhh!'

Jay took a step back and Bruce barked.

Benicio continued his rant. 'Eight months I've been working on this and for what? For you two clowns to bumble in here and balls it all up.'

Nora waved her arms. 'I don't know what you're talking about. I wanted to help you, that's why I came.'

Jay leaned forward and held up a finger. 'And I was worried about her so I followed her.'

'I don't think we deserve to be called clowns,' said Nora, feeling put out.

Benicio ran his hands through his unwashed hair. 'The other houses on this row are marijuana grow houses with a street value of about a million quid.'

'Bloody hell, Benicio. What have you got yourself mixed up in?' Nora's mind was racing. This was serious stuff.

He sighed heavily. 'I'm an undercover cop and you've just singlehandedly—' Jay cleared his throat and pointed at himself, making Benicio's eyes open wider. 'You *two* have wrecked the whole operation. The aim was to bring the people at the top of this to account.'

'Oh,' said Nora, unsure what else to say. 'How long have you been a policeman?'

'Eight years on the force. Three on the serious and organized crime team.'

To say this was a shock to Nora was an understatement. All the time they had dated he'd been in the police and she'd had no idea. She didn't know what to say.

'That's impressive,' said Jay. 'I thought about going into the police but—'

Nora gave Jay a nudge to shut him up. Now was not the time for small talk.

'But, Benicio, you're OK?' She just wanted to check.

Benicio shook his head. 'Yeah, great. Thanks for tracking me down like a stalker to ask me.'

'I think maybe we should go,' said Nora. Benicio didn't seem bothered either way.

'Sorry if we inadvertently messed things—' But Jay didn't get to finish his sentence because Bruce was already pulling him down the stairs.

13

Dixie had a dilemma. She could call a garage and get the van towed. But given the apartment was now rented out, where would she ask them to take her? It was a sad reality that she had very few options and Nora was really the only viable one. And while Nora was lovely, she couldn't stay with her indefinitely. She sighed as it dawned on her that the only sensible thing to do was to call her parents. Dixie looked at her phone. Her dad would say it was all right but she'd hear the disappointment in his voice. And her mum would be a flurry of activity as she sorted everything out for her. But that wasn't what she wanted. For once she had hoped she could stand on her own two feet.

Outside, the blue of the day was being rubbed out by the gentle lilacs and pinks of a cloudy sunset. The van was at least watertight, thanks to Renee's expert welding. She had all she needed, for a while at least. Maybe she didn't have to decide right now. She could give herself some time to think. Perhaps there was another option.

Dixie locked up the van and went for a wander. By

luck she had parked in a truly beautiful spot and now the smoke had stopped pouring from the van she could see all the different colours. Granted, they were basically multiple shades of green, but they were pretty all the same. She was glad she was wearing her trainers because her flip-flops would not have coped well with the undulations and debris of the woodland floor. There was a large stump nearby that she had to inelegantly climb over. She caught her toe and tripped, banging her shin on the stump.

'Bastard stump,' she snapped. She sounded like Renee. On closer inspection the stump was teeming with bugs and creepy crawlies, making her recoil and frantically brush all manner of mini creatures and dirt off her hands. There was no obvious path to follow and it didn't look like anyone had been through this way in quite a while. Excitement rushed through her. She was like an epic explorer discovering this tranquil place for the very first time.

She did a little filming for her followers and made out that it was a planned stop to enjoy the wilds of the countryside and maximize her experience of being at one with the natural world. Zooming in on the biggest mushrooms she'd ever seen growing on the side of a tree, she advised her followers not to eat such things in case they were poisonous. It was nice to think she was providing them with something informative as well as fun, plus she didn't want anyone suing her.

Slightly side-tracked by some pretty pink flowers,

Dixie found herself in an area where the trees weren't as dense and she could see fields stretching out beyond. Something else struck her. Dixie spun around to face the woodland. In the growing dark there was no sign of Elsie. She'd been walking for over thirty minutes and now she wasn't entirely sure which direction she'd come from.

Dixie gave herself a mental shake. She wasn't lost exactly, she just didn't know how to get back. The worst thing she could do now was panic, although at the thought of it her pulse unhelpfully picked up its pace. She had visions of Elsie coming to life, her headlights blazing as she made her way through the trees to find Dixie like the car in Harry Potter. But that wasn't going to happen. No one was coming to her rescue and that was good because for once she had to sort things out for herself. That, or they would find her emaciated body in a few months' time.

She knew it was the flowers that had brought her on this last section of her journey so she followed them in reverse, taking her deep into the wood, which was much darker than before. She was about to put her phone torch on when it flashed up it only had 10 per cent battery left. A few deep breaths were meant to calm her but they weren't really doing the trick.

'Don't be a wimp,' she said out loud. 'What would someone else do?' She thought of her friends. Renee wouldn't be fazed and seemed to have limitless skills so she would likely set up a shelter from bracken and ferns and sleep there after a gin nightcap. What would Nora do? She would have calculated the odds of getting lost and not ventured out in the first place, or laid a trail to follow back. The gift of hindsight was a wonderfully useless thing. The real question was: what was Dixie going to do?

She turned to the internet for counsel. Her happy followers liked a poll and they seemed keen for her to sleep under the stars. Lots of suggestions to switch on Google maps but there was no Wi-Fi and patchy network coverage. Someone else seemed to think she was Lara Croft because they suggested she machete her way out. But most commented on the pretty colours of the flowers. It was nice that she had these supporters in her phone. Even if their comments weren't that helpful, it made her feel less alone.

If she closed her eyes and listened . . .

Shit, no, that's dark and *scary!* she thought.

Closing her eyes was not a good idea. However, she was now aware of the distant thrum of road noise. From where she'd left the van, the main road was probably less than a mile away, so if she headed towards the noise she should be heading in roughly the right direction. It was a revelation and it filled her with confidence. She positioned herself and set off confidently. Immediately she tripped over a root and faceplanted a tree.

She stumbled around for the next forty minutes until it was completely dark. She glimpsed a sliver of moon before it was engulfed in cloud. It certainly wasn't enough to light her way. She'd not noticed before but it was getting colder. Enough to make her shiver and add to her low ebb. The scent seemed to have subtly changed from sweet and earthy to damp and decaying. This was no longer a fun adventure. Her phone began flashing insistently at her that she was almost out of battery. Best to save in case of emergency, she thought as she reluctantly switched it off. Now she felt totally alone.

*

Nora and Jay had not said much since leaving the house and the journey home had been particularly quiet, a silence thankfully broken every so often by Bruce, who liked to bark at things he saw out of the windscreen, like a furry canine sat nav. A police car with blue flashing lights and siren blaring came up fast behind them, making Nora grip the steering wheel and Bruce bark louder than before. For a moment she had a nasty feeling it was chasing her. Was destroying a police investigation an offence? She feared she was about to find out but the police car flew past. A glance in the rear-view mirror and Jay's wide eyes gave her the feeling he'd thought the same. They continued in silence. It wasn't that she was cross with Jay, it was more that it had all been such a lot to take in that it was easier to keep her thoughts to herself until she'd properly worked out how she felt about it all.

At last she pulled up outside Jay's place.

'Thanks,' he said, getting out and coming around to unbuckle Bruce. The dog flopped down on the passenger seat, reluctant to leave. 'Look, you don't have to talk about any of what happened today if you don't want to, but equally if you wanted to then . . .' He pointed at his front door. 'Maybe get a takeaway?' Jay and Bruce looked at Nora with similarly tilted heads and hopeful eyes.

What did she have waiting for her at home? A chameleon who was far more interested in crickets and the occasional episode of David Attenborough. She had recently noticed that he would train one eye on the TV if that was on.

'I mean, *I'd* quite like to talk about it,' said Jay.

'I definitely don't want to talk about it,' said Nora.

'No, nor me. Best forgotten. But did you fancy a pizza? The one you like with the little meatballs?' Bruce's tongue lolled out of his mouth. 'If not, I'll be eating it cold for breakfast so you could at least save me from that.'

'Yeah, go on then,' said Nora, taking the keys out of the ignition and opening the driver's door. Bruce decided he preferred that exit and got on Nora's lap in an attempt to get out of the car at the same time as her.

Jay hung on and found that he was about to be pulled on top of Nora. 'Here, you have his lead, that might be easier.'

'I can only see fur,' said Nora. 'Phht – and now I can taste fur.'

'Sorry.'

Nora took the lead as Bruce walked over her and out of the car, whacking her in the face with his tail before attempting to pull her out with him. She followed them into Jay's house, plucking fur off her top and out of her mouth.

She took off Bruce's lead and harness while Jay pretended to hunt for the takeaway menus but she suspected he used them more than he let on. They ordered pizza and Jay went to the utility. Bruce was there in an instant.

'It's his dinner-time too. I swear one day he'll eat the bowl. Watch this,' said Jay. He put a measured scoop of dry food from a bag on the worktop into a clean bowl and Bruce went up on his hind legs to try to snatch it. Jay held it above his head at the same time as he made a sort of yelping noise.

'You OK?' asked Nora.

'No I'm not. Look at him. I can't even put the bowl down.'

'You're getting him all excited,' said Nora, watching Jay and Bruce dance with each other like week one *Strictly Come Dancing* contestants.

'Bruce!' said Nora with authority. The dog spun in her direction. 'Sit.'

Bruce seemed torn between Nora and the bowl. 'Give me the food.' Nora took it from Jay, which meant she then had Bruce's full attention. He tried to jump up but she turned her back on him. 'Down. Sit.'

'Sorry, he's not big on commands,' said Jay.

'Only because nobody has taught him. Or he thinks he can get away with ignoring them.' Nora tried turning around but Bruce kept jumping up. However, Nora didn't give up easily. After five minutes Bruce seemed to be cottoning on and was now sitting and calming down. When at last she managed to put the bowl down without Bruce intercepting it, she told him, 'Good boy.' Bruce inhaled his meal in record time.

'Wow. Just wow. How did you do that?' asked Jay.

'Easy. Don't give in and don't be intimidated by him.'

'OK. I can do that,' said Jay, pulling back his shoulders. All he needed was a cape and he would have had the look of a superhero. He had thrown himself into dog ownership and she loved that he was looking for ways to overcome their issues.

The doorbell sounded and Bruce lurched at where Jay was standing, making him yelp and dive out of the way. The superhero moment was short-lived.

'Yeah, that may take some work but you'll get there,' said Nora, going to answer the door to the delivery man.

They munched their pizza in silence while Bruce chewed a toy and watched them closely.

'Did you hear about that job?' asked Nora, trying to extricate a slice of pizza from the box without losing any meatballs.

'I got the truck health and safety gig,' he said with mock pride. 'I'll be expecting a Bafta any day now.'

'Yay, that's good news.'

'Plus *Undercover Bullets* has been edited and they're

working out where it's being released, whether it's a streaming service or cinema. Tasha Blake has now done something with Leonardo DiCaprio.'

'Haven't they all?'

'Exactly. But it might be the publicity we need. And I got a text from Tasha today.'

'Ooh, first-name terms.' Nora grinned at him.

'Actually, I think it was from the publicist because it referred to me in the third person. But we're going to meet up when she's next in the UK.' He tried to cross his fingers and fumbled his pizza slice, getting sauce on his hands. Jay wiped his hand on a wet wipe. 'I feel like I need to explain why I was at the cannabis farm today.'

'It's OK,' said Nora.

'I'd kinda like to explain, if that's all right.'

Nora shrugged so Jay continued. 'I wasn't following you. Honestly I wasn't. Well, not intentionally. I wanted to go towards the pet store but Bruce was having none of it. He pulled and tugged and then he lay down. When I finally gave in, he took off and it was all I could do to keep hold of the lead and match his pace. I think he might actually be part greyhound. Anyway, Bruce dragged me to a park, where he was distracted for a couple of minutes with sniffing around trees and weeing . . . Anyway, while he was doing that I spotted you in the distance.'

'And that's when you decided to follow me?'

'Nope. No. Absolutely not,' said Jay. 'It was him.' He pointed at Bruce. 'He spotted you about ten seconds after I did. I then got dragged along. I'm amazed I have any soles left on my trainers. There is no stopping him. He's like a furry warhead. Personally I'm just glad he didn't see a squirrel because I would probably be stuck up a tree right now.'

Nora laughed. 'It's OK. I'm not cross that you followed me.'

'I know it's not OK because we messed everything up with Benito. But thank you for not blaming me.'

'It's Benicio,' she said. 'And I guess there's a lot I need to unpack about him.' She took a moment to eat a bit of pizza and order her thoughts. 'We dated for six months and he said he was a trouble-shooter.'

'Not a complete lie,' said Jay, although he was pulling a face.

'It *was* a lie, but I understand he couldn't tell me he was an undercover cop. But it still smarts that I didn't work it out. I didn't have a clue he was lying to me. That makes me wonder what else he lied about. Plus he never had time for me and would disappear without warning. And he definitely wasn't pleased to see me today.'

'To be fair, we had just blown his operation,' said Jay with a wince.

'I reckon he could front that out. We obviously weren't the police. I only went there because I thought he was homeless.' Nora dropped her pizza crust back in the box, making Bruce sit to attention.

'Oh right,' said Jay. 'I thought you went because he was one of your post-37 per cent?'

'Oh yeah, that too, he was number six.' It seemed like

a good moment for a recap. 'Salvador was number four. He's happily engaged with a baby. Hugh still has rampant toenail fungus and Benicio lies for a living.'

'So you must be done tracking down ex-boyfriends . . .' Jay was watching her closely.

Nora started to shake her head.

'. . . or almost done by now?' he asked.

'Nope. The rule is that after you've ditched the first 37 per cent you carry on reviewing each next option until you find a viable one. Which means there could be a lot more to check out,' said Nora.

Jay blinked.

'Well, not *a lot* exactly. Some. A few.'

Bruce lay down with a huff and Jay leaned back against the sofa making a similar noise. Nora pulled out another slice of pizza and sank her teeth into it. Now she was itching to update her spreadsheet.

14

Dixie hugged herself for both warmth and a little comfort. A blood-curdling screech behind her made her shriek and start running. Terror gripped her tighter than her own fingers digging into her sides. Only a madman would make a sound like that. She gasped for air. Both terror and running were impacting her breathing. She was going to die. But as a barn owl swooped silently past her she realized her mistake. Dixie stopped and bent over as she tried to catch her breath. A fit of the giggles didn't help but it was a release. Leaning back against a tree, Dixie waited until the laughter had subsided. She was a silly goose. What was she afraid of? There was nobody here. Probably no one around for miles. It was just her and the woodland animals. That was a nice thought. It sort of made her feel like a modern-day Snow White.

She carried on strolling through the wood, her eyes still struggling to see, even though they had adjusted a little. It made her more aware of things, like the sound of her trainers on the woodland floor, although the sound of a crunch wasn't a pleasant one. It wasn't an emergency but she did want to see what she'd trodden on so she whipped out her phone to have a quick look. Lifting her foot revealed a snail with a crushed shell. 'Whoops, I'm awfully sorry,' she said. She wondered if the snail would grow another one or if he'd now become a slug.

She waved her phone around for a couple of seconds and saw the plate-sized mushrooms on the side of the tree that she'd spotted before. This was definitely the right direction. The boost she got from this was like a natural high. Perhaps she wasn't completely useless. She hadn't thrown in the towel, she had sorted things out on her own and that made her incredibly proud of herself. A few more steps and she stumbled over a couple of logs, dodged the stump and there was Elsie. Dixie greeted her like an old friend. She was still congratulating herself when she heard a rustle in the bushes behind her. There was no breeze. Fear gripped her insides as she frantically unlocked the van, jumped inside and slammed the door shut. Her heart was racing as she peeped out of the window to see a fox trot by and disappear around the back of the van. Perhaps she wasn't quite Snow White yet.

Dixie awoke to the most beautiful birdsong and she felt privileged to hear it. Although a little more of a lie-in might have been nice. She'd survived the night and that was cause for celebration. Thanks to her power bank she now had a full phone charge but she was going to use it sparingly. While she was buoyed by her overnight adventure, she now had a decision to make. What should she do? The logical thing was to admit defeat and get the van towed, but the elusive alternative she had been hoping for began to seem possible. She could simply stay where she was. Elsie had almost everything she needed. A quick search on her newly charged-up phone showed her that she was less than three miles from a service station that had all manner of facilities, including free charging and the promise of a shower – it was a revelation.

Dixie brushed her long hair and applied the merest hint of make-up before doing a quick vlog about her decision to stay and explore the area. She had wandered off-piste a little when she began telling her followers that she would be foraging for food but she could probably argue that a trip on her scooter to the services shop was very similar. She unfolded her scooter and locked up Elsie. She was about to set off when she noticed something had been tucked under the windscreen wiper. Dixie automatically looked around. There was nothing and nobody for miles. Goodness, those leaflet advertisers went to great lengths to get your business. She pulled the piece of paper from under the wiper to find it was in fact a handwritten note:

This vehicle is parked illegally. Please remove it immediately.

There was an illegible scrawl underneath.

'Goodness me. How rude,' said Dixie, still looking around. She wondered when someone had put the note there. Perhaps it had been when she was asleep, which felt a bit creepy. Or perhaps someone had walked past when she had been out on her extended woodland trip last night. The paper was lined and torn on one side as if it had been ripped out of a notebook. Perhaps it was a joke. A dog-walker, perhaps, who thought it might be funny to leave a note like that. Because who else could it be?

*

Nora had had a full-on Monday at work and fancied a climbing session to de-stress. But first she was doing some searching for the next ex on her list – Liam. She'd not been able to find him on social media but he did have a LinkedIn profile that was quite impressive. Since they had dated he had got his accountancy exams and was now working for a big tech company. It was a promising start. She dropped him a casual message along with her contact details. All she could do now was wait and see if he replied.

There was no sign of Jay in the car park and he wasn't about when Nora came out of the changing rooms, even though he'd confirmed the night before that he'd meet her there. She'd put her phone in a locker, otherwise she would have messaged him. As she pondered whether to put her climbing shoes on or go and fire off a quick text to Jay, a large hand was waved in front of her eyes.

'Are you mesmerized by me?' asked Trent, flexing a biceps.

'No, but it's reminded me to defrost some chicken legs for dinner.'

There was a moment where Trent looked stern but when Nora smiled he began to laugh. 'You're funny. I like that you tease me. Banter is the same as flirting.'

'No, no it's not,' said Nora, going to get a harness.

Trent joined her and leaned in a little too close. 'Have you thought about my offer?'

'What offer was this?' she asked. 'Is there two for one on the cheap sausages at Aldi again?' She gave him a cheesy grin. She hoped he'd eventually get the message.

Trent pointed at her. 'Another joke. That's funny. But we could be—'

'Hiya,' said a flustered Jay, joining them. 'Sorry I'm late. I wasn't sure if I could come because I don't know how long I can leave Bruce.'

'Is he your boyfriend?' asked Trent, followed by a squeaky laugh that in no way matched his sturdy physique.

'It's his dog,' said Nora. 'He's a rescue. Before Jay, nobody wanted him. A bit like you, Trent.'

But Trent was distracted by a woman walking by in cropped Lycra.

'Do you think he'll be OK?' asked Jay, biting at a hangnail.

'Yeah, Trent has thicker skin than a stegosaurus.'

Jay gave her a long-suffering look. 'I meant Bruce.'

'Yeah I know. I'm sure Bruce will be fine too,' said Nora, tying her rope.

'But right now he could be eating his way through my furniture.' Jay seemed agitated.

'I didn't notice that he'd damaged anything at yours. Has he been chewing stuff he shouldn't?'

'No, but he's not really been left on his own before.' Jay leaned in as if about to confide something. 'But there are times when I have gone to another room and I walk back in and he sits up quickly and has a really guilty look about him.'

'Can a dog look guilty?' asked Nora, clipping on and handing the belay line to Jay.

'Absolutely. He also frequently looks like he wants to eat me. You saw how he was with his dinner. He could devour me in seconds if he wanted to, and he and I both know it.'

Nora laughed. 'I think sometimes you can be a bit of a glass-is-half-empty kind of guy,' she said, starting her ascent.

'Because the glass probably contains poison,' muttered Jay. 'And I think you'll find it's more to do with attending drama school, darling,' he added in Shakespearean tones.

She liked how Jay made her smile. He had a lovely way of lightening her mood.

Trent re-joined them and began climbing with the auto-belay at speed. He went for a hold at the same time as Nora and she almost lost her grip on the wall.

'You OK?' called up Jay.

'I am fine, thank you,' called back Trent.

'Arse,' said Nora.

After what turned out to be a fun session where Nora was pleased with a couple of the trickier routes she'd taken and Jay had done his usual steady climb, they were putting the equipment away. Trent was doing some lunges, his thighs bulging with the effort.

'Do you think anyone could make themselves look like that?' asked Jay.

'Why would anyone want to?' asked Nora.

Jay nodded at the three women glued to Trent's every move, although they appeared to be mainly looking at his backside. 'There have been a couple of roles recently that I didn't get and I wondered if maybe I need to bulk up a bit. Do some sculpting. That sort of thing.'

'You have no idea what sculpting is, do you?' asked Nora with a smile.

'Not a clue,' said Jay. 'But maybe a few more muscles wouldn't hurt.' He flexed his biceps under his sweatshirt and both he and Nora stared at it, waiting for something to happen.

'Yeah, maybe a bit wouldn't hurt,' she agreed.

15

They had all agreed that Crafting and Cocktails night should go ahead despite Dixie's absence and that they would take the cocktail-making in turns. Tonight Renee was in the hot seat and Nora already feared for her insides.

'I went for a classic,' said Renee, pouring from a large flask. 'Dirty Martini,' she added with a flourish.

Nora stared at the olive bobbing in her drink. A little swirl and the liquid adhered to the sides of the glass. 'It smells strong,' said Nora.

'Wait till you taste it,' said Renee with a sparkle in her eyes. 'Chin chin!' she added, closing her eyes as she took a sip. Nora and Jay waited. Renee smacked her lips together. 'Heaven in a glass.' The other two were still eyeing theirs suspiciously. 'Bloody hell. Come on. Bottoms up!'

Jay took a swig and started choking. 'Can't breathe,' he spluttered.

'Give him a pat on the back. He'll be fine,' said Renee, savouring another mouthful of her cocktail.

'You OK?' asked Nora, once Jay's hacking had reduced to a wheeze.

'See, I wasn't joking about the glass being half full of poison,' he said, still sounding hoarse.

Renee pointed at Nora. 'Are you not even going to try it?'

Nora felt it would be rude not to. She took a sip and the alcohol burned as it went down. 'Good grief. There's not much mixer in that.'

Renee chortled. 'It's gin and vermouth and the tiniest hint of the brine from the olives to make it dirty.'

'That's it?' asked Jay. 'No mixer?'

'Indeed,' said Renee, looking proud. 'And isn't it splendid?'

'Lethal, more like,' said Nora. 'I'll not be able to knit if I finish that.' She'd made the decision to reduce her slightly ambitious goal of a jumper for her dad's birthday down to a sleeveless sweater vest, but it still needed to be finished. 'I wonder if the Brownies next door have any lemonade I could put in it,' she added, thinking out loud.

Renee gasped. 'Damn sacrilege!'

'Or you could have mine.' Nora pushed her glass towards Renee.

'I'll not see it go to waste.' Renee swiftly tipped it into her own glass.

Jay put his cocktail down carefully as if he feared it would spontaneously ignite, which would not have surprised Nora. She was grateful the Brownies weren't having a campfire in the vicinity.

'Have you heard from Dixie?' asked Jay, glancing at Nora.

'Have you not been following her adventures in the Instant Gram?' asked Renee.

'You've signed up to Instagram?' asked a wide-eyed Jay.

'Absolutely. It's a fascinating thing. I have four Keanu Reeves accounts and a Prince Harry who keep telling me how beautiful I am.'

'You have to block those,' said Jay. 'I've had some weird ones recently. Probably bots, at least I hope they are.'

'I'm not worried,' said Renee. 'Worst case I'll get a restraining order. It won't be the first time,' she said with a wink.

'What has Dixie posted?' asked Nora.

'She's made her first stop and seems quite taken with the outdoors,' said Renee. 'Forests here are much safer than North America, no chance of bear or puma attacks. Dolly Parton and I once had our tent trampled by a rampant elk in the rutting season.'

'And one of the many reasons I prefer Leicestershire,' said Jay.

'I've had a few texts from Dixie.' Nora felt a little guilty that she'd not been following the Instagram posts, but she had messaged Dixie each morning and she'd sounded like she was enjoying every minute. They'd stuck to texts to preserve Dixie's limited battery life on her phone but Nora missed chatting to her friend.

She was pleased for her that she was living her dream, or one of them at least. The one where Dixie invented something better than the air-fryer was still probably some way off. Nora decided she'd give her a call when she got in.

It turned out Renee could actually knit faster after a few drinks and while she was meant to be showing Nora how to do the tricky bits around the neckline, before she knew it Renee had virtually finished it and all Nora had left to do was sew it up. Nora and Jay had both insisted on walking Renee home because after a flask of Dirty Martinis they weren't sure how she was still upright. That left them closer to Jay's place than to Nora's.

'You need to go that way,' said Nora, as Jay was still alongside her.

'It's OK. I'll walk you home.'

'There's no need to go that far out of your way and Bruce will be waiting for you. Go on, I'll be fine.' She could see he was reluctant to leave her. But it wasn't late so it was still light and there were people about so Nora calculated that her odds of being attacked were remote.

'If you're sure.' He bit his lip.

'Certain. I'll see you at climbing,' she said and she started walking off. After a few steps she checked over her shoulder and Jay was jogging towards his house. He'd obviously been keen to see if Bruce had done any damage. Nora smiled to herself and strolled on. It was a lovely evening and while she hadn't finished the Martini, the small amount of cocktail she had consumed had given her that chilled-out feeling. Her phone beeped and she was smiling as she pulled it from her pocket because she was sure it would be Jay checking she was OK. It was an unknown number. She stopped walking to investigate further.

She opened the text.

> Hey Nora, Long time and all that. I agree it would be good to reconnect. How are things with you?

She was surprised and delighted. The message was from Liam, who was ex number seven.

She pinged back a quick reply.

> I'm good. Still playing with numbers, which I see you are too. I've got my own place which is a bit odd on my own but I'm getting used to it. How are things with you?

She'd not gone far when her phone rang. Her stomach flipped. She'd not been expecting to speak to Liam. She took a deep breath and answered the call – it was Jay.

'What's up?' she asked. 'Has Bruce eaten your sofa?'

'I have no idea because he won't let me in my own front door. Listen.' Jay must have held the phone nearer to the door as all Nora could hear now was ferocious barking.

'He thinks you're an . . . Jay?' All she could hear was

barking. 'Jay! I can't have a conversation with Bruce.'
She waited longer than she would have liked to for Jay
to come back on the phone.

'Did you hear that?'

'Yes, he must think you're an intruder. Have you tried
talking to him?'

'I can't hear myself over that racket and I doubt he
can either. I don't know what to do.'

'It's OK. We'll figure it out. I'm heading your way
now.' Nora turned around and it wasn't long before she
reached Jay's house, where he was lying on the front
path trying to talk to Bruce through the letterbox that
inconveniently was at the bottom of the front door.

'Thank goodness,' said Jay, looking relieved as he got
to his feet. Bruce was still barking inside. 'Look at this.'
Jay put his key in the door and had only opened it a
crack before the door was slammed shut by the force of
the dog on the other side.

'You have to admit he's an excellent guard dog,' said
Nora. 'In some areas it's thought that homes with dogs
are a third less likely to be burgled.'

'Very reassuring,' said Jay, raising his voice to be heard
over Bruce. 'But I'm not a burglar.'

'Here, give me the keys and let me try.' Nora crouched
down to the letterbox because that was as far as she was
prepared to go. She opened it. 'Bruce.' The dog continued to bark. Nora leaned a little closer and shouted,
'Bruce!' The barking paused.

'That's amazing,' said Jay. Which set the barking off

again and Nora glared at him. Sorry.' Jay held up his palms and backed down his own front path.

'Listen, Bruce. I'm coming in and you need to be a good boy.' The barking stopped. Nora put the key in the door and opened it a fraction. A big black nose instantly appeared. 'Get ready to grab him if he runs out,' said Nora to Jay, who took up an exaggerated goalie pose. Nora put her hand through the gap in the door and started petting Bruce while talking to him gently. She then slipped inside the door and shut it behind her. Bruce tried to jump up but she commanded him to sit. When he eventually did, she gave him a big fuss.

'You are such a good boy.' Bruce flopped on to his back in the hope of a tummy rub. 'Let's see how much of the house you've eaten.' She went to investigate and Bruce followed dutifully at her side.

'Er, hello,' came the faint voice from outside. 'Any chance you could let me in please?'

Nora shut Bruce in the kitchen and came back to let Jay in. 'Oh thank goodness,' said Jay, seeming genuinely relieved. 'I thought he'd eaten you.'

'Bruce is a pussy cat.'

'I wish he was. Actually I wish he was a guinea pig. I'm sure they're a lot easier to manage and far less likely to gnaw on my leg bone while I'm sleeping.'

'You still having that dream?' asked Nora.

'Yeah,' said Jay with a whole body shiver.

Sometimes Nora couldn't help smiling at Jay. 'The good news is Bruce hasn't done any damage. Well, none that I can see. Relax. You've got this.' She handed him back his door keys. 'Night.'

'Bye,' said Jay, holding the keys to his chest.

'Night, Bruce!' called Nora and the dog started barking. She took that as her cue to leave. As she stepped outside her phone beeped with a reply from Liam.

I'm single too. It sucks.

*

Dixie was almost tearful at the sound of Nora's voice. It had only been a couple of days but she was starting to understand why lonely people went to the supermarket daily just so they could speak to someone. Dixie was a talker. Sometimes she overshared but she was one of life's chatty people and spending hours alone in a defunct campervan was not something she was enjoying.

'Nora, how are you? How was Crafting and Cocktails? How are Jay and Renee?' she asked.

'That's a lot of questions,' said Nora with a chuckle. 'I'm good. I had a bit of a drama with Benicio and a cannabis house but I'll tell you about that in a mo. I've tracked down another ex called Liam. Renee made a lethal Martini that could strip paint so when you get to that stage with Elsie, let me know and we'll send you some. Jay is having a battle of wills with Bruce and the dog is currently winning by a mile. I think that's everything from my end. How about you?'

Dixie stalled for a second. She had a choice to make. Nora was her closest friend. Could she tell her the truth? She certainly felt like offloading everything would make her feel better. But was it going to help? She feared Nora would try to fix things and the only way to do that was for Dixie to give up and she definitely didn't want to, well, not just yet anyway. Although sitting there with only a tealight for company, she suspected she wouldn't be able to hold out for much longer. She took a deep breath and put a smile on her face. She'd once worked briefly in a call centre where they insisted that everyone smile while they were on calls because they believed it made a difference to how you came across. It was the weirdest place she'd ever worked. Rows and rows of depressed minimum-wage individuals all grinning into space.

'I am still fabulous. We're great, me and Elsie. We are enjoying escaping the rat race and appreciating the simpler side of life. It's quite a revelation, being on my own. Although, I'm not entirely sure I am on my own because I keep finding notes under the windscreen wiper. I've had two so far. One told me to move Elsie and the second one threatened to have her clamped. How rude is that?'

'Um, it's not nice, but I'm thinking that maybe you should just move on to somewhere friendlier,' suggested Nora.

'But that would be giving in to the system,' said Dixie with conviction. 'I won't be bullied by the patriarchy.'

'Is it a man leaving the notes then?'

139

'I don't know, but they have that sort of arsey-bloke tone about them. Clearly it's some old man dog-walker who doesn't like me parking here. But it's a public right of way in a woodland so he can't stop me and I won't be intimidated.'

'Good for you. But do be careful.'

'I am. You don't need to worry about me,' said Dixie, finding it hard to maintain her call-centre smile.

16

Nora loved her parents but they were like wasabi – best in small amounts. It was her dad's birthday, which meant her mum would have been cooking all day and the house would be full of their friends and neighbours. The noise levels were already quite high when Nora got there and her arrival only added to the cacophony. Her mother welcomed her and announced to everyone that Nora had arrived like she was the entertainment. On some level she often felt like she was. She found her dad hiding in the garden.

'Happy birthday, Dad.' She threw her arms around him, and he hugged her back.

'I am so pleased to see you. You are my most favourite person.'

Nora was suspicious. 'Why?'

'Because your mother, she tell me I can't have a beer until Nora is here.'

Nora gave him a look. 'I've got presents for you. They're better than beer.'

'Are they wine?' he asked, looking hopeful.

Nora playfully thumped him on the arm.

'I will love them whatever they are,' he said, taking them from her. She hoped he was as good as his word because she'd put a lot of time and effort into the sweater vest. Her mother came outside to join them.

'Ali, you have guests,' scolded Una.

'I know. That is why I am out here,' said Ali, pulling a face.

But her mother was better practised at the art of communication using only a look, and the one she was giving them at that moment had them both bustling inside without further comment.

Ali perched on the arm of the sofa and Nora found a place to sit on the floor. Una shooed next door's children out of the chair so she could sit there and they joined Nora on the rug but Nora still had a good view of her dad. First he opened her safe present. She could never go wrong with coffee. It was like a sacred ritual in their house. Ali nodded sagely at the coffee beans Nora had bought him and his favourite biscuits to have with his coffee. He opened his card and passed it straight to his wife, who carefully read every word of the verse. Nora had tried to explain that nobody really paid a lot of attention to the verses in cards but her mother didn't agree. 'If that was the case, then why are they there?' her mother had argued. Nora had learned that a well-chosen card could have her mother shedding a tear, which always meant extra Brownie points for Nora. She was torn between watching her mother read the card and her father opening his next present.

Ali completed his task first. 'What do we have here?' he asked, as he carefully removed the woollen item from its wrapping paper. He held it up and studied it. His expression seemed to be still asking the same question. He looked around the garment to Nora for an explanation.

'It's a sweater vest. A tank top. It's like a jumper but without any sleeves,' she said. The many faces in the room looked at her blankly. 'You can wear it over another top like a shirt.'

'OK,' said her dad. She could see he was trying hard to be positive about it.

'I made it. I knitted it all myself.' She wobbled her head. 'With a bit of help from a friend but mainly I did it on my own. It's the first thing I've ever knitted,' she said to the assembled faces. 'Try it on, Dad.'

Her dad's expression changed to one of utter pride. He got his head and arms in all right but then it ground to a halt. Perhaps Nora had misjudged the sizing. 'Give it a tug,' suggested Lilian-from-next-door, who was sitting next to her father. She helpfully pulled the garment down. While the intention was to pull it down, it first needed to go over Ali's rotund middle section – something Nora hadn't accounted for. He had embraced life in Melton Mowbray and was a regular at Ye Olde Pork Pie Shoppe. She could see her dad was holding his breath. He looked like he was wearing a knitted corset and she feared for the sweater vest when he finally breathed again. There was a tear on her mother's cheek

143

but Nora didn't know if it was from the card or the state of her daughter's knitting.

The rest of the evening was filled with chatting, laughter and many cups of coffee once they had managed to wrestle Ali out of his sweater vest without doing him or the top any permanent damage. Nora's phone pinged with a text from Liam and she was about to read it when her mum flicked the light switch and plunged them all into darkness. Nora would have to read it later. Una carried in a cake with a single candle on top and started a round of a traditional Bosnian birthday song that only she, Ali and a couple of others there knew, so everyone else just sang happy birthday. Ali blew out his single candle and everyone clapped.

Nora had a quick look at her phone.

Hey how's it going?

It was a good sign that Liam was messaging her unprompted. She fired back a quick reply.

Visiting my parents. How about you?

Slices of cake were passed around and Nora had just taken a large bite of her piece when her mother asked the dreaded question. 'So, Nora, how is the husband-hunting going?'

Everyone stopped to listen. It was like those moments in werewolf films when the stranger walks into the busy local pub and it goes completely quiet, only here there was cake and no mythical beasts. It was made worse by the fact that Nora needed to speedily finish her mouthful of cake before she could answer. There was a nanosecond where she considered revealing the 37 per cent rule but she dismissed it. Her parents would likely not understand but, more importantly, Nora did not want to reveal to them just how many boyfriends there had been.

She slapped on a smile, then worried that she might have chocolate cake on her teeth and stopped. 'I'm not husband-hunting, Mum, and you know that. I'm fine as I am.'

'Alone?' said her mother.

'But I'm not alone because I have Oliver.'

'Is that the praying mantis?' asked Lilian-from-next-door.

'Yes,' said Una with a sorrowful shake of her head. 'What message does that give to a man? I'm going to gobble you up.'

'It gives no kind of gobble message to anyone.' Nora blinked a few times due to the horror of finding herself repeating 'gobble' in a sentence to her mother. 'And Oliver is a chameleon.'

'It's the same thing,' whispered Una to Lilian, as she indicated swirling eyes.

'No, it's not. *He's* not.'

'He's also not a man though, is he?' said Una.

'Dad, help me out here,' said Nora, but Ali was suddenly

fascinated with his sweater vest and was either trying it on for a second time or was trying to hide inside it.

*

Jay decided he was going to take the bodybuilding plan seriously. Perhaps with a beefier physique he would have more leading-man potential, and it could only help when it came to impressing women. Muscly legs would also be a bonus for climbing. And there was the other incentive – he might actually be able to manage his dog.

According to the dog behaviour gurus on the internet, proper exercise seemed to be the answer to all of their problems. A tired dog was a happy one and apparently less likely to pull when on the lead and more likely to respond to commands. Jay was up for giving it a try.

A short drive brought him to a farm and for a small fee Jay had been shown to a huge empty paddock. Armed with treats, which he had let Bruce sample, he took a deep breath and let Bruce off the lead. Bruce raced off and in between sniffing he bounded about. Jay decided to see if he could get Bruce to come back on command. He got out the treat and called his name. Bruce stopped sniffing whatever he was sniffing and looked in Jay's direction – progress indeed. Jay waved the treat and called him again. Bruce began trotting towards him and Jay felt like the dog whisperer. But it was short-lived. Something caught the dog's eye, or nose, and he raced off to the left. Jay wasn't worried because this was a fully enclosed space. Apparently Bruce hadn't read that part because in a stride and a scramble he cleared the fence and was gone.

'Shitting hell,' said Jay, breaking into a sprint.

Jay ran around the farm, looking and calling for Bruce. He was also keen to find the man who had eagerly taken his money because his secure field was no such thing. He saw someone near some stables, quite a way from the dog area. By now Jay had a stitch, which was making him walk like that time he'd worn high heels on stage in a production of *The Rocky Horror Picture Show*. He waved as he got closer and the man waved back. Jay's waving became frenzied and with a frown the chap came over.

'You're not meant to leave them on their own,' he said.

Jay took a moment to catch his breath. 'I didn't. He left me. Over your secure perimeter.'

The man seemed astonished. 'Really?'

'Yes, why else would I be looking for my dog? He could be anywhere.'

'Don't worry. We'll find him.'

After another twenty minutes of searching, Jay was frantic and losing hope. They found themselves back at the secure dog-walking area. 'Did you actually see him escape?' asked the man.

'Well, obviously I did. I was watching him when he . . .' But Jay didn't finish the sentence because the man was pointing into the middle of the paddock where Bruce was lying down, panting.

'What the hell? He wasn't there before. He definitely escaped.' But the man was already walking off, shaking his head.

Great. Was there nothing Bruce wouldn't do to make him look like an idiot? 'Heel, Bruce,' said Jay, getting out the treats, although he had no idea why he was rewarding his behaviour. Bruce raced to Jay, devoured the treat in a nanosecond and ran off before Jay could grab him. On his way past, Bruce brushed Jay's leg. Jay felt the sensation of something dripping down his calf. When he looked down he could see it was a brown liquid. It was at about the same time that he smelt it.

'Good grief. What the actual . . . Bruce!'

Jay scrambled around to find a tissue to wipe the offending substance off his leg. The dog came back to sit in front of him. He looked happy. His tongue was lolling out of his mouth. 'Bruce, you reek!' Jay clipped on his lead. Now Bruce was closer he was not only smellier but Jay could also see that his once black dog was now more black with a wet coating of brown.

From outside the area the man came striding over. Jay waited in anticipation for the moment the smell hit him. 'Shit!' said the man, recoiling.

'Exactly what I think it is too. So you tell me how he's got covered in it if he didn't leave the secure area?' Jay folded his arms and then remembered the poo-soaked tissue in his hand so unfolded them quickly.

'Where on earth . . .' Although the expression on the guy's face changed to that of someone who had worked something out. 'Oh dear. I think he's been for a swim in our cesspit.'

Jay wanted to forget everything about the journey home and the state of his car boot. It would be a long time before he would be putting his shopping in there. The smell would wilt any salad. And now he had got Bruce home he had to work out how on earth he was going to get him into the bath, which was up a flight of light grey carpeted stairs. Bruce glared at his owner.

'Don't look at me like that. You did this. Why would you go for a swim in someone else's poo?' Jay couldn't help the involuntary retch that followed the sentence. He'd been doing that all the way home, even though he'd had all the windows open.

Bruce barked his reply. There really was only one way to get him upstairs and that was for Jay to carry him.

He steeled himself and faced his poo-drenched nemesis. Bruce's nose twitched and he looked around, sniffing the air.

'The smell is you, mate. You absolutely honk,' said Jay, his gut churning. It was no good, he'd have to hold his nose. But then how would he lift the dog? Jay took a clothes peg and attached it to his nose. It pinched a bit but it definitely helped. Bruce gave him a quizzical look. Now all he had to do was pick the dog up.

Jay approached the canine in the same way he had once tried to lift a barbell weight at the gym. Legs apart and almost in a squat position. Jay was quite pleased with his posture. Bruce backed away. Jay waddled a couple of steps towards him, making his thighs start to burn. 'Stay still,' instructed Jay. Bruce dodged. This was useless.

17

Dixie returned from her almost daily trip to the service station. Going on her scooter was probably a good workout but it was only exercising one leg and she had fears that she'd end up lopsided with one chunky leg and one skinny one. She picked up the scooter and walked the last few metres into the woodland. It was too bumpy to ride over anyway. Up ahead, through the trees, she thought she saw a flash of colour. A bird perhaps. Or was it a dog-walker? Dixie crept up to the side of Elsie and peered through one side of the cab. Her view was a little grubby but there was nothing to see. That was until something else grabbed her attention. Another note on the windscreen.

She stomped around the van and snatched the piece of paper. The note read:

Either move this vehicle or I will inform the council and have it towed away. You have 48 hours to comply.

And there was a scrawly signature on the bottom. Heck, thought Dixie. Maybe this was more serious than she'd realized. But it was still very rude. She did a short video showing the note and expressing her dismay at the powers-that-be trying to end her adventures, and hastily posted it on social media. Perhaps if she could find the person who had been leaving the notes she could have a sensible conversation with them and explain her situation. She would like to move the van but that wasn't currently possible without her feeling a failure and disappointing her parents. At least if she could manage to make her adventure last a bit longer it wouldn't look like she'd given up at the first hurdle. And now she had used the showers at the services she felt she could definitely manage a few more days. She put the scooter in the van, locked it up and with the note in her hand Dixie set off to find who was leaving the rude messages.

It was a glorious day and the way the sun came through the trees in bright rods was fascinating. She walked at a brisk pace in the hope that she would catch them up but that was only going to work if she was heading in the right direction, and apart from the tiny flash of colour she'd seen she had no idea if she was on the right track. Scanning the trees ahead it was clear there was no sight or sound of anyone else. After a while she slowed her pace and became distracted by nature. In the past she had paid to be this zen. She'd done quite a few lovely retreats: yoga, meditation, wellness and even ayahuasca. There were similarities between her current situation and the ayahuasca retreat. That one had been held in a forest near Torremolinos, where they slept on straw in open tents. It had been sort of like all the other retreats put together but with cleansing drinks containing plant medicines and led by a shaman called Galaxy, although she had overheard other staff call him Stan. With hindsight, it may not have been completely legit. There were parts of that week she didn't remember at all, but she could vividly recall being chased by a giant blue marshmallow. Living in a wood with Elsie was definitely better than that, and cheaper too.

Dixie came to the area where the trees thinned out and she could see further ahead. There was no sign of anyone else. Her shoulders sagged a little. She didn't want to get towed away and she was sure there was an easier way to resolve the problem. Something caught her eye and distracted her. A squirrel. Dixie stayed completely still so as not to upset the creature. She watched as it sniffed the ground, dug a hole and then moved on. It looked like the poor thing was searching for food. A pigeon landed nearby and spooked the squirrel and it disappeared up a tree at lightning speed. There was nobody here except her and the wildlife.

Back at the van Dixie had an idea. If she left a nice reply under the windscreen wiper, hopefully when the person returned and read it they would be mollified and a little more understanding. She set about writing a note. It took a few goes but she was pleased with the final version.

To Whom It May Concern, I am truly sorry if I have upset anyone by staying in this beautiful spot. I'm afraid I am not here by choice. My campervan is old and ailing and sadly chose this peaceful place to rest for a while. I am behaving in an eco-friendly manner and I'm disposing of my rubbish responsibly. I respect the green cross code and nature. I am hoping that you will understand my predicament and let me stay here a little longer while I enjoy the tranquillity and serenity of the woodland and work out how best to get my van fixed. Yours truly, Dixie Pike.

She reread it and added her mobile number because she had yet to be there when any notes had been left. This way they could contact her without having to leave another snotty message. Dixie folded it up and tucked it under the wiper. That was one job done for the day. What to do now? She had got talking to the lady in the shop at the services, who had told her about a farm not too far away that had a makeshift shop at reasonable prices. Dixie loved the idea of food straight from the farm and as she literally had nothing better to do she decided to track it down.

*

Nora had laughed so hard she was struggling to get her breath. Jay was sitting on her sofa waiting patiently for her to get things under control.

'That's not even the worst of it,' said Jay, who was retelling the poo-nami story. 'While I was trying to work out how to lift him, he trotted into the hallway and he shook himself. Like proper full-on, top-to-tail, shake-all-that-he-owned shook himself. And all I could do was watch as he redecorated my walls with someone else's poo.'

Nora tried to stifle the laughter but it was impossible. 'That's awful,' she said at last.

'Awful? You have no idea.' Jay splayed his hands for emphasis. 'The stench. The coverage on everything.'

The thought of it made Nora feel less giggly and more sympathetic to Jay's situation. 'I bet it took hours to sort out.'

'It did. It took absolutely ages. But I had to leave it initially—'

'To ferment?' asked Nora with a splutter.

Jay rolled his eyes. 'So that I could wash Bruce.'

'How did you get him clean?' She was already quite impressed that Jay had taken on bathing the dog by himself.

Jay's head flopped to one side. 'In the shower.'

'You gave the dog a shower?'

'Well, I had to get in there with him. He can't operate it on his own and he needed a proper shampoo. That coat was full of . . . liquid. It took half an hour of constant cleaning and half a bottle of doggy shampoo.'

'Were you naked?'

'What sort of perv would that make me? No, I had my rubber duck swimming shorts on.'

Nora was laughing again thanks to the image this

155

conjured up. 'I'm sorry but that is the funniest thing.' A quick look at Bruce and he appeared to be grinning at her.

'I'm pleased someone is finding it funny. I'm sure I will too, in about thirty or forty years,' said Jay. 'I think I've got some sort of shit PTSD because I swear I can still smell it. Can you smell poo?' Jay leaned forward. 'Be honest.'

Nora sniffed the air. She inched a little closer and sniffed harder. 'Nope, you smell poo-free.' He actually smelled really nice.

'Thank goodness for that. Anyway, how's things with you?'

'I got totally ambushed at Dad's birthday as to why I am still single. But Dad loved his sweater vest. I might make it for him again but a few sizes bigger so that it actually fits him.'

'Good idea,' said Jay, nodding sagely. 'And the ex-boyfriend strategy. How's that going?'

Nora felt a squiggle of something in her gut. 'I tracked down Liam and we've been messaging.'

'Liam, is he the one who dumped you, like the only person who has ever dumped you?' asked Jay.

'Not the only one. There was Nicholas Badcock.'

Jay snorted a laugh. 'That's not a nice nickname.'

'Badcock is his actual surname. And anyway we were twelve so I can't comment on his anatomy.'

Jay got himself comfortable. 'OK. Let's start with Nicholas. Why did he dump you?'

'Abby Hobbs offered to share her doughnut with him if he went out with her so he told me I was chucked.'

'Shallow Master Badcock. Although . . .' Jay pouted. 'What sort of doughnut? Because if it was jam and fresh cream then I'd do the same.'

Nora whacked him with a cushion. 'It wasn't fresh cream. It was that awful bright white plastic-tasting stuff.'

Jay tilted his chin. 'Still, any doughnut is pretty good,' he said, taking another cushion to the head. 'And why did Liam end your relationship?'

Nora took a moment. 'Because I put weedkiller on his sticky willy.'

18

Nora didn't want to rush things with Liam but she also didn't like waiting. Since she'd tracked him down he had been occupying a lot of her thoughts. Being dumped by him had been a shock and an unhappy time in her life. She'd often been compelled to end relationships at the merest hint that things weren't perfect for fear of being dumped herself. Perhaps it was a reaction to frequently being dropped by girls at school. Walking away first was a way to control the outcome, so it was a shock to have it happen to her. But that was a while ago and as long as she could look past Liam ditching her then perhaps there was something there. He was a good person and she was certain that he no longer held a grudge against her for what she did. Well, almost certain.

She had had to explain what happened to a rather concerned Jay, who had instantly crossed his legs at the mention of her killing her ex's sticky willy. Liam's sticky willy, otherwise known as a cleavers plant, was growing in a tub in his garden. Nora had always assumed these plants, so loved by schoolboys for sticking to school jumpers, were weeds. This one was big and bushy and occupying a nice corner. She thought she would kill it off and buy him something prettier to go in its place. Nora didn't get as far as choosing a replacement because Liam was distraught that the plant he'd grown from one at his beloved great-nana's house had mysteriously died. When she had owned up to killing it he'd called her a murderer and demanded she leave. Apparently he had fond childhood memories of him and his cousins playing with the sticky weed and hoped one day his children would be able to enjoy the same. Even a couple of days to calm down didn't change his feelings about the dead plant or Nora, and he'd dumped her.

That was all behind them and now they needed to arrange a much-needed catch-up. Perhaps if she suggested a daytime meet-up they could have a coffee and she could start to assess if there was anything worth pursuing. If it hadn't been for the sticky willy incident, who knows how their relationship would have gone? From the look of Liam's profile picture, he was hotter than ever. Looks were definitely not the most important thing but they were a nice bonus. In the photograph he was very corporate-suit but it helped that she already knew the muscular physique underneath. Actually, she quite liked the idea of dishevelling his corporate image. She shook that thought from her mind. She was getting ahead of herself.

It was late evening and she was in bed. It was a hot

night and she'd taken to sleeping in just her pants. She had nobody else to think about and she always put on her dressing gown before she went downstairs so she wasn't likely to scare Oliver or the neighbours. It started to rain against her window – perhaps that would take some of the heat out of the day. Nora mulled over what to say to Liam and if it would come across as desperate. She didn't want to scare him off. It was best not to think too much about it so she quickly sent Liam a message.

How about we meet up for coffee and a catch-up sometime soon?

She pressed send before she could overthink it.
An almost instant reply popped up.

Sure. Remember this?

And there was a link. A click took her to his Instagram and a picture of the bar they used to go to. She checked out his Instagram grid. He wasn't using his real name – he was FootyfanLiam. No wonder she'd not been able to find him. She liked the post and began casually scrolling through his feed. A message arrived from him but this time it was via Instagram. It was basically just a row of beer emojis. Was he suggesting they go out for a drink? She replied:

I'm more of a cocktail person these days

And then she waited. And she waited. If he was out he'd likely be drinking so perhaps she'd not get a reply tonight. Nora yawned. She must have started to nod off because she felt her phone slipping from her grasp. She gripped the phone and blinked a few times as she came to. She looked at the screen. It was moving. What was she watching? It was Liam in a dark room. His mouth was moving but there was no sound. And he was pointing frantically at the screen. That was when she noticed the tiny square in the top corner that was her. When she'd gripped the phone she must have inadvertently started a video call. There she was, video-calling with Liam – topless.

'Shit!' She panicked and ended the call.

*

The weather had taken an unfortunate turn from the wall-to-wall sunshine Dixie had been enjoying and was tipping it down with rain and blowing a gale when she returned to Elsie. She'd been back a few hours before she had realized the note she'd left had gone from the windscreen. What she didn't know was whether it had blown away or someone had removed it. She'd dashed out of the van to check if it was on the ground nearby and was quickly soaked to the skin. But the note was nowhere to be found.

Dixie spent another lonely evening in the van. Her damp clothes hung over the front seats, making the windows steam up. She'd made herself a sandwich, which was now her main food source, and tucked herself up in bed, trying hard not to feel sorry for herself. The sound of the almost tropical rainstorm outside was a bit creepy but she had no choice other than to stick it out.

She thought of Nora. Nora hated storms. That was all the motivation she needed to ring her.

'Hiya, Dixie,' said Nora. 'Is everything OK?'

Dixie was so happy to hear her friend's voice. 'Sorry it's late but I know you hate storms so I thought I'd give you a call and check you're OK.'

'Is it raining much where you are?' asked Nora.

'Yeah, it's torrential,' said Dixie, although that was a bit of an exaggeration because now she was peering behind the threadbare curtains it didn't actually seem that bad. Perhaps the sound was magnified by the van.

'It's raining a little but it's still pretty warm here,' said Nora. 'Are you OK?'

'I might be a tiny bit homesick but I'll be fine.' Dixie swallowed hard to stop getting overemotional.

'I'll cheer you up,' said Nora. 'You'll never guess what I've just done to Liam.'

The next morning Dixie was woken by birdsong. Outside the window the sun was shining and the sky a flawless blue. It was as if the storm had never happened. Chatting to Nora had cheered her up. She'd made Dixie laugh about accidentally flashing one of her exes, which made Dixie feel better about things. Frequently she felt she was the silly one in any given group of people. The person most likely to say or do the wrong thing. It was always reassuring when someone considered to be the sensible one messed up. Dixie was still smiling to herself as she checked her Instagram. Her followers had been increasing steadily. They definitely seemed to be liking the nature posts, but for some reason the post of the angry note had got some serious engagement, and she had to blink hard to take in how many followers she now had. A lump formed in her throat. Almost five thousand people were now following her Instagram account and countless more had liked the post, with many commenting with support and solidarity and quite a lot of swearing too, which she thought Renee would approve of.

Outside the window something moved quickly and it caught Dixie's attention. She pulled back the curtain to have a closer look. It was a squirrel. She had no idea if it was the same one from the other day. They all looked the same to her, although now she watched it happily bounding about and scratching at the ground, she noticed that its head was more of a reddish colour than its grey body and the end of its tail was blunt. She pulled out her phone and started filming. This was the sort of content her followers loved. And now she had so many, there was pressure to keep them entertained.

The squirrel obliged and hopped gymnastically about before digging something up and eating it. Its front paws were like little hands – it was adorably cute. Dixie decided that she would take something out for the squirrel to eat. She checked her food supplies. It was unlikely that squirrels ate sourdough crackers or tapenade so she settled on a couple of grapes.

Dixie opened the sliding door slowly in an attempt to keep the noise to a minimum. Previously she'd not really paid too much attention to the sound the door made but now that she wanted it to be quiet it sounded like a small train trundling along a track. Opening it just enough to squeeze herself through the gap, she crept around the side of the van but the squirrel was nowhere to be seen. She locked up and decided to see if she could track down the squirrel and give it the grapes. Perhaps she could even tame it. That would look great on social media and was the sort of thing that regularly went viral.

As she tiptoed through the wood she saw plenty of birds but no sign of the squirrel. She stopped skulking about and strolled on, keeping an eye out for any cute woodland creatures she could befriend. She'd not gone far when she felt the plop of raindrops on her skin. Not a drizzle, it was proper big sploshes and she knew she needed to head for cover. It was time to turn around and leg it back towards Elsie. She could see the van and was almost at the stump when the squirrel appeared. Even though it wasn't great timing Dixie wasn't going to miss a chance to get good quality footage. She pulled out her phone as the rain got heavier. The squirrel scampered across a large tree trunk then sat on the stump to study Dixie. Dixie zoomed in and it looked great. Maybe she could get closer. She crept towards it and the squirrel's tail twitched. Then it started making a horrid screeching noise in ear-splitting bursts. This wasn't the cosy content she was after.

Perhaps if she tried to coax it she might be able to give it a grape. 'Psst, psst, psst,' said Dixie, trying to sound friendly. The squirrel seemed startled and leapt towards her. 'Argh!' screamed Dixie and she backed away and stopped filming. She daren't turn and run in case it attacked her from behind. She reversed away until she backed herself up against a tree. The squirrel hopped a little closer and screeched at her in between wagging its tail. It was not the cuddly encounter she'd been hoping for and now she was feeling trapped.

'Hey!' shouted someone, making Dixie look up. It was like a scene from a film as a gorgeous man strode through the woodland, pushing branches out of his way and stepping over fallen logs. 'Are you OK?' he asked, when he was still a few feet away. 'Was it you I heard screaming?'

'It was just the one scream,' said Dixie. 'But yes. I was being attacked.'

Her rescuer looked concerned so she hastily clarified.

'Not *attacked* exactly. But this squirrel is rather tetchy.' She pointed to where the squirrel was staring her down. Its tail still twitching violently.

The man started to laugh. 'Oh, right. Don't worry, squirrels are harmless.' He clapped his hands as he approached.

The squirrel jumped but instead of running off it turned to glare at the intruder. Perhaps it felt threatened between the two humans, Dixie didn't know, but even though it was only small, the squirrel wasn't going to be intimidated. It charged at the new person and ran up his trousers like they were a tree.

'Argh!' shouted the man. Dixie saw her chance and fled towards the van without looking back.

Fumbling with the key but eventually unlocking it she whipped the door open and dived inside. She was about to shut it behind her when the man dashed in after her and shut it for her.

'Hey!' she said. 'What do you think you're doing?'

He held up his palms. 'Sorry!' he said. 'But that thing is aggressive.'

The van seemed to halve in size with him in it. What had once seemed like a homely space was now cramped and a little claustrophobic. They both peered out of the window but there was no sign of the squirrel. 'Do you think it's got some mental disorder, or rabies perhaps?' asked Dixie.

'Not rabies but it's certainly pissed off.' The man looked cautiously in all directions.

'I think it's gone,' said Dixie.

The man was still staring wide-eyed out of the window. Not quite the hero material he had first appeared. Dixie cleared her throat, making him turn in her direction.

'Right. Sorry. I'm Ned.'

He really was rather hot up close. Dark wavy hair,

brown eyes and a strong jawline. He was watching her and she realized this was where she was meant to introduce herself. 'I'm Dixie.'

'Hello, Dixie,' he said with a smile that made a dimple appear. 'And what do you do, apart from antagonize wildlife?'

'I'm a social media influencer.' She very much liked how that sounded and Ned seemed impressed. 'I'm recording my journey with Elsie.'

'There's more than one of you living in here?'

Dixie chuckled. 'No, it's just me.' She patted the cushion next to her. 'This is a seventies VW campervan and her name is Elsie.'

'You've not got much in the way of facilities. Would you not be better on a campsite with mod cons like running water?'

It made her look around. Elsie's interior was sad and unloved. Dixie had been so caught up in her breaking down that she'd lost sight of all the other things she was going to do to improve Elsie. 'I've not got round to renovating yet as I am enjoying communing with nature. Going back to basics. Learning to live off the land and be environmentally friendly. So what are you doing in the middle of nowhere?' she asked, trying to deflect the questions.

'Woodland management,' he said, then moved his head from side to side as if weighing things up. 'Learning really. If I'm being honest, I'm totally out of my depth, but I guess that's the challenge and I like something that's going to test me. Mainly because I like proving people wrong.'

'Oh, me too,' said Dixie. 'That's really why I'm here. I'm showing my parents they're wrong about me and that I can be successful without them. And I need to prove that to myself as much as to them.' For a second she worried that she'd overshared but Ned was nodding.

'I can totally relate to that,' he said.

Maybe she was imagining it, but in that second something passed between them. A mutual understanding perhaps? But the moment was soon broken by a thud on the roof of the van.

'Heavens, we're under attack from above now,' said Dixie. There was the sound of movement across the top of the van then a furry face appeared upside-down at the windscreen.

'I think this is my cue to leave,' said Ned, heading out the door. He opened his mouth as if he was going to add something, but he shook his head and got out, pausing for a moment. 'Look, perhaps we . . .' While he was talking, Dixie noticed movement behind him. Movement of the bounding-squirrel variety. She didn't want to see Ned savaged by a marauding squirrel. A distraction was needed. She threw the two grapes she still had in her pocket. Unfortunately, one of the grapes hit the squirrel square on the head and it immediately raced towards Ned, screeching loudly.

'What did you do that for?' yelled Ned as he took off into the woods.

19

Dixie watched through the window as Ned hurdled the stump she had now formally named Bastard Stump, raced off through the woodland and disappeared into the greenery. The squirrel went as far as the fallen tree, jumped up and screeched for a bit, flicking its tail violently. It turned around quickly, making Dixie gasp and let go of the curtain. If this had been a horror film she knew exactly who would be next to die. But in a flash the squirrel's demeanour changed. It hopped to the ground and began searching for food like nothing had happened. After a few minutes things were restored to peace and quiet and the birds were idly twittering again.

Dixie had planned to make it to tomorrow and then arrange to get towed back to Melton Mowbray, but it felt like things had changed. Her number of followers had risen dramatically and that was all down to the predicament she was in. If she left now her followers would lose interest and most likely a shedload would unfollow her. This was all bigger than her now, so she had to stay.

She realized that just because she couldn't drive Elsie

didn't mean she couldn't do all the other things she'd planned to do, like making cute curtains and matching cushions and generally refitting and updating the inside. For one thing, it would make use of the items she'd brought for repairs and free up some much-needed space. It was also excellent online content. There was probably a nature angle she could include as well. Visions of the squirrel helping her popped into her mind. That was possibly a long way off but she did still really want to see if she could make friends with the squirrel. They'd got off on the wrong foot. She made a mental note to look for something it would like at the service station so that she could begin winning it round.

While she didn't like to admit it, there was also Ned. Their meeting had been fleeting but he'd made an impression. Perhaps that was because she'd been deprived of human contact for so long, apart from the lady at the service station, who she now knew was called Lesley. The thought of Ned made her feel less alone. Maybe if she stuck around she might see him again and that would be useful because someone who was managing the woodland would know about plants and flowers. Ned would make excellent content and he'd also help her to avoid poisoning herself when she was foraging. And the other thing was that if she went now the person leaving the mystery rude messages would think they had won. There was no way she was going anywhere.

*

Jay and Nora met up to do a bit of bouldering together. Jay had said he wanted to improve his strength and he definitely needed to work on his holds so the low-level climbing activity seemed the perfect answer.

'You boob-flashed him and now he wants to meet up?' asked Jay, summarizing Nora's late-night video call with Liam. 'I can't imagine why he wants to do that.' He gave her a look.

'It's not because I . . . it wasn't boob-flashing. That's something people do on purpose. This was accidental.'

'OK, got it,' said Jay. 'Accidental boob-flashing.'

Nora shook her head at him. 'Anyway, it's just a coffee and it was me who suggested it before the boob . . . incident. But we've not put anything in the diary because he's busy with work. I might catch up with Mickey before then.'

Jay gave her a rather puzzled look. 'Are you two-timing your exes?'

'No, because I'm not seeing either of them, or anyone for that matter. It's simply not efficient to not overlap the research.'

'I'll mention that when I'm dating more than one woman. I'm just being efficient.' He winked. 'Tell me about Mickey,' he added, struggling to get a climbing shoe on. He hopped a couple of steps, toppled and Nora grabbed him to keep him upright.

'Mickey is a personal trainer.'

'I've been thinking about getting one of those,' said Jay, finally succeeding in getting his foot in his shoe.

'I could ask him if he's taking on clients but then I don't think he's local any more because we're meeting in Skegness.'

'I love Skeggy,' said Jay, clapping his hands together and making Nora smile. Jay saw the look and quickly reached into his chalk bag and slapped his hands together again as if he'd been spreading chalk all along. The chalk made a cloud of dust and Jay breathed it in, making him cough.

'Are you OK?' asked Nora, unsure whether patting him on the back would make things worse or better.

'I'm fine,' he spluttered, pulling out his inhaler and taking a puff. 'You were saying,' he wheezed.

'I wasn't really saying anything. I'm catching up with Mickey in Skegness in the next couple of weeks.'

'I wonder what Bruce will make of the seaside?' said Jay, his voice intermittently sounding like his own.

'You can come if you want. To the beach, I mean, not to meet Mickey, obviously.'

'Obviously,' repeated Jay. 'But yes please to a day out at Skeggy. Thanks.'

They decided to climb on two different sides of the bouldering room and Nora was quite in the zone. There was something freeing about climbing without a harness, and the extra thick mat below her gave her the reassurance that the odds of seriously injuring herself were minimal. She understood why some people chose to free-climb but the chances of having a major accident were far too high for her liking. A thud behind her made her check over her shoulder. Jay was lying flat on his back on the mat.

'Are you OK?' she asked.

'Yep, fine. Just missed that tricky hold.' He pointed at the wall. 'I think I'll take a break. You carry on,' he added as he got to his feet.

Nora traversed the room and had a go at the tricky overhang. This was her nemesis. It took a lot of upper body strength to get around it.

'Hey, Nora, have you seen this?' called Jay.

Nora lost concentration, let go and landed safely on the mat.

'Sorry, did I put you off?' he asked.

'It's OK.' Nora walked over to where Jay was studying the noticeboard.

'There's a climbing mini-break next weekend and they need two more people or it's cancelled. What do you think?' he said.

Nora skim-read the notice. Hostel accommodation, lots of outdoor climbing and abseiling, country walks and hearty meals. 'Statistically outdoor climbing is more dangerous,' she said.

'Yeah but a weekend away would be fun, right?'

'What about Bruce?'

'Bugger,' said Jay.

The weekend climbing trip came up again at the next Crafting and Cocktails. Nora had to admit she had been thinking about it but felt she couldn't go on her own.

That would be unfair, given it had been Jay who had told her about it. It had been Jay's turn to sort the cocktails so this week they were having Piña Coladas.

'It's in the Forest of Dean,' said Jay. 'I've always wanted to go there.'

'It's a bloody beautiful part of the country,' said Renee. 'Unfortunately after I stayed there for a folk festival with a travelling community they introduced a bylaw to stop you sleeping in tents and caravans in the national parks. Shame, I love Cockadilly.'

There was a pause in conversation while Nora and Jay were processing what Renee had said, pondering whether Cockadilly was a place or a euphemism, while Renee had another sip of her cocktail.

'It's nice, Jay. Any chance you brought the rum with you?'

He shook his head.

'I'll have Bruce for the weekend,' said Nora, double-checking the measurements on the pattern for a man's jumper, this time for one that had enough space for her dad's two spare tyres.

'But then you wouldn't be able to come too,' said Jay.

'I know, but you want to go more than I do.'

'Very selfless,' said Renee. 'But I'll look after the dog, then you can both go.'

'Thank you,' said Jay tentatively. 'But are you allowed pets at Wrinkly— I mean Brinkley Place?'

'Kenneth Sturgeon has a sparrow in a cage. He says it's a pet-shop finch, which is piffle because any fool can see it's a sodding sparrow, and Audrey Kennet has a geriatric Persian that pisses in the vegetable patch, and everyone turns a blind eye to those. But you're right, officially they don't allow pets.'

'Bruce is a bit bigger than a sparrow and his bark is louder than a car horn. You'd not be able to smuggle him in,' said Jay. 'But it was really kind of you to offer.'

Renee stopped knitting and fixed them with a steely gaze. 'I could get him in. I know things.'

Jay and Nora swallowed in unison under Renee's steely gaze.

Renee shrugged a shoulder and went back to clicking her needles. 'But it'd be easier if I stayed at your place with the dog. Less disruption for everyone.'

Jay scrunched up his features. 'He's really big, Renee. He's more bear than dog.' Nora wondered if he'd had visions of Renee being knocked over by an overenthusiastic Bruce.

'That's fine. I can handle a bear.'

Jay spluttered a laugh but Renee didn't look like she was joking.

'I used to work in a pub just outside Romford. They had a bear,' said Renee.

'What? An actual bear. Like a grizzly?' asked Jay, his eyes wide.

'Big furry black one she was. Ahhh, lovely old Rhani. I didn't like that they kept her in a cage. Ruddy health and safety.' Renee shook her head. 'I used to share a pint and a packet of crisps with her during my break.

I had the occasional wrestle with her too.' She paused her knitting again. 'And my friend Tippi Hedren had a lion called Neil who lived in the house. The rotter used to take up all the bed and he didn't like it if you kicked him off. He used to make a right fuss, the snarly pussy cat. So if I can manage a bear and a tetchy lion, then a dog definitely won't be a problem.'

Nora looked at Jay. He had the usual, slightly dazed expression he wore when Renee was sharing one of her anecdotes. She hoped he was mulling over the offer because Renee looking after Bruce seemed like a good solution. But then, it wasn't her handing over her house keys to Renee. 'OK,' said Jay, nodding vigorously as if trying to convince himself. 'That'd be great. Thank you.' He smiled at Nora.

There was a tap on the open door and an older gentleman with thinning grey hair stepped in. 'Is this the wellness class?' he asked.

'It's usually next door,' said Renee, 'but the teacher is off sick. Ironic really. Sit yourself down and have a Piña Colada instead. Welcome to Rafting and Cocktails,' she added.

20

Nora was having a catch-up with Dixie and bringing her up to date on the goings-on, such as they were, at Crafting and Cocktails.

'I've been replaced by a retired dentist,' said Dixie, sounding glum.

'Not at all. He just got roped in by Renee, you know what she's like. We'll probably never see him again,' said Nora. Renee had put forward a strong argument that crafting was all about improving your well-being and known for its stress-reducing properties. Nora wasn't entirely convinced by Renee's stance that cocktails were good for you because alcohol contained antioxidants, and antioxidants helped fight the effects of high blood pressure and blood sugar. Plus they also increased good cholesterol and could fend off type two diabetes and Alzheimer's. Renee had also argued that cocktails frequently contained fruit juice, which she claimed counted as one of your five-a-day.

'I miss Crafting and Cocktails,' said Dixie. 'I might have to recreate it with Arnold.'

'Who's Arnold?' asked Nora.

'I've named the squirrel Arnold Schwarzensquirrel. He was giving off early Schwarzenegger vibes. And naming him makes him seem friendlier.'

'I'm not sure he'll be up for crafting or cocktails but I did love the video,' said Nora, who was curled up on her sofa with a cup of tea. 'It had loads of likes and views too.'

'I know, it's been my second most successful post to date. Someone even said it was like *The Blair Witch Project* meets *Countryfile*! I mean, that's an accolade right there.'

'When are you moving on?' asked Nora, mentally crossing her fingers. She didn't like the thought of her friend taking unnecessary risks.

'I can't,' said Dixie.

'Oh no, has Elsie broken down again?'

There was a slight pause. 'She has, so I literally can't move, but also metaphorically I can't move on either. I feel like I need to make a stand for the common man against the establishment.'

'And in this scenario, who is the establishment?'

'I don't know exactly, if I'm honest, but I feel a stand needs to be made all the same. And I'm going to make it. Plus my five thousand, seven hundred and eleven followers also want me to.'

Nora wasn't sure this was a good idea. 'Maybe we should do a bit more research and find out who does own the land that you're currently occupying. That way you'd know what or who you were up against. If the person leaving the notes is legit then you will need to get Elsie moved, and if he isn't and it's owned by the council or it's designated nature reserve, then whoever is leaving the notes is doing it for kicks, which is all kinds of weird and you definitely need to get the hell out of there. I mean that's cabin-in-the-woods territory,' said Nora, almost spooking herself.

'Don't say that,' said Dixie. 'Campervan in a shady glade sounds so much nicer. And I appreciate your concern but this trip is all about me doing things for myself.'

'I thought it was about making your parents proud?'

'It is, by showing them that I can survive without their support and that I can do something worthwhile with my life. Being an influencer might not be a conventional job but I'm enjoying it and it's bringing pleasure to others. And while I do want to make my parents proud, I think it's probably more important that I feel worthwhile as a person.'

Nora was instantly worried for her friend. 'Oh, Dixie, you are worthwhile. Please don't ever think that you aren't. You are the kindest, sweetest, wackiest person I know. Well, second wackiest after Renee. And by wacky I mean unique and in a good way. Are you sure you're OK?'

'That's a lovely thing to say. I don't think my parents see wacky or unique as good things. I think they thought I would have worked my life out by the time I got to twenty-six.'

'I disagree. They are business people so they know that you have to stand out from the crowd and that is what you do. Plus most entrepreneurs start their businesses in their forties and are more successful for it.' She didn't have the stats to hand but Nora hoped that sounded positive.

'Thanks. I thought that for now I would focus on how I feel about me,' said Dixie.

'That sounds like a plan. And, apart from worthwhile, how do you want to feel?'

'Hmm, that's the part I've not entirely figured out yet but I'll get there. I have time.'

Nora sipped her drink. From what Dixie had told her, if the notes were serious then time was exactly what she was running out of.

The morning of the climbing weekend came around and Nora was waiting at the pick-up point for Jay to arrive when Trent swaggered over.

'Nora, I was so pleased to see your name on the list. Have you had a change of heart about us?' he asked with his hand on his chest as if he was about to break into the American national anthem.

'Nope, no change of heart. Jay suggested it and I thought it sounded like fun.' He didn't need to know that she'd been checking the stats on outdoor climbing ever since she'd agreed to go and as they made hair-raising reading she had been having a lot of second thoughts, assuming you could have more than one second thought.

'If you get scared, you only have to call and I will be there.'

'We're staying in a hostel so, apart from bed bugs, what would I be scared of exactly?' she asked, thinking that really all there was to worry about was Trent, and the last place she'd feel safe would be anywhere near him at night-time.

Trent's eyes darted about as if seeking inspiration. 'The dark?'

'I'm not five. I'm not scared of the dark. Are you?' she asked with a smile.

Trent laughed, his usual tinkle that in no way matched the rest of him. 'Me, I'm not scared of anything.'

'That's good then. Watch out for wild animals. Oh, and especially the bats with rabies, you should definitely keep an eye out for those.' Technically the UK was rabies-free but there were occasionally cases of lyssavirus, a rabies-like virus that affected the native bat population, so it wasn't a total lie.

Trent was looking suitably terrified. 'What? Flying rabies carriers? Are there any in the Forest of Dean?'

'Who knows?' said Nora. 'Look, here's Jay.'

Jay got out of an Uber and the driver heaved a massive rucksack out of the boot. Nora went to give him a hand. 'That's a lot of stuff,' she said, attempting to lift the backpack. 'Blimey, Jay. What's in here?'

'I didn't think there was that much but I guess it all adds up and you don't know what you're going to need.'

'Have you smuggled Bruce along? Or maybe Renee hopped in when you weren't looking?'

'Ha, ha,' said Jay. 'It's Renee's fault that there are a

few extra things in there.' He scratched his head. 'I've no idea why she said I needed to bring an inflatable pillow and a hair turban.'

Nora snorted a laugh. 'You own a hair turban?'

'No.' He looked mildly insulted. 'Renee gave me one to bring. But the inflatable pillow is mine.'

'How did she get on with Bruce?'

'She's the dog whisperer. He literally did everything she said and walked alongside her like he was in the obedience ring at Crufts.'

'Wow. Is there anything she can't do?' Nora was constantly amazed by Renee. Partly because her life had seemed so full of adventure and also because she was still living life to the full.

'Maybe, but I've not discovered it yet, and she can definitely do dog-sitting. She said she was trained by Barbara Woodhouse?' He shrugged his shoulders.

'Never heard of her,' said Nora.

'Nope, nor me.'

Someone clapped their hands and Nora and Jay were herded on to a minibus with Trent and seven other people. Thankfully they had more seats than they needed, otherwise there would have been nowhere to put the luggage, and Jay's overstuffed backpack was already proving to be a problem. He was trying to shove it into the small overhead storage while Trent was struggling to get past him, his eyes firmly set on the seat next to Nora.

'Jay, put your bag next to mine and sit down. People are trying to find seats.' Nora patted the seat next to her.

Jay put his backpack beside Nora's, then turned to come face to face with Trent still trying to move past him along the tiny aisle.

'Sorry,' said Jay, pointing at Nora as he wriggled to try to free himself.

'No, you can sit there.' Trent nudged Jay into a spare seat.

Nora was flustered. The last person she wanted to sit next to was Trent, plus the seats weren't that big and with his big thighs and likely man-spreading she'd be cramped for the whole journey. She put a hand up to stop him sitting down. 'I get travel sick and Jay said he'd hold the sick bag while I vomited,' she said.

Trent recoiled, giving Jay enough space to squeeze by and plonk down next to Nora.

Trent huffed and moved on to where another lone female was sitting and made himself comfortable there.

'Thanks,' whispered Nora.

'My pleasure,' said Jay, holding her gaze.

Nora noticed the rich depth of colour of his eyes. She hastily looked away.

'I do have a sick bag if you need it,' said Jay, pointing at his backpack. 'And I'd hold it for you.'

'I know you would,' she said. It was bizarre how comforting it was to know that.

It took them two and a half hours to get to the hostel in the Forest of Dean. Nora and Jay chatted happily, got the giggles over something silly and shared too many Jelly Tots. It was like the best bits of a school trip with a best friend, although she was aware that due to the small seats Jay's thigh was keeping hers warm. She didn't mind; it was quite nice really. When they got to the hostel there was just about time to have lunch, which was homemade tomato soup with warm rolls, and a safety briefing before they were bundled back on to the minibus and taken to their first climbing spot of the weekend.

The sun was shining and the climbing company they were using had already been and set the route up a gnarly cliff face. Nora was both excited and apprehensive. This was her first time climbing outdoors. Unhelpfully, her brain was providing her with the many odds of all the things that could go wrong – perhaps it hadn't been a smart thing to look them all up in advance.

A hand on her shoulder made her jump. 'Sorry,' said Jay. 'I didn't mean to startle you. You were looking a bit . . .' He mimed being freaked out.

Nora laughed. 'I am a bit.' She held out a shaking hand.

Jay wrapped her hand in both of his and something zinged through her.

'There, it's stopped,' he said with a smile. 'I feel the same. Totally cacking it.' He let her hand go. 'That's probably not that reassuring, is it?'

'It does make me feel better though.'

They put on their harnesses and, while people were still checking kit, Trent was already making his ascent.

'There's a surprise,' said Nora and they both watched Trent's muscles flexing as he stretched to the max to find a hold. 'I take it he knows there's no prize for being first to the top.'

Jay nudged her and pointed at two women glued to Trent's every move. 'There might be a prize of sorts,' he said. Trent let go with one hand so that he could properly look over one shoulder and wink at his adoring audience.

'Please concentrate on the climb,' said one of the climbing leaders, making Trent grumble something.

Nora and Jay were last to take a turn so the climbing team offered to belay them both so they could climb together and it would save time. It was a wide area and there was plenty of room and holds for both of them. Once she'd started she began to relax. She knew she was safe and she did know what she was doing. It was just outdoors and she had to find the hand and foot holds for herself, although the climbing leader was good at shouting out instructions for where to reach to.

There was something comforting about climbing with Jay at her side, or rather a couple of feet below her and to her left as he was a bit slower than she was. Nora took her time and made certain she had hands and feet in good secure positions before she moved on, although she did get herself in a bit of a pickle over one foot hold, at which point Jay carefully overtook her. He was a slow and steady climber and frequently had his tongue stuck out of the side of his mouth in concentration. Meanwhile, Nora was getting herself into quite an awkward position.

'Now push really hard with that foot and stand up,' called the leader from below. She could do this. She watched Jay for a moment as he tapped the top of the cliff and received a round of applause from everyone below. He gave her a happy thumbs-up and then started to abseil down. Nora took a breath and put all her weight on her right foot. She straightened out her leg and for a moment she was upright. But then there was a slight shift and her foot slipped a fraction. It felt like her heart stopped. She took stock – she was perfectly fine and still attached to the rock. Unfortunately she realized her right foot was very attached to the rock as her climbing shoe had become completely wedged into the crevice. Nora wriggled and tugged but she couldn't free herself.

She looked down. People were congratulating Jay. 'Um, I think I'm stuck,' she said.

'What?' asked the leader.

'My foot's stuck!' she called back.

'OK. Stay calm. Someone will come up to free you,' he shouted back.

Why did her fingers instantly start to feel tired as she gripped the rock?

'You OK?' called Jay.

'Yeah. Just hanging around!' She tried to smile but her muscles wouldn't let her. She was focusing hard on not panicking. Her ankle was not happy about the angle it was now forced into, which wasn't helping matters.

'Don't panic!' shouted Trent.

'I'm *not* panicking!' yelled back Nora, more than a bit

annoyed. Maybe she could free herself. She had another concerted effort at pulling her shoe out of its wedged position. With one big tug her foot came straight out of the climbing shoe. 'Shit!' Now she was hanging on with just one foot. She tried to stick her foot back in the shoe, if only to hide her Cookie Monster socks, but it was at too much of an odd angle.

'Stay there!' shouted Trent.

'Not got much choice!' Nora concentrated on getting her foot back into the shoe. She was aware of shouting below but was a bit preoccupied with her challenge. When the shouting increased, she tuned in.

'Get down. That's incredibly dangerous!'

Oh great, that was all she needed. And not exactly helpful because she couldn't get down and she'd not pulled her foot out of her shoe intentionally. She slowly moved her head to the other side and that was when someone grabbed her right ankle. 'Shit!' The unexpected contact made her instinctively kick out, which was when she kicked Trent in the face. He yelped and let go of her but he also let go of the cliff and, as if in slow motion, she watched him fall.

21

After almost two weeks in the wilderness Dixie was tackling life with fresh enthusiasm. She couldn't completely gut the van and rebuild it like she'd seen some people do in YouTube videos because she was living in it, but she could still transform it. Plenty of video clips and photographs of the before stage highlighted to her how much she needed to do. It felt like she'd accepted the state Elsie was in and now it was time to change that mindset and do something about it. She had already brought with her what she needed in the way of fabric and sewing equipment, as well as a few things she might not need, which were all rammed into any free space, including the passenger footwell. All she needed to do was work out what to do first.

It was a sunny summer's day and she was sitting in her fold-up chair outside, studying the instructions for fitting the utensil rack she'd bought, when she saw movement in her peripheral vision. She turned slightly to see Arnold the squirrel. Dixie stayed still. She had toyed with the idea of putting out some of the walnuts she'd bought from the service station for him, but had decided that she wanted him to know who they were from, otherwise he'd just think it was a lucky find and would have no gratitude towards Dixie. The least she deserved was to take the credit for supplying them.

Slowly she took out her phone, zoomed in on the squirrel and began recording. He hopped a little closer so Dixie took a walnut half from her pocket. Walnuts had been all they had at the service station, apart from wasabi-coated peanuts and she knew he wouldn't like those. She held it up and Arnold stopped what he was doing. His tail immediately went into angry wag mode.

'I brought you food. Don't get cross.' Dixie waved the walnut. Arnold stared her down. 'Fine. Here, have the nut.' She tossed it in his general direction, making him flinch and back away. 'Sorry!'

There was a stand-off for a couple of minutes. Dixie stopped filming as it wasn't the most exciting footage and viewers had short attention spans. Arnold inched closer, keeping eyes on Dixie. He moved cautiously towards the walnut, grabbed it in his mouth and raced off. Success! But she'd forgotten to film it. A couple of minutes later Arnold was back and eyeing Dixie warily.

'It's OK, I won't bite,' she said, setting her phone to record.

'But she might,' said Ned, making her jump.

'Goodness me! You scared the life out of me. Oh, and Arnold.' She pointed to where the squirrel had been.

'Arnold?'

'You can mock but since I named him he's been much friendlier,' said Dixie.

'Not mocking,' said Ned. 'It's just that Arnold is a girl.'

'What? Really?'

Ned nodded as he sat down on the doorplate of the campervan. 'When she was sitting up with her paws in front of her like she was about to start knitting, you could see her, um, teats.'

'Well, that's a turn-up for the books. She's surprisingly aggressive.' Dixie would have hoped for a little female solidarity.

'She's probably got kits somewhere nearby. She'll be on red alert for anything that would be a threat. Plus she'll be defending her feeding grounds.' He was clearly knowledgeable about wildlife.

'Then I'll cut her a bit of slack. But I'll keep the name. She still looks like an Arnold to me.'

'Fair enough,' he said with a chuckle. 'Sorry for running off the other day.'

'I'm sorry I angered the squirrel,' said Dixie. 'Kettle was boiled not long ago. Did you want a mint tea or anything?' She felt her hostess options were somewhat limited.

'Please. Have you been foraging?' he asked as she went inside the van.

'Only as far as Marks and Spencer,' she said, waving the box of mint teabags.

'I can show you where there's wild mint growing if you like.'

'Yes please. I think properly foraging for my food would be so cool. It's what we should be doing, right?'

'I guess it is. Are you vegan by any chance?'

Dixie pulled a face. 'I'd really like to be but you see I love bacon . . . and eggs . . . and cheese is an essential food group for me. If only vegan cheese didn't taste like poo.'

Ned snorted a laugh. 'I agree with you on the bacon. You can't beat a bacon sandwich in white bread. It's the perfect hangover cure. Not that I drink to excess.'

'Don't worry, I run a weekly cocktail club,' she said, handing him a mug.

'Shall we go for a forage once we've drunk these then?' he asked.

'I'd love that,' said Dixie, feeling that things were heading in the right direction for a change.

*

Nora was frozen to the spot. She heard shouting and anxious voices below her. She clung to the rockface, turning a fraction to look down. Trent was lying on his back with everyone around him. Her breathing was fast and her pulse even faster.

'Is he OK?' she called and a few faces glanced in her direction.

Trent let out a groan. 'He's fine,' said Jay. 'Just winded himself probably.' But the number of people running about implied otherwise.

'Shall I bring her down?' asked her belayer.

'But my shoe is stuck in that crevice,' she called, but nobody replied.

'Do you want to let go of your holds and abseil down?' called up the leader.

'On one leg?'

'Yeah.'

It didn't seem like Nora had a lot of choice but it was a relief to let go of the rock, she had been gripping so tightly her fingers were cramping. She was worried about Trent. He'd fallen a long way and while he still had his helmet on, he could have done untold damage to the rest of his body. She pushed herself awkwardly away from the cliff with one foot until she landed at the bottom and thanked her belayer.

'Are you all right?' asked Jay, who had been waiting for her. He steadied her with strong hands and immediately set about getting her out of her harness.

'I'm fine. I just lost a shoe,' she said, but her shaking hands and rasping breath told a different story. She couldn't pull her eyes away from Trent, whose face was scrunched up in pain. Panic gripped her. 'He's in a bad way, isn't he?'

Jay paused what he was doing for a second. 'Let me look after you. There's an ambulance on the way for Trent, they'll take good care of him.'

'How the hell are they going to get an ambulance up here?'

A few minutes later her question was answered as

the sound of a helicopter got louder and louder. Nora wasn't sure how long she'd been sitting on a rock with a foil blanket around her shoulders. It had probably been a while, given the state of the piece of Kendal Mint Cake in her hand that someone had said would be good for shock but had made her a little queasy. The air ambulance landed nearby and Trent was soon stretchered away. She felt awful – she hadn't meant for him to climb up but because he had it seemed like her fault.

Jay came over to her. 'Here you go,' he said, handing over her climbing shoe.

'I didn't see you get it.'

'I didn't, one of the professionals went up for it. I belayed for them.'

'Thanks,' she said, taking the shoe. How had a single piece of footwear caused so much drama? Jay crouched in front of her, watching her closely. Was it the shock? Or was it the light on his face, highlighting his features and making him look every inch the leading man? 'Why was Trent free climbing?' she asked.

'Hang on,' he said. 'I need to stand up because my thighs are burning.' He made an O shape with his mouth as he straightened himself. He sat down next to Nora. 'You know Trent. He was trying to be a hero.'

'He didn't deserve that though. He could be paralysed.' The thought took her breath away.

'Nah, he was moving his legs. Mainly when he was being told not to, but still. The first-aider said they think he's badly bruised but he's got off lightly. Anyway, let's get you back to the minibus. It's three-bean chilli for dinner,' he said and they both pulled a face.

Back at the hostel everyone else seemed on some sort of weird high following the excitement of Trent's accident and subsequent carting off in the air ambulance, which Nora found a little disturbing. She was sitting in the corner of the communal area and all the chatter around her, which she tuned in and out of, was about what had happened. Those who had witnessed it were keen to tell their version of events and those who missed it were desperate for information. Someone had made her a very strong, sweet coffee, which was utterly disgusting, but she worried it was bad form not to drink it so forced it down in little sips. She'd never sleep tonight. She'd be wired from the caffeine and more hyper than a toddler on Haribo thanks to all the sugar in it. But there was another, bigger reason why she'd likely not sleep. Nora kept reliving the climb and the scene of her kicking Trent off the cliff and him falling. The look of shock on his face as her Cookie Monster sock made contact with his cheek and the terror in his eyes as he fell would stay with her for a long time.

'Hey, how are you doing?' asked Jay, appearing in front of her. She had no idea how long she'd been staring into space.

She jiggled her head. 'So so. Still a bit freaked out, if I'm honest. Don't want to be a drama queen or anything.'

'Oh, *I* would totally be a drama queen,' said Jay,

sitting on the arm of her chair and making it creak in protest. 'It's basically what I do for a living. Anyway, this is for you.' He handed her his water bottle.

'Thanks but I'm OK.' She held up her half-drunk coffee.

Jay took the mug from her and swapped it for the water bottle. He leaned in and whispered, 'The hair turban came good.'

'Is that some sort of code? Because I have no idea what you mean.'

'Renee had wrapped a tin of ready-made gin and tonic in the hair turban so I've decanted it into my water bottle. Drink it, it'll do you good. Well, it probably won't, but it might make you de-stress a little.'

'Thanks.' She undid the cap and took a swig. It was strong and she almost choked on it.

'It said on the label it was double strength. Probably should have mentioned that.'

'And you found it inside the hair turban?'

'Exactly, it was all bundled up. I must say I did wonder why she'd made me bring that but I found it really useful. It stopped my wet hair dripping all over me while I was trying to dry myself. I would definitely use one again and would recommend it to others,' he said.

Nora couldn't help smiling. 'You don't think the hair turban was just a ploy to smuggle in a gin and tonic?'

For a moment Jay seemed perplexed. 'Well, *now* I do,' he said.

22

Nora was hugely relieved when the climbing leader called them all together to tell them that Trent had incurred only minor injuries, which included extensive bruising, two broken ribs and a broken little finger, but they were keeping him in for observation overnight just to be on the safe side.

'That's good news,' said Nora, unable to stop the huge sigh escaping.

'Not for the nursing staff,' said Jay.

'Don't be mean,' said Nora. 'Poor Trent. I know they called them minor injuries but he's broken three things and has extensive bruising. None of that sounds like fun.'

'He'll be telling them all an elaborate story how he came to save you. They'll all think he's a hero and he'll come out with enough phone numbers to fill a telephone directory. You mark my words,' said Jay. 'He'll likely thank you for kicking him off the cliff.'

'Oh don't! I still feel awful.' The familiar nausea bubbled in her gut.

Jay gave her shoulder a squeeze. 'Stop beating yourself

up. That was literally a knee-jerk reaction. You couldn't help it. He shouldn't have been grabbing your leg, let alone free-climbing up there to do it. He was just showing off and it backfired.'

'I keep seeing it happen. Him falling. My fingers gripping the rock.' Nora wondered if her clinging to a rockface was a metaphor for her life, or perhaps it was the part where she kicked him away. She looked Jay in the eyes. 'It's me,' she said.

'What's you?'

'It's always my fault. All the failed relationships. They are all down to me.'

As she had expected, Nora didn't sleep well. Mainly because of her brain going over and over Trent's fall but also because she was a bit distracted by thoughts of Jay – he'd been so kind, she didn't know what she'd have done if he'd not been there. She decided to go back over her ex-boyfriends. Focusing on the 37 per cent rule would at least occupy her mind. However, she kept returning to her earlier epiphany that she had in some way caused the end of all her relationships, either by choice or by her actions. On top of that, she had the bunk below a pretty, petite young woman named Gabriella, who every time she turned over loudly broke wind – proving that nobody's perfect.

The next morning Nora was nursing a foggy head, although she did have a renewed determination to focus on the 37 per cent rule because it now felt far more likely that 'the one' was in the pile somewhere, given her tendency to kick men out of her life. Breakfast was porridge or toast and most people seemed to be filling up on both, even though neither looked that appetizing. At least the coffee was drinkable.

A round of applause broke out as Trent entered the breakfast room like a returning war hero, switching between dramatic winces and humble waves to his adoring public.

'It's OK. It takes more than a fall off a forty-foot cliff to break me,' he said with a sage expression on his face.

'Forty feet?' whispered Jay. 'He's at least six foot tall and his feet were barely ten feet up the cliff when he reached for you. And people say I exaggerate.' He rolled his eyes.

'You do,' said Nora, and he playfully dug her in the ribs.

'Nora!' called Trent, frowning as he made his way in her direction.

Oh great, here we go, she thought. 'Good to see you back on your feet again,' she said.

Trent took both of her hands in his with a theatrical grimace. 'I don't want you to feel bad about hurting me because . . . I forgive you,' he said without blinking, which was rather off-putting.

Part of Nora wanted to repeat what Jay had said, that it was all Trent's fault for being a show-off, but deep down she did feel to blame.

'That's good. I'm sorry I kicked you and that you fell and hurt yourself.' She squeezed his hands and he crumpled. 'What?'

'My broken finger,' he squeaked.

'Shit. I am so sorry.'

'It's OK,' he said, his jaw tight as he walked away.

Jay grinned at her.

'Stop it,' she said. 'That's not helpful. As if the poor man wasn't already in enough pain.'

'He's fine. Look at him.' Jay tipped his head in Trent's direction, where all the other women were fussing over him. 'He's milking it. He'll probably get a BAFTA before I do.'

'Hmm.' It didn't stop Nora feeling awful.

'Apparently we're climbing above a gorge today,' said Jay, sitting down next to her. 'And the forecast is dry.'

'I don't think I can do that,' said Nora.

'Sure you can. You are a way better climber than me. One of the climbing instructors said the views from the top are unreal.'

'No, Jay, you don't understand. After what happened yesterday, I can't climb. The thought of it is making my neck prickle.'

He nodded his understanding and chewed his toast thoughtfully as they watched Trent lapping up all the praise and sympathy from others. 'I get where you're coming from but here's the thing.' He pointed at her with a piece of limp toast and marmalade. 'If you don't give it a try today it might grow into a phobia-type thing and you don't want that. Plus, if you're not climbing, you're staying here and spending the day with Trent.'

What a choice.

*

Dixie had felt very proud of herself as she ate her foraged mushroom and garlic omelette. Granted, the eggs were from the farm shop, but she had, with the help of Ned, found the mushroom and the wild garlic herself. The mushroom was one of the ones growing on the side of a tree that Ned said were called chicken of the woods and were safe to eat. With his help she'd cut down one of the smaller ones and she still had loads left over. They had also found the mint so she could have fresh mint tea as well as some elderflower and wild strawberries, the latter of which were surprisingly tasty. It had made her feel like a proper adventurer, like she had in her grandparents' orchard as a child.

Strolling through the woodland with Ned had been both lovely and productive. He'd looked gorgeous on camera and come across very well, as evidenced by the high number of inappropriate comments and people she was now having to block from her Instagram account. When she wasn't filming they had chatted a little about nature but had also spent time listening for the birdsong. It had been her best day since she'd left Melton, especially as there had been no message left on the van when she had returned. Perhaps the note-writer had given up, or did it just mean they were getting ready to evict her? She desperately wanted to stay now she felt she was settling into van life.

It had also galvanized her plans. She needed to make whatever time she had at the woodland count in case she was forced to move on. It was important to vary what she was filming so that she kept her followers interested. Although she got the feeling that if she just posted shots of Ned that would keep most of them happy. What she really wanted was for people to engage with what *she* was doing and come on the journey with her – Ned was just the sprinkles on the cupcake. After making some notes, she tucked herself up in bed full of happy thoughts and a little of the gin Renee had given her, and slept soundly.

A tapping noise made Dixie stir. 'No, Arnold, not now,' she muttered and she turned over. The tapping persisted. She opened her eyes and tentatively pulled back a little of the curtain and was startled by the face peering in at the window. 'Argh!'

'Good morning!' said Ned.

Great, she thought. An early visit from the local hotty.

She hastily rubbed at her eyes to get rid of any sleep, checked her chin for dribble and tried to pull a brush through her hair but it got stuck, so she quickly put her mop of hair in a hairband.

'Hi,' she said, pulling open the rusting van door.

'Sorry,' said Ned. 'Did I wake you?'

'Nooo,' lied Dixie, but a giant yawn she couldn't stifle

gave her away. 'Maybe a bit.' She pulled self-consciously at her rainbow pyjamas.

'I can come back.' He turned to leave.

'No. It's fine. As long as you don't tell everyone what a fright I look first thing.'

'No one to tell,' he said.

Dixie did a double-take, making Ned jolt as he realized his faux pas.

'Not that you look a fright. Because you don't. I look much worse in a morning. I'm all stubbly because I need to shave. And you obviously don't. Maybe I should stop talking now,' he said.

She liked how awkward he seemed. That was how she felt a lot of the time. 'It's OK. I don't easily take offence,' she said. There was an uncomfortable silence where they both looked at each other and looked away. 'Anyway, come in.'

'Thanks.' Ned climbed inside and came face to face with the underwear she was drying on a string across the middle of the van.

'Oh heavens!' She grabbed the first pair of pants, making the clothes peg fly off and hit Ned in the eye.

'Ow!'

'I am sooo sorry,' she said speedily gathering the other garments, rolling them into a ball and shoving them under her duvet.

'It's OK,' said Ned, blinking rapidly. 'Actually that hurt. If you've got some ice.'

'Sorry, no freezer. But I can put some cold water on a

piece of kitchen roll,' she suggested, already grabbing a sheet. 'There you go.' She handed it to him. 'It's like at school when a wet paper towel cured all ills.' She giggled self-consciously.

'Thanks,' he said, looking at her with his one good eye.

Dixie desperately wanted to give her hair a proper brush because she now had visions of the back of her head looking like a bird's nest. 'Sorry, was there something you needed me for?' she asked, unable to stand the tension any longer.

Ned became animated. 'Yes, well, more something you might need me for.'

Dixie raised her eyebrows. It was early and she really wasn't sure what Ned was offering.

'When I was a teenager I used to tinker with a kit car.'

'That's nice,' said Dixie, still none the wiser.

'So I know my way around a vehicle and thought that maybe I could help you fix Elsie.' He bit his lip as he waited for her reply.

She could have hugged him but restrained herself. She wasn't sure what she was more pleased about – Ned offering to fix her campervan or him referring to her as Elsie.

23

Nora now had a deeper understanding of the expression 'caught between the devil and the deep blue sea'. In her scenario, the deep blue sea was actually a craggy cliff face that leaned over a gorge, and the devil was a tight-shorts-wearing lech who went by the name of Trent. She had chosen the rock climbing. Now she was standing at the base of the precipice she was more than a little uncertain about her choices. With a steep cliff above her and a sheer drop to the side of her, she gulped.

'Stop overthinking it and definitely don't work out the odds of dying. Just go for it and it'll be fine,' said Jay with a smile.

'Was that meant to be reassuring?' asked Nora.

'More motivational.' He looked slightly hurt. 'Try and look on the bright side.'

'I can only see a downside.' She peered tentatively over the edge at the long drop to the river Wye at the bottom.

Jay stood in front of her. Initially he was a bit too close and had to back up. 'Look at me,' he said.

'Not a lot of choice if you're going to stand there.'

'I'm serious,' he said, changing the tone of his voice and also squaring his shoulders, making him appear a little stern. 'When life presents you with challenges, the last thing you do is show your weaknesses.'

'Are you acting?' she asked.

'Yeah,' he said, reverting to his usual gentle demeanour.

'It was very good,' said Nora.

'Aww, thank you.' Jay put his hands on his chest. He shook his head. 'We've got side-tracked.' He ran his palms up and down a few inches from his face as if resetting his features and making Nora concentrate. 'Focus. I'm here for you. Today, tomorrow and every day I'm going to be cheering you on. I know in my heart there's nothing you can't do but we all have wobbles and that's when we shore each other up so that we can take the next step, knowing that someone we trust has our back.'

'Acting again?' she asked with a smile.

He shook his head.

'Oh.' She was working out what to say when the leader called to get everyone's attention.

'Who wants to go first?' he asked.

'Me!' shouted Nora. From somewhere she had found the courage and gumption she needed. She also wanted to get the climb out of the way because the longer she had to think about it and work out death odds, the worse things would get. Like that time at the fairground when she worked out the odds of getting whiplash on the dodgems. By the time she had got to the front of the bumper cars line she was petrified, so she'd shared the information with everyone in the queue. Looking back that had actually turned out well because, apart from an irate fairground attraction owner, she had the dodgems to herself and a risk-free ride.

'You've got this,' said Jay. 'And I've got you.' This time she knew for certain he wasn't acting.

Last-minute safety checks were made and Nora found herself staring at a wall of rock. Her heart was thumping in her chest and her mind was full of unhelpful statistics. Jay leaned in and whispered in her ear.

'This is the bit where you start climbing.'

'I don't think I can,' she replied in a hushed voice. It wasn't so much that she was matching his whispers or that she didn't want the others to hear, it was more about her not wanting to admit it out loud.

'Take a deep breath,' he suggested.

Nora tried but her breathing was all shaky. 'My brain is so close to going into flight mode.'

'I take it you don't mean when you flick that little switch on your mobile before you jet off to the sun, do you?'

She shook her head. 'No. This is full-on being-chased-by-a-T-Rex run-for-your-life mode. I can't do it.'

'Yeah, you can,' said Jay. 'Here's a little trick I use when I can't remember my lines. I hum a favourite tune.' There was a long pause. 'What's your favourite song?'

'I can't think,' said Nora. She felt like a computer being hacked. Jay was asking her for information she didn't seem to have access to.

'That's OK. How about we go with "Boom, Boom, Boom" by the Vengaboys?' Nora spun around. 'I'm joking,' he said with a smile on his lips. 'I think a bit of McFly is what we need. Ready?'

'No,' she said, but there was something about the look in his eyes that made her want to try.

She stepped forward and put her hands on the first holds she could see, doing her best to ignore her thudding heart. Behind her, Jay started to hum the opening bars of 'It's All About You' by McFly and she found herself joining in. The humming automatically steadied her breathing and she began to climb.

Nora concentrated hard on humming while the words to the song filled her mind and she looked for each hold one at a time. Below her she could tell Jay was trying to hum louder, though he was becoming distant. Each grab for a crevice felt like a little victory, every push up a win.

'Last one is on the right,' said someone above her and it pulled her attention. The smiling face of one of the climbing crew was looking down at her from the top of the cliff and pointing to a nearby hand hold. She reached out with renewed confidence. 'That's it. You're almost there,' he added.

As Nora climbed the last few feet and scrambled on to the clifftop she heard Jay break out into full voice for the last verse, although together they must have hummed the song all the way through a few times to get her to the top. He had a great singing voice but it was the words that were speaking to her. She felt a rush like nothing she'd felt before and Jay's proud face at the bottom made it feel extra special. With Jay's support she'd done it and she was elated.

*

Dixie was thrilled that Ned was up for helping her to fix up Elsie. It gave her another little boost. She was starting to realize that while peace, quiet and meditation were wonderful for her mental health, she was also the sort of individual who needed to be around people. She was missing Nora far more than she had expected to. They messaged all the time, but it was no substitute for having a good natter. She also missed Renee. It wasn't that she was a stand-in for her granny. Her own grandparents lived in the wilds of Cornwall where they seemed to spend an inordinate amount of time reading the newspaper and walking. No, there was something about Renee that gave her an energy boost. Perhaps she was the very model of how Dixie would like her later years to pan out, although that would be setting the bar rather high and she definitely couldn't handle her alcohol the way Renee did, but perhaps that came with age. Renee was a living legend and that was a status Dixie was unlikely to achieve. But in more subtle ways she pushed Dixie and the others to be braver.

She was finishing tidying up when there was a knock on the side of the van and a smiling Ned held up a large toolbox. 'I'm ready.'

'Excellent. The table in here is awfully wobbly.' She demonstrated. 'That's a priority. I'd like to re-cover the door panels with this fabulous sticky felt I bought.' She held up the roll. 'But getting the panels off is a right faff. I bought some utensil storage which needs putting up and I don't know one end of a screwdriver from the other.' She moved through the van. 'I thought about here.' She pointed above the sink. 'Or maybe better here.' She pointed to the left of the sink area. And then down a bit. She pursed her lips as she pondered the many options.

Ned was giving her an odd look.

'If that's OK?' she asked.

'The table is your priority?' he asked slowly.

'Definitely. I almost lost my salad last night. It's like eating on the side of the Eiger.' She let out a giggle. 'I think my friend Renee has a story about Ursula Andress and a trip up the Eiger.' Dixie shook the thought away. 'Anyway, if you can fix the table I'd be very grateful.'

'OK, if you're sure,' said Ned, and with a casual shrug he came inside.

This time it didn't seem as claustrophobic with him in the van with her, although he did take up quite a lot of space.

'Shall I make us drinks and then I'll get out of your way,' suggested Dixie, getting out her gas ring and kettle. She had just enough water in one of the 1.5 litre Evian bottles. She'd need to get another one on her next visit to the garage. She didn't like bringing back water because it was heavy but as there wasn't a handy stream or waterfall nearby she had no choice.

'Coffee with milk and two sugars please,' said Ned.

'Ah, I probably should have been more specific. I can offer black coffee with no sugar. Did you still want one?'

'No, it's OK. I was only being polite. Are you sure you're managing OK living here?'

Dixie was a little affronted. 'Just because I don't have milk and sugar doesn't mean I'm not managing.'

'But there's no running water or toilet facilities,' he said, failing to hide his mild disgust at the thought.

'I have a port-a-potty. I mean loo. It's very discreet and hygienic.' She didn't mention her concerns for its capacity.

'OK. That's good then.'

'Do I smell?' She put her hands on her hips but then realized that exposing her armpits might not be the best way to demonstrate her point so she crossed her arms instead.

'Goodness no, of course you don't. I wasn't saying that.' Ned glanced around as if looking for an escape from the hole he'd dug himself into. 'I'm sorry. I'd best get on with the um . . . table.'

Dixie busied herself with making a single cup of black coffee even though she didn't want one either. Things were decidedly frosty all of a sudden.

24

The climbing weekend went by in a flash and they were soon back in Loughborough and unpacking their stuff from the back of the minibus. Obviously Trent was still playing the hero and now had his arm in a makeshift sling so that nobody further damaged his broken pinky finger by mistake. He had made a point of staring at Nora when he'd explained to everyone why he was wearing the sling. She was too tired to care. All the climbing had taken it out of her but the sense of achievement remained. There was also a feeling of being closer to Jay somehow, but then trips like this were all about bonding over shared experiences.

Nora and Jay decided to get an uber back from the drop-off point together. Jay seemed quite keen that he wasn't alone when he entered his house. Nora had a feeling Jay was worried that he might find Renee half eaten by Bruce. Instead they were met by a smiling Renee and the smell of home cooking.

'Something smells amazing,' said Jay, putting his stuff down in the hall before freezing as if sensing something was amiss. 'Where's Bruce? What's happened?'

Renee waved her hands in a calm-down motion. 'Don't panic. Everything is fine. He's on his rug. Dinner's on. Are you stopping?' she asked Nora as she gave her a hug.

'Er?' Nora looked at Jay. She'd only really come as back-up in case Jay's wildest nightmares had come true.

Jay nodded. 'You might as well stay, unless you need to get home for Oliver or anything?'

'A shower is at the top of my list,' said Nora, trying to subtly sniff her own armpit.

'Take the weight off and I'll fix us all an Espresso Martini. I've been working on them this weekend and I've almost perfected it,' said Renee proudly. 'You can be my guinea pigs,' she added before heading off to the kitchen.

Jay was still putting things down and Nora was taking her shoes off. 'See, she's fine,' whispered Nora. 'And Bruce hasn't come to bark at us. That's all good. Isn't it?'

'He's probably spaced out on Espresso Martinis.'

'He's on his rug.'

'He doesn't have a rug,' said Jay, throwing his hands up.

In the living room they found Bruce lying on a sheepskin rug with his legs in the air. Jay inched towards the dog and Nora took a seat on the sofa.

'Here we are. Try these cheeky little buggers,' said Renee, putting down a tray and decanting three crocheted coasters and three coupe glasses.

'I like your coasters,' said Nora, nodding at Jay.

'They're not mine.'

'I couldn't find any and I got a bit bored so I made you a set to match the cushions,' said Renee, sitting down.

'I don't have cushions,' mouthed Jay at Nora with wide eyes.

'Cheers,' said Renee, taking a sip of her cocktail and smacking her lips together.

'Thanks,' said Jay, looking puzzled. 'They're not my glasses.'

'I couldn't find anything suitable for cocktails so I ordered in.' Renee looked at them both. 'Drink up!'

'Renee,' said Jay. 'What's wrong with Bruce?'

They all stared at the dog, who looked like he was doing a dying-fly impression, although motionless with his tongue lolling out of his mouth.

'I've been doing some relaxation techniques with him and he's picked them up a treat. Brucey, Daddy's back,' said Renee and he seemed to come to life. He rolled over and lay there with his head on his paws. 'Give him a fuss then. He's been looking forward to you getting home.' Renee stared at Jay.

'Oh right. Um, OK. Hello, Bruce.' Jay leaned tentatively forward and patted the dog on the head.

'He can barely feel that. Have you seen how thick his coat is? Give him a hearty rub, that's what he likes.'

Jay swallowed hard. 'A hearty rub. OK.' Jay's fingers disappeared into the dog's coat as he made more of a fuss of him.

'That's better. Now do tummy tickles. He bloody loves that, he does,' said Renee. 'Brucey, roll over for Daddy.' Bruce immediately flipped on to his back, making Jay whip his hands out of the way. Renee pointed at the dog's middle.

Nora was trying not to laugh. Jay's fear and discomfort was palpable. 'What's with the rug, Renee?'

'He needed a space that was all his,' she said.

'He has a dog bed,' said Jay, trying to look at Renee but clearly not wanting to take his eyes off the dog as he rubbed his tummy.

'He doesn't like it. It's probably been used as a punishment by his previous owners. Go to your bed,' snapped Renee, making Nora and Jay jump and for a second Nora thought Jay was going to make for the stairs. 'The rug is much nicer for him.'

'I think you've done an amazing job with Bruce,' said Nora, sipping her cocktail and making an O shape with her mouth because it was potent. She still wasn't used to Renee measures. 'Are the cushions new?' she asked.

'Yes,' said Renee and Jay together – the tone of each of them quite a contrast.

'The place needed a bit of colour,' said Renee. 'I hope you don't mind.'

'Well . . .' Jay was pulling a face.

'I love them. Teal is the perfect colour for this room and it goes with the painting,' said Nora, studying the beautiful picture of a café on what looked like a Paris side street.

'What painting?' asked Jay, swivelling his head in different directions until he spotted it.

'Oh that's nothing. I whipped it up in a morning,' said Renee. 'I was briefly Salvador Dalí's muse,' she added. 'Lovely man. The locals frowned upon him taking his anteater out in Montmartre. Groovy times.' Nora wasn't sure if that was a euphemism or not and couldn't hide her giggles but Renee hadn't noticed because she seemed to be lost in the painting for a moment. Jay continued to look bewildered as he stroked the dog, who was the most chilled-out Nora had ever seen him.

'Renee,' said Jay, 'have you drugged Bruce?'

Renee cackled. 'Good heavens. Of course not. What do you take me for? And anyway I wouldn't waste the good stuff on him,' she said with a cheeky wink. 'There's no witchcraft. It's just good manners and a little chicken.'

Bruce lifted his head. 'Brucey, come here, please,' said Renee. The dog got up and came to sit in front of her. 'Thank you. Brucey, lie down, please.' Renee held out a piece of chicken and moved her hand towards the floor. Bruce lay down and gently took the chicken as his reward. 'Good boy,' she said, giving him a rough rub on his head.

'Wow,' said Jay.

'He definitely has had some training before. I just tapped into the fact that he'll do anything for a piece of chicken. Now all I have to do is train you,' she said.

Jay looked alarmed and Renee started to laugh.

'I need to train you how to command Bruce. Not to lie down!'

'Oh OK,' said Jay, looking relieved.

'Right. Dinner time!' Renee knocked back the rest of her drink. Bruce quickly righted himself. 'Not you, Bruce. You stay here. There's a good boy.'

'I'll feed him,' said Jay, getting to his feet.

'No you won't,' said Renee. 'He's learned that he has to wait until we've had ours. Then it's his turn. He's the beta.'

'Does that make me the alpha?' asked Jay, looking chuffed.

'You'll get there.' Renee ushered him to the table, where they found a new tablecloth and a lovely floral centrepiece.

Nora pointed at the flowers and Jay shrugged. Renee definitely had an eye for interiors and she'd brightened Jay's place up a treat. 'I really like what she's done,' whispered Nora.

'I think I'll need a few days to get used to it.' Jay's eyes darted about as if searching for any other alterations.

'I especially like the conservatory she's added on,' said Nora, making Jay spin around to face the back of the house.

'Oh very droll. Although I wouldn't put it past her. She'd have probably dug the foundations herself.' They both laughed.

'What's the joke?' asked Renee as she ferried lasagne and salad to the table.

'We're impressed with what you've done this week-end,' said Nora.

'Gotta keep busy,' said Renee.

'You've definitely done that.' Nora was amazed by what Renee had achieved in such a short space of time. 'Did you make this too?' she asked as a waft of rich pasta sauce floated in her direction.

'Goodness, no. Life's too short for fannying around with lasagne. I bought it from Marks and Spencer. Red or white?' she asked, holding up two bottles. Nora could only admire Renee's priorities.

They were interrupted by the doorbell. Bruce ran to the hallway and barked once. 'Good dog,' said Renee. 'Right, that'll be my taxi. You too have fun. Don't do anything I wouldn't do, which gives you quite a lot of scope.'

'Are you not staying to eat?' asked Jay.

'Sorry. It's illicit poker night and I'm hosting. Cheerio.' And with that she picked up her bag and left.

Nora and Jay looked at each other. 'She's exhausting,' said Jay.

'I think she might be an animatronic.'

'That would make more sense,' said Jay, pouring them both a glass of white wine. 'Thanks for a lovely weekend,' he added, raising his glass, which Nora clinked.

'Ditto. You got me through it.'

'Nah. You don't need me.' Jay began serving the lasagne.

Actually I think I do, thought Nora. The ping from a text interrupted her thoughts.

Jay pulled his phone out and his face lit up.

'Anything exciting?' she asked.

'It's Tasha Blake. She's in London tomorrow night and she's free for dinner if I'm still up for it.' His face dropped. 'I can't leave Bruce again.'

'I'll look after Bruce. It's definitely my turn,' said Nora.

'You're the best,' said Jay, putting away his phone and looking happier than if he'd won an Oscar.

*

Dixie had been feeling decidedly lonely. Ned had fixed the table for her but had made some excuse about needing to be somewhere else and had left swiftly. The atmosphere had been uncomfortable after they'd had words about her living arrangements but she had felt worse once he'd left. It seemed an awkward silence with someone was preferable to one on your own. She'd not even seen Arnold for a while and Nora's phone was going straight to voicemail so either it was switched off or she was out of range. She had mentioned going away for the weekend so perhaps that was why Dixie couldn't get hold of her. For a moment Dixie thought how nice it would be to go away for the weekend, then she looked around and sighed. She was away, although she was stuck in one place. Things really weren't panning out how she'd hoped.

She made a start on swapping the cushion covers but her heart wasn't in it. For some reason she thought about the notes that had been left on the van windscreen by the angry landowner. She'd not had one for a few days. Even that person had stopped bothering about her. Everyone was deserting her. There was a moment where she had a wobble. The pull of normality was strong. A Waitrose dinner and a nicely chilled Pinot Noir called to her. But she simply couldn't give up, although it was now Sunday so technically she had reached the mini milestone she had set herself of surviving for two whole weeks. The goalposts had only changed when Ned had appeared. She tapped her lip with her fingertip as she thought. She was torn and she wasn't entirely sure why.

Why had Ned's words and his reaction affected her so much, she wondered? She could admit that Elsie was a bit basic but it was no worse than camping, not that she'd ever been camping. Her parents had a couple of second homes and they frequently visited the villas of other family members so rarely holidayed in the UK. She suspected the one time she'd been in a yurt didn't count as that had had its own wine fridge, double bed and shower tent. But it wasn't her fault that her parents had been able to take her on nice holidays.

Maybe she felt defensive of Elsie. She wondered if Ned would be back. The thought that he might not made her feel sad. Well, sadder than she was already feeling.

What she needed was to snap herself out of the doldrums and get back on track. The important thing was to make her campervan habitable for her and if Ned did ever come back then she could look him in the eye and say 'Yah boo sucks!' Maybe she'd come up with something a little better than that given time.

25

Monday's Bruce-sitting went by without incident. Getting him to comply was surprisingly easy now that Renee had shared her top tips. Nora spent all evening wondering how Jay was getting on with Tasha. When he finally walked in at almost midnight she was curled up on his sofa watching *Aquaman* and switched it off quickly. Jay would only rant about the naffness of it but Nora quite liked it. Mainly because it starred a half-dressed Jason Momoa – what was not to like?

'How'd it go?' she asked as Jay appeared in the living-room doorway and Bruce went to greet him. Jay looked tired but still every inch the film star, having put in contact lenses and dressed up specially to meet Tasha. It was a big change as she was used to seeing him in his trackies.

'It went OK. I guess. Bit weird really.'

'Did you show her the ear-wiggling too soon?' she asked with a grin.

He pretended to look shocked. 'I'd never do that before a third date. What do you take me for?' He flopped on to the sofa. 'The thing was it was me, Tasha and Tasha's PR, Anastasia.'

'Oh,' said Nora, feeling quite pleased and then feeling a little guilty that Jay's date hadn't turned out to be one at all. She changed her expression to one of consolation. 'That's a shame. Did you and Tasha have any time together?'

'Only when Anastasia went to the loo.'

'Not a great night then?'

'It was nice enough. Food was good. And they have lots of plans for publicity for *Undercover Bullets* so that's cool and we got mobbed by photographers when we left the restaurant.'

'Is that good?' asked Nora.

'It's all publicity,' said Jay, who was fussing Bruce without looking as if he was worried about losing fingers.

'Look at you, throwing caution to the wind.'

'Sometimes you have to take a risk.'

How true that was.

Jay had been quiet at the start of Crafting and Cocktails on Tuesday evening but after a couple of Renee's newly perfected Espresso Martinis he perked up. But when he checked his phone for the umpteenth time, Nora had to say something.

'Is everything OK?'

'Hmm.' It took him a moment to pull his eyes away from his phone. 'Just some weirdos on social media. There seem to be more and more of them for some reason.'

'Is it the paparazzi photos?' Pictures of Jay and Tasha leaving the restaurant had been all over the internet.

'Yeah, I guess that's what it is.' Jay put his phone away and went back to his knitting.

'That's why Liza Minnelli used to love Monaco. No paparazzi allowed.' Renee laughed. 'It's a bloody good job really given the things we got up to.'

Renee began telling a story about Jackie Stewart winning the 1966 Monaco Grand Prix but Nora found she was distracted. Jay had something on his mind, and it hurt her to see that it was troubling him.

Wednesday whizzed by as Nora was meeting Liam after work in the pub they used to like to go to when they were dating, the Anne of Cleves. It was in Burton Street and had an olde-worlde charm without being kitsch. Nora was first to arrive so she got herself a Diet Coke and pondered whether to sit in the corner by the fire like they used to do. Was that too obvious? Then again, the odds of him remembering were probably slim and too obscure for even her to work out. She was standing by the bar with her drink in one hand and a gift bag in the other when Liam walked in. He'd always been handsome but a few years had made a big difference. His hair was shorter and neater but his boyish good looks were now more chiselled. He had matured and so had his dress sense. A crisp white shirt under a casual jacket looked good on him and a huge improvement on the tight T-shirts he'd favoured when they'd dated.

'Hey, Nora.' He put his arms out but immediately seemed unsure of what should happen next. They gave each other a peck on the cheek in an uncoordinated fashion. 'What are you drinking?'

'Diet Coke. But I've already got one.' She raised her glass as evidence.

'OK. I'll join you. Did you want any peanuts? Do you still like peanuts?'

'I do but no thanks,' she said. 'I'll grab a seat.'

'The one by the fire is free,' he said, pointing keenly. It seemed he did remember. This was a great start.

When Liam took off his jacket and sat down she could see he'd kept himself in good shape. She put the gift bag on the table and pushed it towards him. 'I probably should have done this a lot sooner. But anyway, there you go.' She pointed awkwardly at the bag.

He peered inside. 'A sticky willy!' he said, possibly a little louder than was necessary as it made the woman at the next table spin around. She didn't hide the fact she was checking them out in a very judgemental manner.

'Because I killed yours and I'm sorry,' Nora said. 'Better late than never and all that.'

'You didn't need to,' he said, but he hadn't taken his eyes off the plant since he'd been presented with it. 'I was a bit of a dick about the whole thing. I think I was going through an angsty emotional phase at the time and you took the brunt of that. I thought about apologizing so many times but never got around to it.'

'Me too.' That had gone a lot better than she'd dared to hope.

Hours flew by. Conversation had quickly turned to reminiscing and the awful lot of shared history they had. They'd quickly settled back into easy chatter. Memories bred memories as they opened doors to shared jokes and funny stories. They had been friends before they had dated, which made it a double blow when they'd split up. That was something she didn't ever want to go through again. Making friends had always been hard for Nora, and life had frequently shown her that letting people get close made you vulnerable. They still shared the same sense of humour and ended up laughing so hard it hurt, making the nosy lady from the next table tut and shake her head a lot. More soft drinks were consumed and they shared a bag of peanuts just like they used to do. When the landlord called time they both checked their watches in disbelief. The evening had whizzed by and Nora's tummy muscles had had a good workout from laughing so hard.

Liam's eyes widened. 'Getting chucked out of a pub, that reminds me of—'

'Sasha's birthday do at the White Hart when you walked out with their flowerpot on your head and nobody stopped you,' said Nora, finishing his sentence before getting the giggles again. When the laughter faded they held each other's gaze. That had been the night they had first kissed. Looking at him now, the details of that kiss were suddenly clear in her mind. It wouldn't have taken much for her to hold his face in her hands once more and kiss him. His features were so familiar and yet he had changed and she wanted to get to know him all over again.

Liam blinked and the moment was gone. 'We'd better get going. But it has been so, so good to catch-up. It's been too long.'

'It has.' Was that it? Were they going to part ways? If they did, it was likely they'd not meet for another few years. Nora was in a quandary. She wanted to see Liam again but only if he wanted to see her. Unfortunately she didn't have much time to work it all out because Liam was on his feet and getting ready to leave. Nora grabbed her bag and followed him into the car park.

'I'm parked over there,' said Liam, squeezing his key fob and making an Audi a few cars away beep and flash its lights.

She sensed his hesitation. 'I can't believe how quick the evening went. We literally only talked about the good old days, which makes us sound ancient. I didn't even ask you about what you're up to now.' She knew he was working as an accountant and was single from their text messages but not much else.

'That means we've got stuff to talk about next time,' he said.

She pointed at him for no good reason. 'You're right. We'd best get something in the diary.'

'I'll message you.' He scanned her up and down. 'Take care, Nora.' He gave her a brief hug and a kiss on the cheek before striding off to his car, leaving her pondering.

As soon as she got in, Nora updated her spreadsheet and called Dixie to tell her all about her evening. She was still hunting down snacks with her head in the fridge while she relayed everything that had happened, and her friend made the right noises in the right places as all good friends should.

'Oh dear. That was a friend-zone goodbye,' said Dixie when Nora reached the end of her story.

'I know, right?' Nora didn't feel any better having her thoughts confirmed by Dixie but it was lovely to hear her voice. 'And he said "Take care". I say that to my nanna after a visit to Bosnia because I fear she might have a fall or choke on a Werther's Original or something before the next time I see her because I don't see her very often.'

'Ouch. That doesn't imply he wants to rip your clothes off or settle into a long-term relationship,' said Dixie.

'Exactly my thoughts.' Nora bit into a large lump of cheddar and shut the fridge door with her bum.

'What now?' asked Dixie.

Nora walked through to the living room and flopped on to the sofa, making one of Oliver's eyes swivel in her direction to watch her thoughtfully chew her cheese. 'I think I'll wait for him to make the next move.'

'Good idea,' said Dixie firmly.

'Unless he doesn't call me, then I'll probably message him in like a week or so.'

'Oh, absolutely you should,' said Dixie. 'I've sort of done the same thing. I hadn't heard from the grumpy-message person so I've left a note under the wiper.'

Nora needed a moment to process what Dixie had said so she munched on a bit more cheddar. 'Isn't it a good thing that they've stopped leaving angry notes on Elsie?'

'It definitely is. Although, when I didn't hear from them it was a bit like they'd ghosted me, plus I felt everything was up in the air and I wanted clarification or closure or both.'

'And leaving a note for someone who wants to evict you will do that, will it?' asked Nora.

'If there's no reply then I think I can safely assume they have given up or died or something else equally final. If there is a response then I'll know where I stand.' The sound of Dixie sighing came down the line.

'Are you OK?'

There was a small pause before Dixie replied. 'I had a tiff with Ned. It was something and nothing but I can't resolve it because I have no way of getting in touch with him.'

'You know that you don't need Ned, don't you?' asked Nora.

It took a while for Dixie to reply. 'I know. It's lonely, just me, Elsie and Arnold. And Arnold's busy most of the time.'

Nora wondered at what point she should start to worry about her friend's mental health if she considered a clapped-out campervan and a bolshie squirrel her closest companions. 'If you want to do this campervan adventure then you need to properly go for it. Get the renovations completed, get someone out to fix Elsie and move on. But if you're done with it all, that's OK too and you can come home. You've proved you can cope without your parents so that box has been ticked. You can stay with me until your tenant moves out.'

'You are completely right,' said Dixie with gusto.

'About which one?' asked Nora, waving a piece of cheese in the air and making Oliver's eye swivel wildly.

'About giving it a proper go. I'll crack on first thing tomorrow with the renovations. That's what I set out to do and I'm going to finish it . . . assuming it's not too hard because the door panels are not easy to get off and I've only ever made curtains once before and that was for my doll's house.'

'You definitely want to stay?' Nora felt she needed to check.

'Absolutely. For the time being anyway.'

'OK, if you're sure,' said Nora and she popped the last piece of cheese in her mouth.

26

Nora went round to Jay's and was surprised to be met at the door by two Jays. The real one and a life-size cardboard cut-out.

'I know that review said your acting was wooden but I think they'll notice if you have this as a stand-in,' she quipped as she took in the life-size replica.

'Haha. It's a present from my stalker.'

'Shit. No way. You've got a stalker?'

'It would appear that I have.'

'Was there a message with it?' asked Nora, studying the grainy image of Jay in jeans and T-shirt.

'No, but given it's me when I popped to Tesco Express last week I think it's safe to say that's a clear message in itself.'

'Bloody hell, this is a bit scary. Are you OK?'

'Let's say I'm really glad I have Bruce at home. I guess this is the price of fame. Not that I've had much of that.'

'Now come on. Those press pictures of Tasha and you leaving the restaurant the other night were all over social media.'

He pulled a face. 'In most of them all you could see of me was my elbow.'

Nora pointed at the cardboard cut-out's elbow. 'And a very photogenic one it is too.'

He rolled his eyes at her. 'Anyway, let's stick this in a cupboard.'

'Do you not want to burn it?' she asked, thinking it was weird to keep it.

'I don't think watching my own effigy go up in flames will be great for my mental health and I can't put it out with the bins in case the neighbours think I bought it. So for now it's living in the cupboard. Maybe if I get famous I'll donate it to charity.'

'One you don't like,' said Nora, and Jay rolled his eyes at her.

Nora relayed her evening with Liam once more for Jay's benefit over a supermarket pizza and received a similar response to the one she'd had from Dixie. At least her friends were consistent.

'What's the plan now?' he asked, getting out a pull-along hoover.

'I'm going to let Liam make the next move and anyway I've got my meet-up with Mickey tomorrow.' Nora watched as Jay plugged in the vacuum. This was weird: he was a bit of a neat freak but they'd not made any mess with the pizza.

'Tomorrow? You're taking time off work to see him? You never take time off work.'

'Which is why I have loads of holiday I need to take.

And a Friday was better for him because he's a personal trainer so he works weekends.'

'Of course he is,' said Jay. 'So a day at the beach then. Weather forecast is sunny. Should be the perfect day for it.'

'It should. Are you working tomorrow?' she asked.

'I wish. But I've an audiobook coming up so no need to sign up for a job pushing supermarket trollies just yet.'

'That's good news.'

'Thank you. And it means tomorrow I will be free as a bird.'

Nora smiled at Jay's unsubtle approach. 'Did you and Bruce still want to come to Skegness?'

'Absolutely, say a time and we'll be ready and waiting. Bruce is a different hound.'

'He did seem calmer when I arrived.'

'I mean, *totally* different. I was considering taking him to the vet to get his microchip scanned in case Renee had got in a stunt double.'

Nora chuckled.

'Don't laugh,' said Jay. 'I would not put it past her and he has no distinguishing features.'

Nora remembered a disturbing conversation she'd had when she'd been telling someone that her childhood tortoise had changed colour while in hibernation and both her parents had started to laugh and all the little traumatic pieces of a twisted puzzle had slotted into place. Nora involuntarily shuddered at the memory. 'Do you really think she's swapped your dog?'

'Nah, he still keeps taking the robovac outside to bury it. I'd not be that unlucky to have two identical dogs who do that.'

Nora watched Jay fire up the cleaner. Bruce came trotting in from the kitchen and flopped down in front of Jay, who started to run the nozzle over the German shepherd's middle.

'Are you vacuuming the dog?'

Jay switched it off and Bruce lifted his head to glare at him. 'Yeah. With his coat he needs grooming daily and this is way easier. He killed the robovac. There was only so much soil it could take on board before it died. I bought this as a replacement. He barked at it so I thought I'd show him it wasn't anything to be scared of, which was when we discovered it doubled as a very effective dog groomer.' He fired it up again and Bruce looked like he was in heaven.

'He does seem different,' said Nora, impressed by how chilled-out Bruce was now.

'See, I told you. Swapped for a doppelganger.'

'Just like you,' she said, pointing at the cardboard cut-out.

The next morning Nora checked the weather before choosing an outfit and as the forecast was sunshine she went for a simple summer dress. She'd already got all her beach things together the previous evening so all she had to do was load them into the car and leave. She always liked to plan ahead; she felt it took out a lot of stress and also reduced the odds of forgetting something vital.

As promised, Jay and Bruce were standing by the gate when she pulled up. Bruce barked excitedly but Jay waved a little chicken in front of him and gave him a command and the dog stopped barking and ate the chicken.

'Impressive,' said Nora, getting out of the car. 'Renee has trained you well.'

'But I will now forever and more smell like a walking deli counter.' Jay pulled a Ziplock bag of chicken pieces from his pocket.

Nora tried not to laugh. 'But if it works that's a good thing.'

Jay mumbled something as he brought Bruce to the car. The dog was determined to get in the passenger seat so there was a bit of a stand-off but the chicken won and Bruce eventually lay down on the back seat, securely strapped in.

'Tell me about Mickey,' said Jay once they had set off.

Nora's mind flew back to when she'd dated Mickey. It had been a bit of a whirlwind. 'I mainly remember lots of sex. Great sex and takeaways.' She was surprisingly comfortable telling Jay honestly about her relationship with Mickey.

'And you classify that as a relationship?'

Nora tipped her head from side to side. 'We had fun. I like someone who can make me laugh. We did other stuff together.' Nora had to rack her brains for what that other stuff was. 'Mickey is big into his fitness so we went jogging together.'

'You jogged?' When she glanced across, Jay was staring at her agog.

'Yes. Is that so hard to believe?'

'Er, yeah. Because you *hate* jogging. And I quote: "If we were meant to run around in circles, we'd all be hamsters."'

'I might have said that. Anyway, we got on well together, enjoyed each other's company and the sex was—'

'Yeah, you mentioned that already. Why did you split up?' asked Jay.

This bit was less comfortable to discuss. 'There were rumours about him cheating on me with the receptionist at the gym. But they weren't true.' She took a breath. 'However, I did walk in on him having sex with the head receiver of a local warehouse.'

'Head receiver? How ironic.'

'Exactly what I said!'

'So he was a cheat and you're considering a long-term relationship with him. Have I got that right?' asked Jay.

'I did consider skipping over Mickey but people are capable of changing and if I'm going to apply the theory then I need to apply it fully.'

'Hmm.' Jay didn't sound like he agreed with her approach.

They got to Skegness with plenty of time to spare – Nora always built in contingency.

'If we find a good spot on the beach we can set up

camp and then I'll go and meet Mickey,' she said, getting the things out of the boot.

'Or we could all grab a coffee and then me and Bruce will set things up.'

Nora gave him a look.

'What?' he asked.

'For one thing, I won't know where you are and there might not be signal on the beach so I'll never find you. And secondly, while Bruce is a very good boy—' The dog wagged his tail at the words, which distracted Nora. 'Yes, he is. He's a good boy. Brucey is a good—'

Jay cleared his throat, which regained Nora's attention. 'And secondly, if you have hold of Bruce's lead in one hand, there's no way you'll be able to put up a windbreak on your own.'

'Windbreak? How posh are you?' Jay gave her a dig in the ribs. 'Come on then, Queen Camilla, let's see where to erect your throne and windbreak.'

The sun was already shining and, because it was a Friday, the beach was relatively quiet. With their arms full they set off across the sand. They circumnavigated a small family where the toddler was hitting things with a spade while his father made an elaborate sandcastle. Nora and Jay chose a spot away from other people, as Jay had brought a long lead for Bruce so he could have a bit of freedom. He wasn't yet confident enough to let Bruce run free. Renee had promised to work on his recall next week.

Bruce was a little tentative stepping on the sand at

first, which made them think he may not have been to the beach before. While they were trying to put up the windbreak, Bruce discovered that sand was excellent for digging, which appeared to be the most fun thing ever. It was lovely to see him beginning to enjoy life. That was until he ran about like a loon doing a number of laps around them both and tying them to the windbreak with his long lead. Jay and Nora were instantly pulled together face to face.

'Wow, extreme close-up,' said Nora with an embarrassed laugh.

'Sorry.' Jay tried to move his arm.

'Ouch,' said Nora as his elbow dug into her ribcage.

They both started to rotate in an attempt to free themselves but this got Bruce even more excited and he raced around them a few more times.

'Maybe if we stay still he'll be calm and we'll be able to get out.' Bruce started to dig a massive hole, showering them with sand. 'Argh!' squealed Nora as sand rained down on them.

'Brucey, come here please,' said Jay, making Bruce stop for a second before trying to eat the sand. Eventually Bruce turned around and tried to get to Jay but the lead was pulling tight. Bruce seemed confused that he couldn't reach Jay so pulled a bit harder, which squished Jay and Nora together a bit more.

'Maybe we didn't think this through,' said Nora, wriggling an arm free and trying to direct Bruce around the other way in the hope of loosening off the lead.

'Are you OK? Can I help?' called the dad from the family with the small child as he strode towards them.

'No thanks,' said Jay. 'We're—'

'Yes, please,' said Nora, encouraging the man over with an odd gesture of her partly trapped arm. The quicker he released them the better. The lower part of one of the posts was quite uncomfortable as it was sticking in her bum cheek and Jay's bent elbow was still digging in her ribs.

'Is he friendly?' asked the man as Bruce started to bark at him. The man stepped backwards and looked as if he was going to run back to his family.

'He's a rescue so he's a bit wary of people,' said Nora.

'But he's not bitten anyone,' said Jay. 'Well, not that I know of,' he added.

The man stared at Jay. 'Do I know you?'

Jay smiled, took a breath and let out the burp sequence he was known for.

The man looked repelled. 'Blimey, mate, there are ladies present.'

'Sorry, I thought you recognized me—'

'You look like my dentist,' said the man. 'But you're definitely not him.'

Nora started to giggle. Bruce continued to strain on the lead and bark ferociously at the man.

'Bruce, be quiet please,' said Jay. The dog looked at him. 'Now he wants some chicken. It's in my pocket.'

The man was still keeping his distance so Nora wriggled her hand back inside the windbreak and started trying to locate Jay's pocket.

'Not there!' said Jay with a high-pitched squeak.

'Sorry. You'll need to direct me.'

'Right a bit . . . No, my right, your left . . . Round a bit further . . . now put your hand in there and pull it out.'

Nora was concentrating but she could see the man sniggering in her peripheral vision. Her fingers met with moist cooked meat. 'Eww, I think I've found the chicken. At least I hope I have,' she said, retrieving her hand. She twisted as much as she could towards Bruce. 'Come here please, Bruce, and be a good boy for the nice man.' She shared some of the chicken with the dog, who wolfed it down. She waved the man closer but he only took one step. He seemed quite cautious around Bruce. 'Here, if you take the chicken he'll follow you anywhere.'

'OK.' The man took the chicken but in the handover he almost dropped it and Bruce darted forward, which made the man dash out of the way with the chicken in one hand and an eager Bruce close behind him.

But at least he was running in the right direction and the lead was soon loose enough for Jay and Nora to escape.

'Bruce, come here please!' shouted Jay, waving another piece of chicken. Bruce put on the brakes, stopped chasing the poor man and ran back to Jay.

'Thank you!' Nora called to the man. 'You can keep the chicken!'

Once the windbreak was up and picnic rugs were down, Jay checked his watch. 'I think I have time to go and grab a coffee if you're all right to wait here with Bruce.'

'No problem,' said Nora, settling herself on the blanket.

'Did you want one?' asked Jay.

'I'll probably get one with Mickey,' said Nora.

'Of course you will. OK. Back in a jiffy.' He went off across the sand sliding in and out of his flip-flops like a drunk surfer, which made Nora smile.

27

J ay hated flip-flops and he wasn't keen on sand either but they were a price he was prepared to pay for a day at the seaside. He had to agree with the Victorians that there was something restorative about sea air. It was hard not to keep checking over his shoulder as he waded across the soft sand but Nora and Bruce were fine, they were lying down together. He nodded to the nice helpful man who had now returned to his family but for some reason they appeared to be packing up early.

It wasn't far to the café and it was a nice stroll along the promenade in the sunshine. On the way he spotted an ice cream shop that looked like it needed checking out later. He ordered a vanilla latte to go and waited near a kiosk window. Jay took a moment to take in his surroundings. He rarely visited the seaside but it brought back memories of family holidays. His mum trying to feed everyone paste sandwiches they didn't want and then not letting them go swimming afterwards for reasons nobody ever explained. His dad spending far too long measuring out a cricket pitch on the sand and desperately trying to get the bails to stay on the stumps even though the merest breeze would knock them off. But despite any squabbles over spades or grumbles about sunhats they were all mollified by an ice cream. Happy days.

He watched a couple walk past him hand in hand and join the coffee queue. He was dark and rugged, she was blonde and petite. He wondered why small women seemed to go for big men. Were they trying to even out the gene pool perhaps? Did that mean there might be a very tall woman somewhere looking for someone exactly like Jay? The blonde woman was very pretty.

They were touching each other in that easy way that lovers do. They were talking quietly and almost every sentence was punctuated with a kiss. He didn't like to stare but it was hard not to and they were oblivious to anyone or anything else around them. All-consuming love, that was what Jay was after. To know someone felt the same as you did, that was the dream.

The man pulled his phone from his pocket and shook his head. 'I am so sorry. That's a client who needs me. I'm going to have to dash but I'll see you tonight, yeah?'

'You getting a coffee?' she asked.

'No time. I need to go right away. And you're going back to the office anyway.'

'OK. You owe me,' she said. The woman looked disappointed but she kissed him and waved as he strode off.

'One frothy almond milk and a caramel latte for Jay?' asked the lady at the kiosk window. Jay didn't like to leave Bruce out and a quick Google had told him small amounts of plant-based milk alternatives were OK for dogs.

'Sorry. Mine was a vanilla latte,' said Jay.

'My mistake, love. Give me a minute.' She disappeared and the petite young woman came to stand near Jay. An Americano for Amelia arrived and the woman walked off into town.

Jay's phone beeped with a text. It was probably Nora wondering where he'd got to. It wasn't. It was a text from an unknown number that read:

Did you get your present? You didn't say thank you.
That's not nice.

He stared at the message. An icy sensation trickled down his spine. Was this meant to be a joke? It really wasn't very funny.

'Vanilla latte for Jay,' said the kiosk lady.

It took Jay a moment to pull his eyes away from the text message. He shoved his phone in his back pocket. 'Thank you.' Jay took his drink and willed himself not to drink it through the lid because he always burned his tongue that way but he really wanted a shot of something to distract his mind from the message. Who had sent him the cardboard cut-out and how had they got his phone number? This was all getting a bit serious. He hoped he'd not been too long as he speed-walked back along the prom.

Nora was sitting up and looking for him when he returned.

'I am so sorry. First they got my order wrong then I got a—'

'It's OK. Tell me later. Mickey is coming to the prom to meet me now anyway.' Nora jumped to her feet. 'How do I look?'

'Gorgeous obviously,' said Jay. Thinking how mad Mickey was to have cheated on her. He hoped he'd changed his ways. 'I'll keep everything crossed for you,' he added, showing her his crossed fingers and almost dropping his coffee. Nora did the same crossed fingers gesture with both hands.

'Wish me luck.' She gave him a peck on the cheek and walked off across the sand. Somehow she didn't seem to slip and slide about like he did.

Bruce sat up and whimpered as Nora got further and further away.

'I know, mate,' said Jay. 'She'll be back. Don't worry. Here, try your no-caff almond latte.'

They watched as Nora reached the promenade and was greeted by a tall, dark man. Jay pushed his glasses up his nose. He was a little way away but that man was very familiar. Then it hit him. It was the loved-up guy who had been with the pretty blonde woman in the café.

Jay gasped but there was no one there to hear him. All he could do was watch them walk away.

*

250

Nora was excited to catch up with Mickey and to see if the old feelings were still there. Although the old feelings had been mainly lust, and she did need something a bit more substantial than that. Meeting up was the first step. It was odd but she felt a bit like she was cheating on Liam, though seeing as she'd not heard from him yet he was obviously not in a rush to set up another meeting so she really didn't have anything to feel bad about. And anyway it was only a friendly catch-up with Mickey and a chance for her to assess if dumping him had been the right decision.

At the time she had been shocked, angry and hurt. Understandably she had not reacted well when she'd found Mickey in bed with someone else. If she recalled the incident correctly she had screamed and shouted at him and he'd tried to get her to calm down, which had angered her further, making her give him the ultimatum of either get dressed or she was going to stick his bedside lamp up his arse and switch it on.

He had opted for getting dressed, as had the head receiver, who had slunk out quickly. There had then followed a string of excuses from Mickey and pledges that it was a one-off and he would never be unfaithful again. But Nora knew she couldn't trust him. Which was why what Jay had said in the car had made her wonder why she was effectively giving him a second chance now.

Perhaps Mickey had changed or maybe he hadn't but that was what today was about. It was a chance to see if Mickey was the next viable option on the list of exes.

And if he wasn't, then she could just move along. But she didn't feel she could skip over him without at least checking. The worst case would be that she wasted an hour over a coffee – she could live with that.

'Hey, Nora. Great to see you.' He gave her a warm hug in greeting. 'Shall we grab a coffee? The café at the leisure centre is pretty good and I get a staff discount.'

'Sounds good.'

It wasn't far to the leisure centre and Mickey filled the time by updating Nora on what he'd been up to since he'd last seen her and the many holidays he'd been on, which was accompanied by a variety of photographs of him topless on lots of different beaches.

As they entered the leisure centre he winked at the receptionist, who blushed and pressed a button so that Nora could follow him through the turnstile. Should she read anything into that? Her spider sense was on red alert. Take a deep breath, she told herself. She needed to relax and not jump to conclusions.

Mickey showed her through to the café, bought her a coffee and took it to a table in the corner.

'What brings you to Skegness?' he asked.

She could hardly say 'you', could she? But she decided to go with something close to the truth. 'I've been reviewing my life and I thought—'

'Ah, mid-life crisis, is it? I had a bit of one of those too. I bought a Porsche. I can show you later if you like.'

'OK. I'm only twenty-nine so hopefully not a mid-life crisis as such . . .'

'I get you. But you've been remembering the fun we had. Am I right?' There was that wink again. She didn't remember him doing that when they had dated. Had she forgotten or had he developed an annoying habit?

'We did have fun,' she confirmed, and an image of his topless body popped unhelpfully into her mind. 'However, it takes more than fun to make a relationship.'

Mickey's expression changed. 'Shit, did I get you pregnant?'

'No.'

'OK great. Phew.' He made a show of wiping his brow. His smile disappeared. 'There's nothing else is there . . .' His eyes travelled downwards. 'You know . . . not a rash or anything?'

'Nope.'

Why did they always have the same thought process? She decided to drink her coffee and then make a decision. It wasn't that she owed Mickey anything but she had been longing for a coffee ever since Jay had mentioned getting one. A picture of Jay sliding along the sand in his flip-flops appeared in her mind and made her smile. Whatever happened now she would have a good day with Jay and Bruce.

'So update me, Mickey. How have things been with you?' she asked.

For the next fifteen or so minutes she sipped her coffee and listened. Mickey's favourite subject had always been Mickey. Although she wasn't paying full attention. She hopefully was nodding in the right places but it was hard to stay focused when Mickey was talking about super sets and EMOM.

'I've revolutionized our HIIT,' he said with a sage nod.

'My mum's thinking about HRT,' said Nora, tuning back in and wondering why Mickey was smirking at her.

'HIIT stands for High Intensity Interval Training.'

'Oh right. That's not the same thing.'

'Look, did you want to get out of here?' he asked, downing the last of his coffee.

She did but not with him, though Nora was too polite to say that, so instead she nodded. They made it to reception where Mickey asked the receptionist to lie about where he was and she giggled.

'You've still got a thing for receptionists then,' said Nora as they walked outside.

Mickey laughed. 'Yeah. It was all a bit awkward with Janette,' he said. 'She got a bit . . .' He twirled his finger at the side of his head.

'That's quite unprofessional,' she said.

'You're right. I said basically the same thing to management but because she made a fuss, I got my marching orders.'

'I meant it was unprofessional of you to say that about a colleague,' said Nora.

Mickey's face went through a number of expressions, a little like the barrels on a fruit machine, until it settled on grinning disbelief. 'Did you still want to come back to my place?' He checked his watch. 'I've got like thirty minutes.' He pulled out some car keys and an ugly white car behind him flashed its indicators, which were oddly in time with Mickey's eyebrows doing suggestive jumps.

'What?' asked Nora, most likely mirroring the look of disbelief but for different reasons.

'You know. Back to mine. Quick . . .' Instead of finishing the sentence Mickey whistled.

'Oh good heavens. Are you suggesting we have sex?'

Mickey looked nervously about as he grinned like a teenage boy. 'Yeah. What else did you come here for?'

'You know, I'm not sure why I came but it definitely wasn't for a hook-up with a dishonest, immoral and unscrupulous chancer like you. So thanks for the offer but you can stick it up your arse along with your bedside lamp!' She turned and marched off.

'Is that a definite no then?' he called.

Nora stopped, turned around and strode back, making Mickey look wary. 'I'm afraid it is, Mickey. And here's some advice for you. When you can be anything in life, don't be an arsehole!'

He looked genuinely confused as she walked away with her head held high. Maybe sometimes things were as easy as toe fungus. Mickey was a player and she wasn't going to put herself through that ever again. If she'd learned anything about herself through this process, it was that she had standards.

28

It was a sunny day and – thanks to her taking down her 1970s orange and brown daisy curtains – Dixie had been woken early by the sunshine. But she didn't mind because she had made a decision to be positive and have a can-do attitude. The latter had been a little tricky when she'd tried to put up her utensil rack and failed dismally but she had instead turned her attention to finishing the sticky fabric on the inside panels and now they looked brilliant – as long as she didn't look too closely. Her followers agreed and that had given her a boost so she'd decided to reward herself with a bar of chocolate from the service station. She also needed to have a shower and lug back some water.

As she approached the van on her return she noticed it instantly – there was a new message under the wiper blade. Dixie dashed over with renewed vigour despite being knackered. She pulled the note out and read it.

Dixie – Thank you for explaining your situation.
Whilst you are trespassing, I can see that you can't

simply drive away. Therefore, I am happy to give you some leeway and allow you time to fix your van and trust that you will move on once you are able to. I apologize if my previous correspondence came across as bullish.

Dixie reread it. The tone was definitely friendlier, although she wouldn't go so far as to say warm. But she did feel a sense of relief that she wasn't about to be evicted any time soon. She carefully folded up the note and put it in her pocket. It wasn't much but correspondence was always nice to receive. And in an odd way it made her feel less alone.

Straight away she penned a reply:

Thank you for understanding. It is very much appreciated.

She decorated it with flowers before popping it under the wiper. At the same time she balanced a few walnuts, ones she'd bought at the service station, on the other wiper blade for Arnold.

Dixie got to work on the curtains because she had pledged to do that but also because she really wasn't a morning person and the thought of being woken by sunlight piercing her eyeballs at dawn again wasn't a pleasant one. It was a long old job sewing by hand, but one thing she did have was time and she needed something to fill it. It took her a while to set up her phone to film it as a timelapse but she'd read that followers liked to have varied content so it would be worth the effort.

She was starting to flag on curtain number two when a thump on the roof of the van made her jump and stab herself with the needle. 'Ouch!'

As she sucked her sore finger she listened to the tiny footsteps scamper across the roof until Arnold's front legs and then tummy appeared at the windscreen. The squirrel slid down until she could reach a nut then retreated. It was a simple thing but it was nice to watch Arnold keep returning until all the walnuts had been snaffled.

Dixie decided to take a break from sewing – she'd definitely earned one. She came out from the van, which must have made Arnold jump, as she was sitting on the roof munching on a walnut. The squirrel instantly started screeching and flapping her tail about. Dixie darted away from the van. The last thing she needed was to be attacked and get a squirrel stuck in her hair.

'The walnuts are from me,' said Dixie but Arnold was still very cross. 'Fine. I'm off for a walk.' She left Arnold shouting squirrel abuse after her and went for a stroll. Dixie loved how the sunlight dappled through the trees and cast patterns on the woodland floor. And how pretty flowers were dotted around. There hadn't been any rain for a few days and the woods smelled different for it. Gone was the earthy, damp smell, replaced by something fresher and slightly floral. Dixie was careful where she walked because she'd been stung by nettles and scratched by brambles before in an area she now referred to as Prickly Patch. Naming the different places made it feel more homely to her. She wandered for a while, pointing out to herself the plants Ned had introduced her to. There was no need to forage today because she had bought some pasta for tea from the services and a sad-looking salad. Plus she still had some chocolate left over.

She reached the clearing and took a moment to enjoy the view. She called this area Tidy Trees because it wasn't the same as the dense woodland: the trees were different and smaller and almost in lines. The wonky rows of trees drew her eyes across to the undulating hills in a patchwork of greens. It really was very pretty. In the distance sheep were grazing. She couldn't see them well, just groups of white dots on the hillside. But somehow it made her feel more alone. Even the sheep had each other. She was about to turn back when she noticed movement at the base of a nearby tree. It was a squirrel. Was it Arnold? It was hard to tell.

Dixie watched as the squirrel dug a hole and pulled something out. She wondered if it was a nut it had buried earlier. But the squirrel had a nibble and then quickly dropped whatever it was before bounding off to dig somewhere else. Curiosity got to her and she went to investigate what the squirrel had discarded so disdainfully. She crouched down and picked it up. It was covered in mud but she knew instantly what it was.

*

Back at the beach, Nora found Jay and Bruce playing tug of war with the bag the windbreak had come in. She waved and saw Jay exchange the bag for a piece of chicken. When she got closer, Bruce spotted her and got excited. Dogs were lovely creatures – always so pleased to see you and consistently loyal, unlike some people. Jay grabbed Bruce's collar and hung on as the dog pulled him along the sand like a water-skier while at the same time bashing Jay's groin with his tail.

Nora sped up to greet them both and received an enthusiastic welcome from Bruce.

'You're back sooner than I thought you'd be,' said Jay cheerily, trying to avoid Bruce's tail, which was now rhythmically bashing into his thigh. 'How did it go with Mickey?'

'Not great,' said Nora. 'He thought we were going back to his for afternoon delights.'

'Not quite the long-term commitment you were looking for then?'

'Ha ha. But at least I know I did the right thing the first time around by ending things. I just feel for the women who get sucked in.'

'I fear there might be quite a few of those,' said Jay. They exchanged knowing looks. 'Oh well. Time for lunch,' he added breezily as he unzipped his large cool bag and began decanting tasty offerings on to the rug. Bruce was glued to his every move.

'I've probably dodged all sorts of nasties if he's still sleeping around,' said Nora, a little distracted, as she sat down.

'Sticky sausage?' he asked.

'Most likely,' said Nora, pulling a face.

'Sticky honey and mustard cocktail sausages,' said Jay, waving a Tupperware container under her nose.

'Oh, sorry. Actually, no. I couldn't face a sausage right now, but thanks.'

She'd had a lucky escape but somehow she felt a little down. Perhaps it was because she had fewer and fewer possibilities in her back catalogue. That was number eight ticked off. Liam was still pending. That left just one more potential match and she didn't like her odds at all.

Nora ate a sandwich while Bruce inhaled some kibble then settled down to concentrate on chewing his roast-beef-flavoured indestructible bone – he loved a challenge. After their picnic Jay did an excellent job of jollying her out of the doldrums with a game of badminton. He'd avoided tennis because he thought Bruce would steal the ball. It seemed a shuttlecock was equally worth pinching as the dog intercepted it a few times and ran off as far as his long lead would let him. But the chicken treats were working because he came back every time to swap the shuttlecock. They didn't have a net, which was also causing some issues.

'There's no way that was over the net,' said Jay, pointing at an imaginary line.

'Let's check with the digital umpire,' said Nora, putting a finger to her ear as if receiving information. 'Umpire says it was fine.' She grinned at Jay, who shook his head.

Jay served and after a few returns Nora hit a drop shot. Jay dived for it and his racquet just connected and tipped the shuttlecock on to Nora's side of the line.

'I win!' declared a puffed-out Jay.

'No way! That was *under* the net, not over it.'

'Hang on.' Jay put his finger to his ear. 'Digital umpire says . . . I'm the winner.'

'But Bruce and I say you're a cheater,' said Nora, tickling Jay's ribs and making him squirm. He was the most ticklish person she'd ever met. Bruce didn't know what was going on but he was keen to join in, and Jay lying down was fair game so the dog piled on top. Nora laughed until she had a stitch and was covered head to toe in sand.

It was getting warm so they decided a dip in the sea would be a good idea and would also help to keep Bruce cool. They stripped off and ran down the beach with Bruce barking at their heels. That was until their toes met the water and all three of them came to an abrupt halt.

'Blimey, that's like ice,' said Jay, creeping backwards.

'It's not that bad,' said Nora, although it certainly wasn't warm.

Bruce licked the water and shook his head. His expression said he'd definitely not tasted seawater before. Nora reversed into the sea and tried to coax him in. The dog looked over his shoulder at Jay. 'Come on, you need to set an example,' said Nora, as a gentle wave kissed her bum cheeks and made her suck in a breath.

'You're turning blue,' said Jay. 'And he's got a fur coat on. I think I'll give it a miss, thanks.' He turned around to head back up the beach. Bruce was watching them both as if torn as to who to follow.

'I thought you wanted to beef up and be an alpha male,' said Nora, making Jay stop.

He turned and pouted at her. 'I don't think freezing off your unmentionables makes you an alpha.'

'We need to stick together or it'll confuse Bruce,' said Nora, and the dog looked at her as she slipped her shoulders under the surface.

'Fine. But if I get hypothermia I'm blaming you.' Jay took a deep breath and ran into the sea. The expression on his face was a picture of shock as the water splashed up around him. 'Argh!' he yelled as it reached his swimming shorts and he dived into a wave with Bruce close behind him. Jay quickly popped up. 'Bloody hell, it's freezing.'

'There's a good boy,' said Nora, as Bruce paddled towards her.

'Thank you,' said Jay.

'I didn't mean you, you fool,' said Nora, starting to laugh.

The three of them splashed about for a bit until Bruce had had enough and swam to the shore where he had a big shake. Nora joined him so he wouldn't run off. They dug holes in the wet sand and watched them fill with water while Jay was swimming up and down like he was doing lengths at the swimming pool. A toddler was happily filling his bucket and emptying it out again as his mother watched from nearby. The similarity between Bruce and the toddler wasn't lost on Nora.

She glanced up as Jay waded out of the water. He pushed his wet black hair off his face and his torso glistened as he strode towards her. It was quite reminiscent of the famous James Bond moment when Daniel Craig walked out of the sea in *Casino Royale*, only Jay wasn't quite as ripped, but still very easy on the eye. Nora was about to look away when Jay tripped over and face-planted the shallows.

'Ow, that hurt,' he said, attempting to get up as another wave engulfed him.

Jay scrambled upright between waves and began hobbling towards them, blood starting to trickle down his leg.

'You've cut yourself,' said Nora, pointing at his knee.

The toddler was watching and burst into tears. His mother marched over and scooped him up while glaring at Jay.

'What did I do?' whispered Jay to Nora as the screaming child was carried up the beach. They both looked down at his injured knee.

'Ouch, that's starting to smart now.'

Nora put an arm around his waist to help him and felt his muscles tense at her touch. 'Come on, Alpha, let's get a plaster on that.'

'It had better be an Incredible Hulk one or I'm going to scream like that,' said Jay, pointing after the toddler.

29

Dixie was surprised when she got back to Elsie to see that someone had opened the engine bay at the back of the vehicle. Her heart started to thump but her fears were unfounded because, as she got closer, Ned appeared, wiping his hand on an old rag. He saw her approaching and waved. She waved back and promptly stumbled over a tree root. It was impossible to stay elegant in the woods. At least she didn't fall flat on her face.

'You came back,' she said.

'Yeah. I thought I'd see if I could get Elsie going. I was worried I'd had a wasted trip when you weren't around but helpfully you'd left the engine bay unlocked.' He pointed at the engine.

'I should probably lock that then?'

'I would. Just in case anyone is in the market for a vintage engine that doesn't work,' he said with a smile.

'No luck then?' she asked, peering at the grubby engine as if checking for signs of life.

'Well, I'm no expert but—'

'It's buggered,' she filled in for him.

Ned laughed. 'I wasn't going to say that.'

'Oh, it's just that my other expert-VW-engine-type person said exactly that and I didn't listen to her.'

'That explains why some parts look recently lubricated.'

'That'd be Renee. She seemed to know what she was doing.' Dixie had been impressed with Renee's know-how, even if Elsie had conked out a few miles down the road.

'I think your piston rings are worn out,' said Ned with a sage nod.

'My pissed-on rings are worn out?' she queried. Was he taking the mickey out of her?

Ned snorted a laugh. 'Piston rings. They keep an airtight seal on your engine so if they go, pow!' He mimed an explosion.

'It didn't explode exactly. There were vibrations under my feet followed by smoke out of my back end. Then it was more of a fast decline of power.'

'Vibrations sounds like something else, flywheel maybe.' He seemed to be thinking out loud. Was a flywheel a real part of a car? She wished she'd paid more attention to what Renee had said because now she had no idea if Ned was winding her up or not. 'I could see about getting some replacement parts, if you like?' he offered.

'Yes please. That would be amazing. Assuming that you're offering to fit them as well.'

'Of course. I can't offer a guarantee, I'm afraid.'

'That's OK. Just let me know what I owe you and I'll transfer it across.'

'OK.' They looked at each other for a little too long and both seemed to realize it at the same time. 'Right, I'll finish up here,' said Ned, scratching his cheek and leaving a small grease mark. It gave him a more rough-and-ready look and Dixie found it strangely attractive. She knew it was a terrible cliché but as a rich girl she was rather fascinated by working-class men. She'd certainly had very little luck with the posh ones.

She stepped closer, pulled a clean tissue from her pocket and handed it to him. Ned seemed confused for a moment. 'There's a smudge on your face.'

'Oh right. Thanks.' He rubbed the tissue on his chin.

'No, higher, other side,' she instructed.

Ned rubbed near his eyebrow. Dixie was becoming frustrated. She took the tissue and gently ran it over his cheek to remove the grease, suddenly aware that it was quite an intimate thing to do. Her pulse had quickened and Ned was staring at her lips. Goodness, it was all a little intense, with an air of Lady Chatterley about it.

'Hey, you!' shouted someone with a posh voice at the same time as a Labrador came bounding through the trees and almost took Dixie out.

The moment was gone. If it was a moment. Dixie wasn't sure. She may have fabricated the whole thing in her head. It had been a while since she'd been in male company, or any company for that matter. She was probably just craving some human contact.

'Hey. You there!' shouted the same woman and Dixie turned around.

'Hello! How can I help?' said Dixie, her accent matching the woman's. She watched as the rotund woman approached, wheezing slightly with the effort of striding through the woods.

The woman seemed startled for a moment. Perhaps by Dixie's accent. 'You can't set up camp here,' she said, jabbing a walking pole at Elsie. 'We don't want undesirables or that ilk turning the place into a fairground.'

'Oh I know. I broke down. Terribly inconvenient. Vintage camper, you see,' said Dixie. 'We were trying to fix it and we think we've identified the trouble so hopefully we'll—'

'We?' The woman was peering past Dixie.

'Yes. Ne—' Dixie turned around but there was nobody there. That was strange. She peeped inside the van but he had gone. 'Anyway, it needs some new parts.' She leaned towards the woman. 'Piston ring and flywheel,' she said.

'Oh I see, how awfully inconvenient,' said the woman.

'Indeed it is. But thank you for your concern. Lovely of you to stop by,' said Dixie.

'No bother at all. Need to keep an eye out for any riffraff, you understand.'

'Oh totally,' said Dixie.

'Cheerio,' said the woman before turning and heading back the way she'd come. 'Hendricks!' the woman hollered somewhat belatedly and the large Labrador dashed by Dixie and off into the woodland.

Dixie did a full lap of the camper and checked inside and even under the seats. Where had Ned disappeared to and why? It was rather strange. A thought struck Dixie and she jumped out of the van to call after the woman but she could no longer see her. Was she the mystery note-writer? Unfortunately she'd missed her opportunity to find out.

*

Nora and Jay bought a stick of rock for Renee and decided they would call in to give it to her on the way back from Skegness. Nora was driving when she heard the beep of a text arriving. 'Can you see who that is?' she asked Jay.

'I'm on it,' he said as he rummaged in her bag. He pulled out her phone. 'Well, well, well,' said Jay and Nora's interest jumped a notch higher.

'What? Who is it?' she asked with a couple of quick glances in his direction.

'Liam wants to know if you would like to meet him for a coffee.'

Nora wasn't sure if she was pleased or not. 'Coffee? That's not a date, is it? Coffee is . . . what is coffee?'

Jay pulled a face. 'Friends have coffee. My nan has coffee with friends.'

It wasn't the response she'd been hoping for but at least Liam had got in touch. She was trying to stay positive. 'Exactly. But it's better than nothing. And he did

271

say he was getting over a break-up. Please can you reply with something casual.'

'I'm not replying straight away. That smacks of desperation,' said Jay. 'I don't want him thinking that I've been hovering over my phone like a saddo. I mean, that you've been waiting for his message. He'll think you have nothing better to do.'

'Good point. There's no rush. He's kept me waiting. I'll reply tonight.'

'We could compose something for you at Renee's.'

'Oh heavens. Can you imagine what Renee would say?' They both burst out laughing.

'Bloody hell,' said Renee. 'Not exactly *Fifty Shades*, is it?'

Nora held her phone in her hands, ready to send a text to Liam. 'That's not what you suggest I put, is it?'

'Nooo,' said Renee. 'Although . . .' She tilted her head as if considering it. 'No. I'd say something like. "Can do, but a large G&T is more my thing. Talking of my thing." Then I'd put those three little dots.'

'An ellipsis,' said Jay.

Nora hesitated with her fingers over the keys. 'That really doesn't sound like the sort of thing I'd say.'

'I think keep it simple,' said Jay.

'Bruce Willis had a great chat-up line. He used to ask, "What are you doing for sex later?"' Renee pursed her lips. 'Very effective, I can tell you.'

Jay was looking impressed. 'You knew Bruce Willis?'

'In between wives only,' said Renee. As if that explained things adequately. Jay opened his mouth but seemed to think better of questioning further.

'How about,' began Nora, '"Sounds good. I'm free any time."?'

Nora looked at the others for reassurance. Jay sucked in a breath.

'Don't imply you have nothing and nobody better to do,' said Renee. 'Even if that is the case,' she added quietly.

'Why is this so hard?' asked Nora. 'Come on. Tell me what to put.'

'Maybe you could say: "A coffee sounds fine. Let me know when you're free and I'll check my diary",' offered Jay.

'I like that,' said Renee, giving him an approving raise of her glass before taking another swig. 'Just the right level of interested, I'd say.'

'Great.' Nora tapped out the message word for word. 'Should I add a kiss?' She looked up at the waiting faces.

'Did he put one?' asked Renee.

'No,' said Jay quickly.

'Then definitely not,' said Renee.

'OK. And send.' Nora pressed the button and immediately swapped her phone for her cup of tea.

'Have you got a one who got away, Renee?' asked Jay.

'Goodness, no. I did it all.'

'How about you, Jay?' asked Nora.

'Far too many to list really. Although . . .' He tilted his

head and looked wistfully off into the distance, which just happened to be a painting on Renee's wall of a naked woman. 'Layla Davis.' He sighed deeply after her name. 'She was perfect. Like she'd walked off a film set.'

'Given your line of work, had she?' asked Nora.

'No. She worked in the sandwich bar at uni. My heart used to properly flutter when she asked me if I wanted plain or seeded.'

Nora failed to suppress a giggle. Jay gave her a look. 'Sorry, carry on,' she said.

'Big eyes. The kind you could look into for hours. And a smile that brightened a room, or in this case the student canteen. After a while she knew my order and would have it ready for me every day.'

'What did you have?' asked Renee.

'Cheese and onion on seeded,' he said.

Nora knew she was scrunching up her features but she couldn't help it. 'But you hate onions.'

'Yeah. She got the order wrong so it used to take me ages to pick the bits of onion out. Happy times.'

'Why didn't you ask her out on a date?' asked Renee.

'No confidence. But I heard she was obsessed with horror movies so I figured if I became an actor and one day starred in one, it would be the perfect story.'

'Bloody hell, Jay,' snapped Renee. 'What a pifflingly long-winded way to go about it! It would have been a lot easier and quicker to just ask her, "Hey, what are you doing for sex later?"'

'I couldn't ask anyone that.'

'And that's just sex,' said Nora. 'It's not a relationship.'

'My point exactly,' said Jay.

'Sex is a relationship, isn't it?' asked Renee, looking at the others. They both slowly shook their heads.

'Hogwash.' Renee seemed to pause for a minute and Nora didn't know what to do. Renee stared into her glass. Nora wondered if all Renee's relationships had been transient sexual encounters, which was quite sad. Renee's head snapped up. 'Oh well, I had a damn good time. Cheers!' and they clinked mugs with her glass.

Renee put a finger in the air and everyone stopped. 'Actually, there was one person. There was one who got away. Mersea Island 1969. Theo Carlisle. Absolute darling. Kind, considerate and smart. Not my type at all. Artist. Painted blurry flowers. Utterly bewitched, I was.'

Everyone was leaning forwards. 'What happened?' asked Nora in almost a whisper.

'Parents,' said Renee. 'They didn't approve. Theo married a teacher and I went on tour with Julie Driscoll and the Brian Auger Trinity.'

Everyone was gobsmacked.

'You must have heard of the song "Wheels On Fire"?' Renee was looking at the blank faces.

'I'm afraid not,' said Jay. 'But I'm sorry about Theo.'

Nora nodded. Renee shrugged but definitely seemed to be carrying a little sadness after what she'd shared. Nora and Jay exchanged glances. Nora felt unexpectedly emotional at the thought that Renee may have missed out on a meaningful relationship. It made her even more determined to complete her review of her exes. She didn't want to be Renee in a few years' time, sitting there with a gin and tonic wondering if she'd thrown something magical away. 'Renee, I'm sorry,' said Nora. 'Don't be. I'd have only messed it up anyway.'

30

Nora had had a busy day squeezing in all the jobs she couldn't do in the week and was looking forward to putting her feet up in front of the TV. What she didn't need was to open her front door to the sound of her parents singing. They were belting out 'Never Gonna Give You Up' by Rick Astley. Rick-rolled by her own mum and dad – what was going on? She stood in the kitchen doorway for a full minute before they noticed she was home. Ali hastily put down the soup ladle he was using as a stand-in microphone.

'Nora! Look, Una, it's Nora. Hello, Nora,' said her dad, switching off the radio.

'Hi,' said Nora, wondering if this slightly smug feeling was how they felt when they'd caught her doing something she shouldn't as a child. Like the time she'd tried to make a cake on her own and redecorated the kitchen with flour.

'We were just . . .' Una flinched and guiltily checked her clothing was straight, which Nora found even more troubling than their singing. What had been going on here? Nora didn't want to think too deeply about that.

'Do you remember the conversation we had about you letting yourselves in and that the key was only for emergencies?' asked Nora.

'And it is an emergency,' said her mum, lifting her chin. Ali nodded.

Nora lost her smugness. 'Why, what's happened?'

'I am making punjena paprika and sogan dolma for the fete and I need your big serving plate.'

These were traditional Bosnian dishes, a variation on the theme of stuffed vegetables, and her mum's versions were always very tasty. 'OK. In that cupboard,' said Nora, pointing behind her dad. 'But what's the emergency?'

'That. That is the emergency,' said Una, getting frustrated. 'Do you think I can cater for goodness knows how many people without a plate to put things on?'

Nora looked to her dad for some signs of sanity but he was busy trying to put the ladle away without being noticed. 'Other than that, there's nothing wrong?' Nora needed to check.

'You are still single but other than that . . .'

Nora glared at her mother. 'Being single isn't an ailment.'

Una pouted her disagreement. 'No male company then?'

Nora was about to say no but she stopped herself. 'Actually I have lots of male company, thanks. In fact, I spent all day yesterday with a man.'

Her parents were silenced but only for a moment. Her

mum narrowed her eyes. 'You took time off work for a man?'

'Yes, I did,' said Nora, warming to her little game. 'We went to Skegness. Had a picnic on the beach, played badminton, went for a swim and ate ice creams walking back to the car.' The last part made her chuckle at the memory of Jay trying to eat his with Bruce walking backwards in front of him in the hope of Jay dropping some – and causing Jay to trip up every couple of steps.

It had been such a great day. She always had a good time with Jay. An image of him striding out of the sea made her feel a bit funny until she remembered him falling over, which made her laugh again. Her parents were now looking a little concerned. 'He's lovely. We had a great time.' She folded her arms.

'That's good,' said her dad. 'I'm pleased for you.'

Una waved his words away. 'She's not said who it is yet.' Her mother mirrored her folded arms, which made Nora uncomfortable.

'I don't have to tell you,' said Nora.

'It's not a relationship,' said her mum, with a shake of her head. 'I know these things. Come on, Ali, where's that plate?'

Her dad began rummaging in the cupboard.

Nora was irked. 'Hang on. It could be a relationship. It could be a very serious relationship. I am capable of having those, you know.' There was another memory of a topless Jay – what was going on there? She couldn't unpack that right now as she was preoccupied with convincing her parents that she was potentially in a relationship when she wasn't.

'We know you are capable,' said her dad. 'Any man or woman or non-gender binary person would be lucky to have you.' His political correctness was a work in progress.

'Thanks, Dad.'

Una shot Ali a look and he stuck his head back in the cupboard in search of the big plate. 'You are playing games, Nora,' said Una, with a disheartened shake of her head.

'I did spend the day with a man,' said Nora. She wasn't backing down yet.

'I believe that,' said Una. 'What I do not understand is how you have not yet found your prince charming. What is it you're looking for, Nora?'

It was a question that had more of an impact than she was expecting.

*

Jay was having a play wrestle with Bruce when his phone pinged. He was finding texts quite triggering since his stalker had started to send him messages. Thankfully it wasn't the stalker. It was Anastasia, Tasha Blake's publicity manager.

The message read:

Need you on a vid conf RIGHT NOW. Link here

She was quite rude and also presumptuous; he could have been anywhere. He messaged back.

Hi Anastasia, Lovely to hear from you. Just in the middle of something but I will of course make my apologies and duck out to join in. All the best, Jay

Jay turned to Bruce. 'Really sorry but I need to join a very important video conference call. By way of compensation, can I interest you in a chew stick? Would that be acceptable?'

Bruce barked and wagged his tail.

'That's awfully understanding of you,' he said, fetching Bruce a chew stick.

Jay settled himself in his office as it was white and nondescript so he could be joining from anywhere in the world. He ran his fingers through his hair and rubbed his lips together a few times to give them some colour and when he felt he had left sufficient time so they wouldn't think he had bugger all else to do, he pressed the link to join the call.

An unsmiling Anastasia greeted him, which only served to make him friendlier, to counterbalance her slapped-arse expression.

'Hi, Anastasia, you're looking amazing. How are—'

'Tasha is joining us shortly,' she cut in.

'Oh OK. Great. Is everything all right?'

Her phone began to ring. 'I need to take this,' she said and turned her back on the screen.

281

Jay was now wishing he'd joined from his desktop because it was uncomfortable having to hold his phone at the same angle. He always found getting the right angle tricky. Too high and it emphasized his forehead; too low and they could see up his nose. He grabbed a few books and constructed a makeshift stand while making a mental note that a proper stand for this sort of thing would probably be a good investment.

He waited and listened to Anastasia's side of the conversation. Whoever had called was getting a roasting. Another box appeared on the screen and a very tiny Tasha appeared.

'Hey, Tasha. Great to see you. How's things?' he asked.

Anastasia spun around and shushed him loudly before turning her back again.

Tasha rapidly stuck up two fingers on both hands in a frenzied revolt, which made Jay snort a laugh. Tasha waved at Jay and he waved back.

'You OK?' he mouthed, emphasizing the question with a thumbs up and a big smile followed by a thumbs down and a downturned mouth to give her options.

Tasha grinned and mimed that she was thinking hard about her reply. She then held her palm flat and wobbled it.

'Aww, anything I can do?' he whispered.

'Buy me more hours in the day?' replied Tasha, matching his low voice.

'Sorry, I'm up to my quota of deals with the devil,' he said with a shrug.

Tasha laughed and Anastasia glared at her over her shoulder.

This was nice. He really liked Tasha. On paper she was his ideal woman and here she was chatting to him, although very quietly, like old friends. It was quite a change from when they'd worked on *Undercover Bullets* and she'd been more than a bit stand-offish.

Anastasia finally ended her call and gave them her full attention. 'I need to run some dates past you. Obviously you need to make film promo your absolute priority, but both your agents have said I need to check first before confirming.' She did nothing to hide her disdain at this.

'OK, great,' said Jay. 'Thanks for org—'

'Launch week, we have press junkets on the Monday. Radio and all day back-to-back interviews across all majors on Tuesday. *Lorraine*, *The One Show* and Graham Norton are the Thursday but Graham's will be aired the following day and I'm trying my absolute hardest to get us a premiere in Leicester Square. So keep the Saturday free. Got it?'

'Oh, sorry, was I meant to be writing it down?' asked Jay, searching for a pen and sticky notes.

'Can you email that to us please?' asked Tasha.

Anastasia huffed. 'Anything else we can utilize? Anything in your personal life that we can get the press writing about? We need column inches. Personal interest. Going off the rails . . . Or a romance between the leads is always a winner.'

'I'm not faking an addiction,' said Tasha.

Anastasia held her palms up. 'Fine, just a suggestion. How about the romance?'

'Fake romance doesn't seem above board,' said Jay.

Tasha sat up straight. 'Jay Pandey, are you saying you don't find me attractive?' she asked, pretty blue eyes staring into the camera.

'Oh goodness, no, not at all. The opposite . . . Well, not *opposite*, I'm not obsessed with you or anything. I'm the right level of attracted to you. If that's all right with you,' he said, wanting Bruce to come in and eat him whole.

Tasha laughed. 'Leave the romance, Anastasia. I think it's better to let the press and public speculate.'

'Actually, that's a good idea,' said Anastasia, looking surprised as she jotted something down.

Jay was nodding along and, if he wasn't mistaken, Anastasia was leaning in and staring at him but it was hard to tell on the tiny screen. 'Jay, what's happening with you?'

'Umm—' he felt put on the spot, 'I've recently got a rescue dog.'

'Aww, how cute,' said Tasha. 'I love doggos. Is he all cute and cuddly? Is he there?'

'No time for that,' butted in Anastasia, 'and not really what we're after. The film is gritty. So something more edgy and dangerous is needed.'

Jay pouted at the screen. He didn't do edgy or dangerous. 'I went on a climbing trip the other week. Oh, and I might have a stalker.'

'That,' said Anastasia, jabbing a dangerously pointy fingernail at the screen, 'that is exactly the sort of thing we need and the public will love.'

'Climbing trips?' asked Tasha.

'No. A stalker. It's worrying. It plays on people's minds and it has the shock factor. It's perfect. I'll brief that into the newspapers.'

'Hang on,' said Jay. 'I was thinking about speaking to the police about it first.'

'No need.'

'But doesn't publicizing it give the stalker the attention they are craving?' he asked.

Anastasia shrugged. 'No such thing as bad publicity.'

Jay was not sure that was strictly true in this instance.

31

Nora arrived early at the coffee shop to meet Liam so she went to the nearby charity shop to have a browse and kill some time. She was examining a glass chopping board with Elvis's face depicted on it in vegetables when Liam walked by the window. Nora dashed from the shop with the chopping board still in her hand.

'Liam. Hi.'

'Hey, you've not paid for that!' shouted the shop assistant, chasing after Nora.

'Good grief. I'm so sorry.' Nora and Liam stared at the depiction of Elvis in aubergines and avocados in Nora's hands before she thrust it at the cross-looking shop assistant.

The woman didn't take it. Instead she folded her arms. 'It's two pounds. We're a charity shop, you know.'

'Er, of course. Right. Sorry.' Nora rummaged one-handed through her bag, looking for her purse.

'Here you go,' said Liam, pulling some coins from his pocket and handing them to the woman, who took the money and shook her head at Nora.

'Oh, um, thank you,' she said, and slipped the ugly chopping board in her bag.

The shop assistant muttered something under her breath in a Muttley-esque way as she stomped back into the shop.

Nora rolled her eyes. 'That was weird. Anyway, hello.' She tried to brazen it out as they walked two shops down to the coffee place.

'Hi. Is everything, um, you know, OK?' asked Liam.

'Yes, it's great. Why?'

'It looked like you were taking that picture from the charity shop.'

'It's a chopping board,' she said, realizing that really wasn't the point. 'It was a misunderstanding. I was look-ing at it for someone else, obviously. Then . . .' Nora had an odd image of Renee in her head saying, 'Whatever you do, don't say you rushed outside in a blind panic when you saw him.' Nora swallowed hard. 'Then I real-ized the time. And I hate being late. *Hate it!*' There was a possibility she was a little too vehement because Liam took a slight step away from her.

Liam looked at his watch. 'We're five minutes early.'

Crap. 'Oh, that's good then. Clearly I need a new watch.' They both looked at her bare arms. 'Anyway here we are.' She opened the coffee-shop door and waved for him to walk through. He hesitated, then slipped inside quickly as if not wanting to pause too long next to Nora.

Brilliant start, she thought. At least it can't get any worse.

They joined the coffee queue and Nora began to relax. This was recoverable. She just needed to act normal. She could do normal. Liam was staring at the chopping board in her open bag. She tried to zip up the bag but it was too tall and Elvis's aubergine hair was still visible as the board stuck out the top.

'How has your week been?' she asked, in the hope of distracting him.

'I secured a new client at work, my cousin had a car accident and my nan broke her dentures.'

'Great,' said Nora, before all of what he'd said had fully registered. 'Oh goodness. Not great at all. Awful. The thing about your cousin and your nan. But yay for the new client.' She punched the air with both hands like a cheerleader who had lost her pom poms. She felt like she was losing her pom poms. She really needed to calm down. Did she used to be this jittery around Liam? She didn't think so.

'How was your week?' he asked tentatively, still taking sideways looks at Elvis.

'Good, thanks.'

They both nodded uneasily at each other. Nora was hugely relieved when it was their turn to give their drink orders. Once they had their coffees, they found a table for two near the window.

Liam kept doing that uncomfortable rolled-in-smile thing he'd used to do when he was feeling awkward. Nora took a deep breath. 'I'm sorry. I know I'm acting weird, and I don't know why. This feels like a first date and as you know I'm terrible at those. Can we sort of delete the bits where I was being strange and start again?'

'Sure. Just one thing though. It's not a date, is it?' he asked.

She wasn't sure how to interpret his raised eyebrow. Was that a 'it had better not be a date or I'll run for the hills' gesture? Or a 'that might be quite OK, if we were on a date'? She had no idea but decided to play it safe. 'It's coffee, Liam. OK?'

'That's good.' He leaned back in his seat and did seem to be relaxing. He smiled. 'Our first date was truly awful, wasn't it?'

'Don't remind me.' Nora could feel heat creeping up her neck at the thought of it. 'I've never had a tummy bug like it. I should not have left my bathroom but I really didn't want to miss out on a date with you and I thought if I cried off you'd think I was being flaky and wouldn't ask me out again.'

'I would have asked you out again,' he said, his eyes full of warmth. This was the Liam she remembered.

'That's good to know.' They held each other's gaze as they sipped their drinks.

A succession of raps on the window near Nora's head made her jump and drop her cup, splashing coffee all over her, the table and Liam. 'What the hell—' She turned to see an unwelcome face at the window. Gareth, her disastrous date from a few weeks ago, was waving at her and gesturing that he was going to come in. 'No!' She waved her hands and splattered Liam with more coffee. 'I am so sorry. This is some random guy I barely know and—'

Gareth barrelled up to her and embraced her in a tight hug. 'It's so good to see you, Nora.'

'Gareth, I'm kind of busy right now,' she said, wiping herself with a very small and already sodden serviette.

'Whoops, was someone clumsy?' he asked as he snorted a laugh. 'How are your bowels now?'

Nora frantically waved the dripping serviette towards Liam. Gareth seemed to spot Liam for the first time. 'Hello there. I'm Gareth.' He offered a hand to shake.

Liam wiped his palm first before shaking hands. 'Liam.'

'And how do you know Nora?' asked Gareth, pulling up a chair, which Nora quickly intercepted and added to the table behind them, making Gareth falter as he almost sat down on thin air.

'We dated . . .' she said.

At the same time as Liam said, 'We're old friends.'

'Ouch,' said Jay, from halfway up the climbing wall.

'I know, right?' Nora was pleased she had Jay's support as she had just divulged all the details of her coffee non-date with Liam.

'Sorry. That was a real burn calling your relationship "old friends".' He winced as he said the word, which Nora felt was a little dramatic. 'I think I might have niggled my groin injury when I tripped over at Skeggy. I'm coming down,' he said.

They'd had a good climbing session but Nora was feeling a little low after her catch-up with Liam.

'Do you need a hug?' asked Jay when he'd reached the bottom. 'Because I think I do.'

'Why, what's up with you?'

He got his phone out of his bag and scrolled to what he wanted to show her. 'What do you make of that?'

Nora read a series of messages sent over a couple of days. The first couple were someone saying hi, and Jay asking who it was. When Jay stopped replying the messages changed:

Hey answer me or I'll get cross

Stop faffing about Mr P

I'm watching you Jay Pandey

Still watching U Mr P

You don't want to end up at the corned beef factory

'Shit, that escalated quickly. Who is it?'

'No idea,' said Jay. 'Some weirdo. Same one who sent me the cardboard effigy, I guess. I keep blocking them but they pop up with a new burner phone. I'm not worrying about it.'

'That's good,' she said, feeling that she would be cacking herself if they'd been sent to her.

'Does that warrant a hug?' asked Jay.

Nora nodded and Jay wrapped her in a cuddle. It was

lovely to be held and feel the warmth of his body against hers. He wasn't some great brute of a man but she felt safe in his arms. 'I think I might give up on the 37 per cent rule,' she mumbled into his shoulder. 'Maybe the past is best left alone.'

'Don't be daft.' Jay held her at arm's length. 'You need to finish this. Then you can move on and look for new possibilities. Don't you only have one more left to check out anyway?'

'Yep, Tyler.'

'Do you want me to come with you?' he asked.

'No, that's a little bit weird.' She paused as she mulled over the offer. It wouldn't be much fun going alone, especially if it was another hopeless mission. 'But I could do with the support if you didn't mind tagging along. I've found where he's working but there's no personal contact details and I don't like to message the company. Maybe we could go over there and see if we can casually bump into him. It'd look less stalkerish if we both went. Sorry, that was insensitive. What with you having an actual stalker and threats and creepy cut-outs and . . . I'll shut up now.'

'It's OK. What does Tyler do?' asked Jay, getting out of his climbing equipment.

'He's a farrier.'

Jay's head shot up and, as he had one leg in the air getting out of his harness, he toppled over and landed with a thud. He lay still for a moment. Nora bent down to him. 'I'm OK,' he said in a small voice.

Nora helped him up and out of the harness, then together they sat down on the bench.

'Did you say farrier as in blacksmith?'

'Yep.'

'It may have escaped your notice but neither of us have a horse. I know Bruce is the size of a baby donkey, but still. He's not a horse. I'm not sure popping by his business is going to work as a credible plan. I mean, I do have access to a high-quality pantomime horse but unless Tyler has the same IQ as a teabag he may see through our cunning disguise.'

Nora gave him a nudge for his cheekiness.

'Ouch.'

'Wuss.'

'You know I bruise like an out-of-date peach,' he said, rubbing his arm.

'He is a farrier but he makes stuff like gates and things. So no horse required.'

'Good. I'll stand down Dobbin.'

There was a round of applause as Trent strode into the centre wearing disturbingly tight shorts. 'Great, just what I need,' said Nora.

Trent was keen to maximize the returning-hero moment. Jay and Nora watched from the bench.

'Good to see you back, Trent,' said Jay.

'On the road to recovery, I hope,' said Nora, turning towards Trent and finding herself face to face with his bulging shorts. She didn't know where to look but given his proximity her options were limited so she put her head back until her eyes met his, but it was a very unnatural angle to have her neck at.

'A few scars physically and emotionally,' said Trent. 'But I will heal.' He held his palms together in front of him as if praying or blessing the top of Nora's head.

'Yep, you do that,' said Nora.

'It's incredible how a near-death experience can be life-changing,' said Trent without a flicker of sarcasm.

'Maybe everyone should try it,' said Nora.

Trent nodded sagely. 'It's an interesting concept that I'd like to explore,' he said. And Nora was pretty sure he wasn't taking the piss. Nora's neck was aching from keeping it fully tilted upwards. As she relaxed it a fraction she came face to face with Trent's tight shorts once again. 'Can I get you a coffee while we talk about it further?' he asked.

Jay leaned into her shoulder and the contact made an unexpected shiver run through her body. He whispered, 'One lump or two?'

'No, thanks, I've got to dash,' she blurted to Trent, grabbing her stuff and skirting past him as she and Jay almost ran for the exit.

Outside they got a bit giggly. She loved how much she laughed with Jay.

'Trent should get an Equity card. He's a better actor than I am.' Nora laughed and Jay waved his arms about. 'That's the part where you say, "Nooo, Jay, there is no greater actor than you!"'

'Sorry. You're right. You are an excellent actor. The best in the business apart from Gary Oldman.'

'Accepted,' said Jay.

'And Idris Elba, Benedict Cumberbatch, Ewan Mc—'

'OK, that'll do. My ego is shrinking with every name and it's about to turn itself inside out. At least you didn't say Steven Seagal.'

Nora pouted and Jay slow-blinked at her.

'Don't even go there,' he said.

'I was joking. Unlike Trent who is very serious about his life-changing experience.' They both chuckled. 'He's definitely seizing every opportunity to milk this. Me getting stuck has kicked off a whole new chapter for him.'

'Talking of new chapters, shall you, me and Bruce track down Tyler tomorrow?'

'Great. I'll finish work early and we can go then but do we really need to bring Bruce? He'll only be an hour on his own, tops.'

'Sorry. Non-negotiable. I'm a responsible dog-owner, and more than that, Bruce is my friend. Plus if things turn ugly you'll be glad we brought Bruce with us,' said Jay.

32

Dixie spent the afternoon finishing off the curtains, which took quite some time. She would need some proper line to hang them on when she made it back to civilization but for now the string would do. She threaded it through and tightened it up. Dixie admired her curtains – she'd made a good job of them, even if she did say so herself. If she ignored the droopiness, they were still pretty, and definitely made Elsie look more refined and modern and a lot less 1970s-reject.

She popped her finished video on the gram and set about cleaning her find from the other day. It was going to be her prize for finishing the curtains. She looked at her sad salad and plain spaghetti. It needed a little something else. It was getting cloudy so she took her torch and a knife and went in search of chicken of the woods and wild garlic.

Dixie discovered both were a lot easier to find when you could remember where they were, as she stumbled over twigs and got scratched by brambles in Prickly Patch. After a few false starts she finally found the right tree in an area she was calling Woody Corner, and cut away a small mushroom from its bark. For some reason she felt guilty. It wasn't stealing but it was still taking something for nothing. 'Thank you, tree,' she said in hushed tones, although there was nobody about. There never was anyone around. At first she'd liked that, but now it just made her miss her friends. It was one thing to be at one with nature, but it turned out that nature really wasn't that bothered about her.

On the way back she had a little talk to herself. She was coping way better than she'd ever thought possible. And she was about to make herself a proper scrummy meal and sit in the campervan and close the new curtains she'd made all on her own and have a look at how many followers she had. Her Instagram numbers were continuing to rise.

Holding the torch and the mushroom carefully, she moved around a large tree where she knew the ground was uneven. She didn't want to trip over and break something, that would be a complete disaster. In the distance she noticed someone. Realizing she wasn't alone, she froze. She wasn't sure why. This was a public right of way. Perhaps it was Ned. Her stomach flipped at the thought, or it could just have been hunger.

But if it wasn't Ned it could be anyone. A dog-walker? An axe-wielding murderer? She peered into the darkness and could see that they were looking inside Elsie. Any reservations she may have had evaporated and she marched on through the trees. Nobody was going to break into Elsie! She held her torch aloft. Renee was right. It would make a good weapon if she needed to defend herself.

Dixie pulled her phone out and had a momentary dilemma whether to put it on to record or to phone the police. Then she began recording, obviously because it was all content, and if it was a burglar rather than a nosy parker it would make good evidence. She almost jogged towards the front of Elsie, where she knew the ground was mossy and there were fewer dry sticks to alert the intruder to her presence.

But then she stubbed her toe on a tree root and yelped.

'Stop! That is my campervan and you are . . . Oh, Ned, it's you. Goodness, you could have said something. You gave me a fright!'

'Sorry,' he said, looking sheepish.

She couldn't hide that she was thrilled to see him and very relieved. 'I'm so pleased you're not a mad axe-murderer. Come in and I'll show you what I've foraged.' She opened up the van and waited for him to come around. Once they were both inside she popped on her battery lights and put down her spoils. 'I've got mushroom. Unfortunately I couldn't find any wild garlic but it doesn't matter because look what I did find.' She picked up her prize from the other day, now thoroughly washed, and held it in front of Ned. But Ned wasn't paying attention. He was looking past her to the front of the van. She turned her head to see what he was looking at. There was another note under the wiper. 'Oh, don't worry. I'll read it later.' She waved her hand in front of his face to return his attention to what she wanted to share with him. 'See?'

Ned pulled his head back and focused on what she was holding. 'Truffle? Goodness, that's posh. Did you venture as far as Waitrose?'

'Wait! There's a Waitrose?' Dixie was momentarily stunned.

'Yeah, it's about five miles or so away.'

Dixie tried to erase the thoughts of avocados and the fresh pastries she was missing almost as much as her friends. 'I may have to check that out. But tonight I have a totally foraged meal. Apart from the pasta and wilting salad.' She said the last part quickly. 'But the mushroom is cut down by my own fair hand.' She wasn't sure why she'd gone all Jane Austen but she quite liked the added drama. 'And I discovered this truffle and dug it up.' She held it on her palm proudly. 'Actually, Arnold found it and dug it up. She had a nibble. See the teeth marks. Or it may have been a relative of Arnold's. It's very hard to tell squirrels apart. Do you think they have the same problem with us?'

Ned picked up the truffle and studied it closely. He didn't appear to be listening. 'Where did you find it?'

'In the middle of Tidy Trees.'

He glanced up from the truffle to give her a perplexed look.

'Sorry. I sort of named the different areas around here. Anyway, there's a bit where you come out of the densest part of the woodland and the trees are neater, almost like they're in rows. I call that Tidy Trees, and Arnold, or a member of Arnold's family, was—'

'The smaller trees before the hill that dips down to the farm?' he asked. His eyebrows were pulled tight together. It wasn't his best look.

'If the sheep are where the farm is then yes, near the hilltop. I found it there. How exciting that there's truffles growing right here.'

'On my land,' he said.

There was a moment. Ned froze and Dixie was a fraction behind him in realizing what he had said. They both turned to look at the note still under the wiper blade.

Dixie was mad. Although that was one of many emotions vying for attention. She was also feeling misled and hurt. Ned had ruined everything.

'Get out now!' Dixie forcefully shooed him outside and closed the van door.

'Dixie, let me explain,' said Ned, from outside the van.

She realized it wasn't like a house or apartment where you could slam the door and walk away. There was nowhere to escape to. Elsie was small and her frame was far thinner than bricks and mortar so it was impossible not to listen to Ned.

'I don't want to hear any more lies!'

'I didn't lie to you.' Ned's tone was desperate.

'Did I miss the part where you said you were the one leaving the notes?'

'Sorry. It just felt a bit weird to own up to it. I felt bad about the tone of the early messages. They were written

301

by my gran. Well, they were her words, but since she got arthritis she's not so good with . . . Anyway, the point is I didn't know you then. And Gran was quite cross.'

'Because Elsie was on the tiniest corner of your land.' A penny dropped. 'That's why you offered to help fix her. Just because you wanted to get rid of me!'

'That's not true. I was trying to help,' said Ned.

'Helping yourself more like.' Dixie thought she'd found a friend in Ned, a likeminded soul. But now it turned out, like every other man, he was only interested in things that benefited him. She'd been taken for a fool.

'Dixie. Please can you open the door? I feel silly talking to a curtain.' There was a pause. 'You made new curtains. They look good but I'd like to see them from the other side.'

'*You* feel silly? How do you think I feel? I've been such an idiot. This whole time you were only playing the nice working-class guy so you could get rid of me without any fuss.'

'I never said I was working class.'

'You have spanners!' she yelled. 'But you don't have to play mechanic any more because Elsie and I won't be a bother for much longer because I'll call my friend. And she'll come and get me.' Dixie dialled Nora's number.

'It's me,' said Dixie. 'I can't get Elsie going again.'

'Are you still talking to me?' said Ned from outside the van.

'Hang on,' said Dixie into the phone. 'Ned's outside.'

'Hello, Ned!' called Nora.

302

'Don't be nice to him. He's the enemy. The patriarchy. The lord of the manor who wants the serfs off his land. He left threatening messages and then pretended to be my friend.' The last word caught in her throat and she had to stop speaking or she'd start blubbing. And she was an ugly crier.

'It's probably best if I go,' said Ned.

Dixie whipped back the curtains so that she could glare at him. 'You should,' she said, vitriolic. 'And me and Elsie will be out of your hair any minute now and you'll never have to see us again.'

'I can only take you. I've no way to tow Elsie,' said Nora from the phone.

This was embarrassing. Dixie's dramatic exit had been thwarted. She could hardly leave Elsie behind. 'But we *have* to go today!'

'You really don't. There isn't any rush,' said Ned.

Dixie felt oddly relieved by his words. But why would she want to stay? She didn't even understand herself sometimes. 'I'll call someone in the morning and then I'll be gone for ever,' she said, but Ned was already walking away.

Dixie watched him go and was surprised when Nora's voice cut through the silence. 'Are you sure you're OK?' She'd never had a friend like Nora before. There were the girls at boarding school but that had all been about knowing who to please, whose pa knew yours, who had the biggest tuck allowance. University had been quite similar. She'd had lots of friends there when she was holding parties in the house Daddy had paid for, but somehow those friends hadn't kept in touch. She knew in her heart Nora would always be her friend.

'Ned's gone.'

'That's good then. What do you want to do now?'

'I'll stay here. I've been here three weeks so another night won't kill me. I'll be fine,' said Dixie. She needed to find a positive out of all this. 'I found truffles.'

'On Ned's land?' asked Nora.

'Yes. But I didn't know that at the time.'

'They sort of belong to him then.'

Dixie just couldn't get a break.

33

It was after work on Monday when Nora and Jay set off on their trip to track down her last remaining ex-boyfriend.

It wasn't far, and she and Jay chatted on the way. 'I saw the look in your eyes when Renee told us about her lost love,' he said.

'I know, right? Theo Carlisle, the artist.'

'You've looked him up too, haven't you?' said Jay.

'Might have done,' said Nora. 'But I didn't find anything. Did you?'

'Not really. There's a couple of Theos exhibiting in the southeast, but he must be a similar age to Renee so it's likely he's not still working, or he could even be—'

'Don't say it,' said Nora. 'But I know you're right. I think we should try a bit harder. See if we can track him down.'

'Meddling doesn't always end well though. It's very unlikely it'll turn out like Davina and her long-lost-family show. What if he's still happily married with umpteen children and a football team of grandchildren? What then?'

Nora ran her teeth over her lip as she thought. 'Maybe you're right. But whatever it is, at least Renee would know.'

'Hmm,' said Jay. 'OK. I'll do a bit more digging.'

'Any more weird messages?'

'Yeah, a couple. They're sick of my faffing about. If I don't reply, things will get choppy. They're saying they're going to share all my secrets. And they still want me to take a trip to the corned beef factory.'

'Jay, this is getting serious. I'm sure stalking is a crime. I think you should report it,' said Nora, feeling anxious on his behalf.

'It's OK. I've spoken to the police about it. Apparently it's classed as harassment. They've said to keep records but they need quite a bit of evidence to actually arrest someone, and seeing as I have no idea who it is, it all gets a bit tricky. They're pretty sure there's no intent behind it and say it's best to ignore them. They sent me a useful information sheet about home security, which was nice.'

'And you're OK with that?' she asked.

'I think I have to be. Hopefully they'll get bored or turn vegan then I definitely won't end up as corned beef.'

Nora crossed her fingers. She hoped Jay wasn't really in any danger. Worry clenched at her gut. The thought of anything happening to him sent a horrible sensation through her body. They both kept their thoughts to themselves for the rest of the journey.

Nora pulled up in a gravel car park where an ornate iron sign declared Bramble Brook Forge. Bruce waited until Jay instructed him to get out of the car and he walked to heel the whole time he was sniffing all around. It was clearly a good place for smells. Through some gates they found a paved courtyard dotted with metal sculptures, from bees on a trellis to a giant palm frond. A welcome sign on a converted barn led them into a shop full of smaller pieces.

Through a split barn-style door with a large red warning sign on it, they could see a furnace and hear someone hammering metal against metal. Unless it was a cleverly positioned soundtrack, in which case it certainly gave the place an authentic feel. Nora wondered if perhaps sometimes she was a little cynical.

'Can I help?' asked a middle-aged man, appearing from outside. He had long grey hair tied back in a low ponytail.

'I'm interested in the garden pieces. Who makes them?' she asked.

'They're all designed and made here on the premises by our local blacksmiths. Was there anything in particular that caught your eye?' She suspected the man could smell a sale.

'I'm still browsing really,' said Nora. 'I'm hoping I'll know the right piece when I see it.'

The barn-style door opened and with a backdrop of the roaring furnace behind him, out strode a bare-chested Adonis of a man.

'Nora?'

'Tyler?'

'Oh, come on!' muttered Jay behind her.

'I thought I recognized that voice. It's so good to see you,' said Tyler. 'I'd better not hug you as I'm all sweaty.'

The light seemed to catch the sheen on his chest as he spoke.

'Yeah, probably not a good idea,' said Jay. 'Pleased to meet you. I'm a friend of Nora's.' He swapped the lead between his palms so he could shake hands, but Tyler only had eyes for Nora.

'Hi,' said Tyler. 'It's so good to see you. My astromancer said to expect good fortune and you must be it. What brings you here?' He wiped his hands on his leather apron.

'My garden isn't very exciting. I thought something a bit different would add some interest.'

'This stuff is definitely different,' said Jay, studying a twisted lump of something unidentifiable on a table that Bruce was sniffing forensically.

'I call this piece "Serendipity",' said Tyler, stepping in front of Jay.

'Like the romcom film?' asked Jay. 'With Kate Beckinsale and John Cusack? I love that movie.' Nora had had exactly the same thought – she and Jay were in tune like that.

Tyler scowled over his shoulder at him and addressed his reply to Nora, who was studying the sculpture with interest. 'It's a celebration of good fortune. Of the joy of unexpected good luck.' Nora had forgotten how engaging Tyler was.

Jay squinted a little as he gave the piece another inspection. 'Which bit is the good luck then?' he asked.

Tyler had an irritated look about him as he addressed Jay. 'It's an interpretation.'

'Huh,' said Jay. 'I like the bees. Did you make those?'

'I specialize more in the intuitive rhythm of life and its manifestation.'

'And then bash one out in metal. Interesting,' said Jay.

Nora was giving him her wide-eyed shut-the-hell-up look. She smiled as she turned back to Tyler and his sculpture. 'I really like your piece,' she said.

Jay sniggered and hid behind the metal structure as best he could.

'Thank you. That means a lot,' said Tyler with sincerity.

'Sorry if I interrupted you while you're working,' she said.

'You are the best kind of interruption.'

Jay mimed being sick from behind the metal artwork.

'This is a bit crazy, but maybe we could catch up some time? If you're free.' Nora watched Tyler closely.

'You know part of me really wants to say yes but—'

'You're already seeing someone?' anticipated Jay, coming from behind the sculpture as Bruce tried to pull him in the opposite direction.

'Ah, no. I was dating this businesswoman. High up in pharmaceuticals. Worked away in the city a lot. But she was seeing other people and that doesn't work for me.'

'Sorry, that sucks,' said Nora. 'Was it a recent split?' She was wheedling, but she hoped Tyler couldn't tell.

'About seven months, two weeks and three days. You

309

always remember the day your heart gets broken into a thousand pieces.'

Jay and Nora were stunned into silence for a moment.

'I'm joking,' said Tyler. 'But your faces were hilarious.'

'So not heartbroken then?' asked Jay. Nora scowled at him. And in response he mouthed, 'What?'

'Not exactly.' Tyler fiddled self-consciously with his leather apron, making Nora think that it was most likely unpleasantly sweaty in the groin area.

'Then you're single,' said Nora, unable to hide a small smile.

Tyler sighed. He had a melancholy look on his face, which made him even more attractive. He was still fiddling with his apron. 'I am.'

'Then we should definitely catch up some time. Hey, here's a thought . . .' She waved a hand as if something had just popped into her head. 'We could maybe go out for a meal.'

They were all momentarily distracted by the clip-clopping of hooves as a horse was led past outside. This really was a rural idyll. Bruce almost dragged Jay to the doorway to watch the horse walk by.

Tyler tipped his head down. 'But, Nora, you see, *you did* break my heart and if you're suggesting what I think you might be suggesting then I definitely can't go through that again.'

'Woah,' said Jay. 'I didn't see that coming.' He pointed at Tyler who scowled at him. 'I'll be somewhere else,' he added quickly. Although it seemed he didn't want to miss the rest of the discussion, so instead of leaving he skulked behind the sculptures.

'I feel bad that I hurt you,' said Nora.

'Don't. I'm fine now after a period of grieving, learning how to activate my light energy and a week of healing therapy in Goa.'

Nora chuckled. 'Joking again?'

Tyler's jaw was tight as he slowly shook his head.

'I thought everything was great between us and I didn't see it coming,' he said. 'It's taught me a lot about my ego and to not take things for granted. And for that I am grateful. I genuinely think I'm a more whole person now than I was back then. And I am better placed to share my light and my love.'

This showed her there was a different side to Tyler. Perhaps it was a clever play on his part.

'I may have been a little hasty in ending things,' said Nora. 'I look back now and all the things I thought were important . . . I've learned that they're not. People are what's important. That's all there is.'

'That is true,' said Tyler.

'I'm sorry I hurt you,' said Nora. Tyler and Nora exchanged weak smiles. There was nothing here for her.

Nora got a whiff of something unpleasant.

'Blimey, that makes your eyes water,' said Jay. Nora and Tyler both glared at him. 'Sorry. Horse.' He pointed out of the open door and began wafting his hand, although it didn't seem to make much difference.

'It's been lovely to see you again,' said Tyler.

'Anyway, my number hasn't changed if you decided you wanted to keep in touch,' said Nora, turning to leave.

'Did you not want to talk about something bespoke for your garden?' asked the older man, popping up out of nowhere and making Bruce bark. Had he been lurking this whole time, she wondered.

'I need to think about it a bit more,' said Nora.

Jay followed her out into the sunshine. 'Are you OK?' he asked.

'Yeah, I'm fine actually.' Although she wasn't sure that she was fine at all. She felt bad for hurting Tyler and didn't want to open his old wounds. But it was making her wonder. She definitely still fancied Tyler, but there was something missing. They had never laughed much, and certainly not as much as she and Jay did. It had been quite serious and intense. Something made her glance at Jay – she liked silly and relaxed. She liked Jay. He was a strikingly good-looking man. Of course she'd known that. He was an actor after all but looking at him now her heart was doing crazy things.

In that moment she realized, like Thor's hammer to her head, that Jay could be the one.

Jay Pandey was everything she wanted in a man and – more importantly – everything she needed. He cared about her, made her laugh and supported her unconditionally. And, quite frankly, he was hot. Not in a beefy macho blokey way but in a subtle, kind and delightfully charming way.

But, with as much force as the Hulk punching her in the face, she also realized that he could never be hers. She valued their friendship too much. Friendships of the sort she shared with Jay were rare. She wouldn't risk that for anything. Once before she'd made the mistake of going from friends to lovers, with Liam, and when they had split it had been devastating. There was no way she could risk that happening again, especially not with Jay. He meant far too much to her to risk losing him from her life.

The devil on her shoulder gave her a nudge. What if you just told him how you felt? What's the worst that could happen? The scenario played out in her head. It could be instant rejection or – worse still – a brief relationship that destroyed their friendship for ever. She could hardly sit and crochet opposite a man she'd bounced up and down on top of. The thought of it made her catch her breath – this was getting out of hand and it had to stop.

'That's good,' said Jay, pulling her back to her sad reality. 'Out of interest, why did you dump Tyler?'

'He was quite high maintenance. Needed a lot of reassuring all of the time. And there was something else.' Nora waited until they were definitely out of earshot before she elaborated. 'That smell . . .'

'The horse's bottom?' he queried.

'That wasn't the horse,' she replied, striding to the car.

It took Jay a moment to process what she'd said. 'Ewww,' he said with feeling.

34

After the drama of the previous day, Dixie woke up feeling remarkably positive. She knew her adventure had to come to an end at some point and now was as good a time as any. After three weeks she wanted to go back to civilization – living on her own had made her read far too much into things with Ned. What she needed was to draw a line under her adventure, savour all the positives from it and move on, emotionally and physically. Her fingers had hovered over the number of the local garage but something had changed her mind.

'Well, bugger me backwards, would you look at this place?' said Renee, setting foot inside the van. 'It's more dapper than dangerous Dave Cameron's shepherd hut!'

'Do you like it?' Dixie knew she was fishing for more compliments, but she needed a little boost.

'You've done a lovely job with it. I admit, I thought it was a pile of shite when you bought it. But it goes to show that while you can't polish a turd, you can roll it in glitter.'

Dixie had a feeling there was a compliment in there somewhere. 'Did you want a sit-down and a cup—'

'Bloody hell no. I'm not dead yet. I want to see the sights and then I'll have one last go at getting this baby running.' Renee waved her crossed fingers in the air.

Dixie followed her out of the van and locked up quickly. 'Be careful, it's uneven underfoot!' she called.

Renee was already strolling through the woodland when Dixie caught up with her. 'It's a lovely spot,' said Renee.

'It is. I'm going to miss it.' Dixie sighed.

'It's only thirty minutes up the blinking road. You can come back any time you like,' said Renee with a chuckle.

'Hmm. I can't really. It's all turned a bit weird with the landowner so I think when I leave I won't be coming back.' Dixie didn't like how much it hurt her.

Renee linked her arm through Dixie's. 'Then leave it up to me and you'll go out with a bang.'

'Now I am worried,' said Dixie.

Their walk took them through all Dixie's favourite places. Renee didn't question the new names she'd given them. The sun was glinting spectacularly through the trees making it feel like they were walking through a piece of art. The familiar, fresh, flowery scents were stronger somehow, and Dixie tried to commit it all to memory.

Dixie pointed out all the natural ingredients she could see and Renee picked up a few others that she recognized as well, including wild thyme and some mushrooms. She was suitably impressed with the truffles, although the only ones they could find were those nibbled and discarded by the squirrels. They stood together on the ridge by Tidy Trees and looked across the rippling hills.

Renee was sucking in a great lungful of air. Had the walk been too much for her, Dixie wondered. 'Are you OK?'

'Fresh air. You can't bloody beat it. Unless you have alcohol, then no contest. Come on. Let's go back and get cooking and then we'll get fixing.'

Dixie realized it was the last time she'd look out over Tidy Trees and walk past Woody Corner and try not to scratch herself going through Prickly Patch or stub her toe on the Bastard Stump and it was hard not to feel sad about it.

'Stop being maudlin! Life's too short for it,' called Renee, snapping Dixie out of her doldrums.

They were chatting about what cocktails Dixie had missed at Crafting and Cocktails when Renee put her arm in front of Dixie to halt her, a lot like her mum had used to do when she was in the front seat of the car and she was braking heavily – Dixie's mum wasn't the best driver. Renee put a finger to her lips and then pointed ahead.

'What is it?' asked Dixie, but she had already spotted what Renee had seen. 'Ned! What the actual f—'

'We'd better go and investigate,' interrupted Renee, her voice low.

They crept closer until Renee gestured for Dixie to go one way around the van whilst she went the other. Dixie did as Renee asked but her mind was buzzing. What was Ned doing back here? Why were they creeping up on him rather than shouting at him?

'What are you doing?' asked Renee, popping out from the cover of the van and making Ned jump.

'Oh, it's nothing to worry about. I'm—'

'We know who you are and what you are,' snapped Dixie, making him jump again as she appeared on his other side. She leaned over and snatched the note from under Elsie's wiper.

'Right, let's see what this says, shall we? "Dear Dixie, I've never met anyone quite like you before. It feels like I've found something I didn't even know I was searching for. You're bold, unorthodox and completely unique. I'd hate things to end like this. Please can we talk . . ."' Dixie stopped reading. She couldn't have been more surprised if Arnold had started to sing opera.

Ned scrunched up his shoulders in his discomfort. 'I maybe should have led with an apology. But you get the gist. Anyway, I—' He waved a thumb over his shoulder.

'Oh no you don't,' said Renee. 'I've got a great recipe and I'm about to whip it up. So you two have a walk and sort out your differences or when you get back in thirty minutes I'll be banging your heads together. Got it?'

Ned looked mildly alarmed by Renee, which was fairly usual.

'This is Renee,' said Dixie. 'She's a very good friend of mine. We'd best do as she says.'

Dixie and Ned walked in silence for a bit. But Dixie had had enough of silence. She'd spent every evening with it for too many nights and it really wasn't something she was going to miss. Ned on the other hand . . . she was very confused about how she felt about him. She'd thought they had been nurturing something but if he'd been trying get rid of her all along then he obviously didn't feel the same but then again he'd left the lovely note that she was clutching. It was all rather befuddling.

'Look. I'm sorry I shouted at you but it was a shock to find out the mean letters were from you. It wasn't nice to discover that someone I thought was a friend was scheming to get me moved on.' She felt instantly better for saying it.

Ned took a deep breath and shoved his hands deeper into his pockets. 'I was scared,' he said.

'Of what?'

'I saw the campervan and I made assumptions about who had left it there. And then I realized someone was living in it so I told Gran and that had her awake at night, worrying that more people would move on to the land and we'd be overrun and they'd never leave.'

'She has quite the active imagination.'

'Yeah. It's not helpful sometimes. Gran made me write the notes because we wanted to stop all of that happening. It was a pre-emptive strike if you like. And then I met you and you were the last person I expected to be living like that. Sorry, no offence.'

'None taken. It is a little unusual and there is the tee-niest possibility that I overreacted,' said Dixie.

'Great – something we can agree on,' said Ned. But he was smiling.

'Then who was the lady with the Labrador?'

'A neighbour. Sorry I ran off that day but I knew she'd tell Gran if she saw me here talking to you.'

'So it's your Gran who owns the land then?'

'She handed things over to me early as she'd had a few bad health episodes and now we're in this odd place where we both think we're in charge but neither of us wants to upset the other one.'

'I get that,' said Dixie. 'You want to be your own boss but also keep things genial.'

'Exactly.' They walked on for a few steps before he spoke again. 'Are we friends again?' He gave Dixie a sideways glance.

'I think so.'

'Then you'll stay?'

'I don't think I can. I'm a bit natured out. It's an awful thing to admit but I miss a proper bed. Elsie's mattress is like sleeping on a bag of spanners. I actually checked the first night in case there were a variety of tools under-neath, it was so uncomfortable. And I miss proper coffee and, most of all, I miss my friends.'

'I understand,' said Ned. 'Because when you leave I'll miss my friend too.'

320

They strolled back in silence. Somehow silence wasn't so bad when she shared it with him. As they neared the campervan, Arnold scurried across a branch above their heads and screeched her annoyance at them.

'Grub's up!' called Renee.

Delicious smells met them as they entered the van where Renee was dishing up mushroom risotto. She grated a little of the washed truffle on top. 'This is quite something.' She waved the brown nugget at Ned.

'Lucky find, I think,' he said.

'Nope,' said Renee. 'By the looks of things you've got a whole truffle orchard down by the ridge there.' Ned looked stunned. Renee nodded at the food. 'Now you're both OK with shrooms, right?'

'I love mushrooms,' said Dixie.

'Great. It's a bit haphazard as it's not the right rice but it'll blow your mind, I guarantee it. Dig in!'

'They don't sell arborio at the garage,' lamented Dixie.

They all sat down and began to eat. Renee was right, it was delicious. They chatted amiably while they ate.

'There's something about this,' said Ned. 'I've eaten a lot of foraged food but there's something I can't quite work out.'

'Wild garlic?' said Dixie.

'No, I'd recognize that.'

'Wild thyme?' said Renee.

'That could be it. Subtle and earthy. It's very good. Thanks, Renee,' said Ned.

'You're welcome. I take it you two have sorted out your differences, then.' She eyed them both over her full fork.

'We have,' said Dixie, realizing she felt so much happier now.

'Then you're stopping here?' Renee raised an eyebrow.

'No, I'm coming home. I think it's time to draw this adventure to a close. And assuming you can get Elsie fixed, then I'll be off today, but it won't be forever.'

'Hmm,' said Renee, checking her watch. 'That might not be possible today.'

Dixie didn't always know when Renee was joking. She cleared everything away and Ned helped her wash up while Renee sat outside on the deckchair and threw nuts to Arnold.

'Were you expecting Renee to fix the van?' whispered Ned as he dried up a plate.

Dixie sat down on the edge of the seating; she was feeling a bit lightheaded. 'She's a dab hand with engines and she can weld. I'm not sure what's happening now though.' Dixie blinked. 'Can you smell green?' she asked.

'Green what?'

'Just green,' said Dixie. Ned's eyes widened.

35

Dixie was feeling calm and happy but Ned was giving her an odd look. At least she thought he was but he now looked partly like Ned and a lot like Ed Sheeran, which was weird because he'd not looked like Ed Sheeran before and she was fairly sure she would have noticed that. Ned waved a hand in front of her face but it was a giant hand and colours were flowing from his fingers. It was quite beautiful.

'Wow,' said Dixie, almost hypnotized by the varying shades spiralling around the inside of the campervan from his fingertips.

'Isn't it marvellous?' called Renee from outside.

'Marvellous is yellow,' said Dixie.

Ned moved around Dixie to perch on the bed and talk to Renee. 'What's happening?' he asked.

Renee waved a hand near him as if trying to pat him but missed. 'Relax and let it take you somewhere incredible. I can see tiny purple elephants!' She moved her hands as if conducting an orchestra in a jaunty beat.

'Oh heavens, have we taken drugs?' asked Ned, his

head turning from Renee to Dixie and back again quite quickly. 'Was that what the weird flavour in the risotto was?' He sounded panicky.

'Nooo,' said Dixie, fascinated by the sound of her own voice. Could she smell that word? 'Renee wouldn't spike our dinner.'

'I did check you were both all right with the shrooms. It's all organic. Nature's charm. The Aztecs called them flesh of the gods. Magic mushrooms were what we called them in the sixties. You can't beat them. So you have to join them,' said Renee, starting to laugh. She got up and began dancing while still conducting an orchestra only she could hear. She beckoned the others to join her. Dixie stepped outside but it wasn't the outside she remembered. This was like walking into a Disney film. Flowers shot up where she trod and each time she lifted up her foot, more pretty coloured petals appeared. 'They smell like Tuesday,' she said. She'd never been so happy. Renee took her hands and they danced in circles with the pineapples.

'Wait! Stop!' Ned waved his arms about, which was fascinating to Dixie because there were so many of them and every one a different colour. She and Renee stopped dancing to watch. 'I thought when you said shroom you had a speech impediment,' said Ned, frowning hard.

'I thought it was just a cute way to say mushroom. Like when people say K instead of OK,' said Dixie, starting to sway to the music she could hear.

'They're just lazy buggers,' said Renee. 'I thought everyone knew a shroom was a magic mushroom.'

Ned frowned at them both. And for a moment the music stopped and the colours faded. But then Ned started to laugh. Just a snort at first but then growing until he was belly laughing. Renee and Dixie joined in until all three were holding their sides. The colours came back and the music was switched back on. Arnold screeched at them and hopped inside the van to help herself to the nuts.

Lots of dancing followed until Renee announced that she and the tallest of the Bakewell tarts were going for a lie-down. Dixie and Ned both tried to flop into Renee's vacated deckchair at the same time. The chair gave way and they landed in a heap on top of each other. They tried to get up but it was quite hard now that Dixie appeared to have flippers instead of feet. But they would be awfully handy the next time she went snorkelling in the Caribbean.

'Shall we just stay here,' said Dixie.

'I wish you would stay here.'

'I meant on the ground,' said Dixie, watching more flowers spring up around her.

'That's OK too,' he said. 'The whales won't see us down here.'

'Good thinking,' agreed Dixie. 'You're very smart,' she added.

'You're very lovely. I especially like your tail.' He swallowed hard. 'I think I love you,' he added in a rush and then he kissed her.

*

Nora and Jay were in Jay's garden enjoying the sunshine while Bruce lay with his legs in the air in the hope of someone scratching his belly. Nora sipped her Diet Coke and relished the rare feeling of warmth on her skin. She had expected to feel different at this point. Her review of her back catalogue of men was complete and she had achieved her goal, although she hadn't. The review hadn't delivered a definitive answer. Had she overlooked the one or had she made sound decisions with all of her ex-partners? There was still a large question mark hanging over Liam but for now she was going to sit with her friend and enjoy the tiny glimpse of summer because you never knew how long it would last.

She'd been thinking a lot about Jay. Mainly puzzling thoughts. She feared she was confusing friendship with something else. They were good together, there was no denying that, but just because they had the same sense of humour and a couple of things in common it didn't mean they should embark on a relationship. Plus neither of them had ever given the merest inkling that they might be attracted to each other. She supposed she could just ask him. That would be the quickest way to find out how he felt, but was that the same as declaring how *she* felt? The last thing she wanted was to make Jay feel awkward if he thought she fancied him but he didn't feel the same. No, she would have to word it in the right way to get away without any impact on their friendship. That was too important to her to lose.

'Just got an email. I might have a lead on Theo Carlisle,' said Jay, interrupting her thoughts.

'Ooh, exciting. Tell me more.'

'Art gallery in Devon did an exhibition a few years back so I've asked if they can pass on my details. I said I was a solicitor in the hope that Mr Carlisle thinks it's worth him getting in touch.'

'Naughty,' said Nora. 'But also genius. I hope he takes the bait.'

Jay's phone pinged and he opened a message, giggled and began speedily responding. Nora peered over her sunglasses at him. 'I'm guessing it's not your stalker?'

'No. It's just Tasha.'

'You two seem to be getting on well.' She pushed her sunglasses back up her nose and turned her face back to the sun.

'Yeah we are.' There was a brief pause. 'She wants us to be exclusive.'

Nora had a sensation like she'd never experienced before. Gutted didn't come close. It was as if someone had ripped out her major organs, dropped them in a blender and shoved the mush back inside, expecting her to carry on as if everything was exactly the same when it wasn't. In that single sentence, everything had changed. All the possibilities had been deleted. If the house had suddenly landed on top of her it would have had less impact. 'She wants what . . . So are you two . . . Obviously you are . . . How long?' It wasn't the most coherent sentence she'd ever put together but considering her discombobulated state she felt it covered the main points. Apart from the burning question as to how come she didn't know anything about Jay and Tasha.

'She was being really flirty the last time I saw her, but I figured I'd gotten it wrong and she was just being friendly. But she's been messaging me ever since, and we have stuff on this week and a thing on Saturday.'

'A thing?' Nora almost spun herself off the plastic garden chair in her haste to see Jay's face. What did he mean by 'a thing'? Was it a serious thing, or just a thing?

'You know?' he said. 'Press, radio and TV interviews. All very dull. And there's the *Undercover Bullets* premiere on Saturday night.' He said it like it was an afterthought. Like when you say 'extra cheese' when you're ordering a pizza.

Nora opened and closed her mouth like a goldfish taking its final gulps of air. 'Premiere? As in posh outfits, red carpet, stars of stage and screen?'

'Nah, not really. It's a bit last minute because Tasha's last film has done pretty well so they're squeezing us in. Like I'll be squeezing myself into my tux.' He snorted and carried on texting.

'Stop. Jay, this is huge.' Nora waved a hand in front of his face.

'Oh, did you want to come? I get a few free tickets. To be honest, we'll probably be glad of bums on seats.'

'But I've got Bruce most of this week, which is why

I'm working from home, plus I've got him on Saturday.'
She'd not realized exactly where Jay had been planning on going when she'd signed up to dog-sit. Her mind had been too preoccupied with ex-boyfriends to question it.

'We can see if Renee's available. Or there's always next time. Let's hope there is a next time,' he said.

Nora felt uncomfortable: a little sweaty and anxious. 'Did I miss something? With you and Tasha?'

He put his phone away. 'If you did, I think I did too. I'm not sure what it is or even if it is anything but hey. It can't do any harm, right?'

Alarm bells were going off in Nora's head. Her biggest quandary was whether to share any of her fears with Jay. Tasha was big right now and he'd fancied her for ages. But how hadn't he realized that he was in a relationship with her sooner? Perhaps she was looking for problems. Or maybe Jay was playing it down. After all, he didn't owe her an explanation. He was her friend and she should be happy for him. She felt bad for not being instantly supportive.

'You could be the next Brangelina,' she said, trying to lighten her heavy mood.

'Without all the kids hopefully,' he quipped. 'What can we make with Pandey and Blake?'

'Blandey,' said Nora. 'Jasha or Bandey?'

'Maybe not then,' said Jay pulling a face.

'You don't seem as enthusiastic as I thought you'd be.' She studied him – the bowed head and sloping shoulders were not the body language of an excited man. 'Or at all enthusiastic, actually. About the film I mean, not Tasha. Obviously you're excited about Tasha because she's the most gorgeous blonde on the planet. Right?' For some reason she pushed her mousey brown hair behind her ear.

'She is.' He sighed. 'You're right about the film. It doesn't feel real. Maybe I'll believe it once it's premiered.'

Something was niggling her like grit in a sandal. 'But this is it. It's what you always dreamed of. The famous girlfriend, red carpet premieres, the big career.' It suddenly brought Nora's little life into sharp focus. Jay was leaving her behind. His life was going to change beyond recognition, and it was very unlikely there would be any space in it for her. Something like panic gripped her and she took a sharp breath, making him look up.

He swivelled around. 'But you remember when my agent got all mega excited about the Blake Seven film and started looking at yachts because that gig was going to catapult me to stardom and make him rich?'

'Yeah. What happened to that film?'

'Last I heard it was on its twelfth rewrite and still had no funding. And my agent still has no yacht. I think for now it's best I manage my own expectations. The life of an actor teaches you to expect disappointment. Then if it's good news it's a nice surprise.' He gave her a half smile.

'That's depressing.'

Bruce jumped up and almost knocked Jay backwards off his chair as he got as close to him as he could. 'Does my boy need a cuddle?' Jay wrapped his arms around Bruce's neck. 'Who knew he was just a big softie underneath?'

'I guess we all hide our true selves to an extent,' she said, but Jay was busy fussing the dog and was probably no longer listening. A cloud moved and blocked the sun's rays. Perhaps summer was already over.

36

A melodic ringing woke Dixie. 'Where are you?' asked Nora.

'That's a very good question,' said Dixie, sitting up and looking around. She lowered her voice. 'I'm lying down in the campervan with Ned and Renee.'

'Please tell me you're not naked.'

Dixie had a quick check. 'We are all fully clothed.'

'Thank goodness for that. Wait. Were you and Ned—'

'Gosh, I don't think so.' Although Dixie ran a finger over her lips. Something was making her body tingle.

'And why on earth is Renee there?'

'She came to fix Elsie.' At least Dixie could remember that, even if everything else was a little fuzzy. 'But we ended up doing leapfrog over giant hotdogs.'

'What?' asked Nora. She sounded as confused as Dixie felt.

Renee stirred next to her. 'Don't squish the pine-apples,' she muttered before going back to sleep.

'Hang on, Renee is sleeping.'

Dixie wriggled off the bed like a caterpillar. She was

going to sit in the deckchair outside but that was in pieces. Pictures of her and Ned danced into her mind. 'I think we kissed,' she whispered.

'Please tell me you don't mean you and Renee.'

'Ha, very funny. No. Me and Ned. We definitely kissed. After we'd been dancing in colours. Hang on. I remember what happened. Renee fed us magic mushrooms. We must have been tripping. Oh thank goodness. At least that explains the giant hotdogs and Ed Sheeran.'

'But you're all OK?' asked Nora.

'I feel fine. I actually feel zen and happy.'

'You're probably still high.'

'Could be.'

'You can't drive like that,' said Nora, sounding all grown-up.

'I know. Plus Elsie isn't fixed anyway. But if Ned and I kissed maybe I don't want to rush back to civilization.'

'Oh . . .' Nora sounded a bit sad.

'Are you OK?'

'Yeah, I'm absolutely and completely fine. I was looking forward to some girly chats. You know. It's just been me and Jay and . . . he's OK . . . actually he's great. But he's still not you.'

'I will be coming back, just not right now. I think maybe I need to investigate this thing with Ned.'

'Of course. You must investigate Ned's thing. Everyone seems to have a thing. And that's great. I am happy for you.'

'Nora, you don't sound right at all.' Dixie was starting

to think that perhaps she should call a taxi and go to Nora's anyway as there was definitely something wrong.

Nora sighed down the phone. 'Jay is seeing Tasha Blake. And that's cool. His film is going to be huge and everything is changing. I need to get my head around it all. I'll have a glass of wine and a pizza and I'll talk it over with Oliver. I'll be fine. Don't worry.'

'OK. If you're sure.' Dixie looked over her shoulder at a dishevelled Ned sitting up. She could tell he was experiencing the same confusion she had but when their eyes met his smile was warm and she knew it was going to be OK.

*

Nora knew it wasn't a good idea to sit at home and wallow with wine and a pizza, however tempting it was. What she needed to do was stop dwelling on the lives of others – Dixie happy with Ned, Jay dating his dream girl – and look to her own. She was happy for her friends, but her own life was not as rosy.

She decided that she was the only person who could solve that. And she knew exactly how to do it.

Nora picked up the phone and made a call. Her future started here.

Nora was early to the Italian restaurant. Mainly because she didn't want any reason to back out. She had reviewed all her exes and now she had made a decision. Einstein had said the definition of insanity was doing the same thing over and over and expecting different results. She had broken the cycle.

The door opened and Nora instinctively turned to see Liam stride in. He looked gorgeous and confident. He was perfect. They had history, a shared love of numbers and he was a good man. There was nothing more she needed. Liam fitted the bill. Now all she had to do was find out if he felt the same about her.

'Hey,' he said, leaning down and planting a kiss on her cheek.

'Thanks for coming,' she said as he took a seat opposite.

'No worries. Is everything OK? It sounded serious on the phone.'

'Shall we order some drinks and then we can chat?' It wasn't that she wanted to delay the discussion, but she really did need that glass of wine now.

'Of course.' Liam nodded at a waiter and they quickly came over. 'Please can we order some drinks?'

'Absolutely, sir. Would you like the wine menu?'

Liam looked at Nora. 'Still like a Merlot?' he asked.

It was nice that he remembered and it put her a little at ease. 'That'll be good.'

'A bottle of Merlot please.'

The waiter nodded and disappeared. Now they were in that awkward in between part where they had no drinks and only the menus to distract them. Nora stared at hers in the hope that Liam would get the message that she wasn't quite ready to reveal why she'd asked him there.

'So . . .'

Nora looked over the top of her menu. Liam was staring at her. 'I've not decided yet,' she said as she raised the menu. She liked lasagne but she could have that at home. Perhaps she'd go for the gnocchi.

Liam gently pushed her menu down. 'I know you. There's something up and now you're starting to worry me.'

She didn't like that he was concerned about her. The best approach was to be brave and just come out with it. What was the worst that could happen? Unhelpful images of him turning the table over and storming out ran through her mind. But he wasn't like that. The worst he would do would be to look embarrassed and leave. 'Right. The thing is . . . Why is there always a thing?'

He raised his eyebrows. 'Is there?' He didn't know about the other things. Jay's thing with Tasha and Dixie's thing with Ned.

'I'm just going to say it. Please don't judge me or hate me. Or—'

'Nora . . .'

'Sorry.' She took a steadying breath. 'I asked you here because—'

'A bottle of the Merlot?' The waiter showed the bottle to Liam.

'Thanks.' They sat awkwardly while the waiter half filled their glasses, which seemed to take ages. At last he put down the bottle and walked away.

Liam had a look of expectation about him. She

thought back to their last outing when Gareth had tried to join them and Liam had said they were friends. That comment was still niggling her. It was the thing that was going to spoil things if that was all he thought of her. That was the red sock in her whites wash.

'Liam. When Gareth rocked up when we were having coffee . . .'

He shook his head but was smiling. 'He was a bit full on. How did you ever match with him?'

'Who knows? Anyway, the thing is, when he asked how you knew me, you said we were old friends.' She waited and watched for his reaction.

'I can't believe he asked about your bowels.' Liam laughed as he perused the menu.

'Liam, are you listening to me?'

He looked up. 'Yeah. I said we were old friends. I thought that was the end of your sentence.'

'It was but what I want to know is . . . is that it? Is that how you see our past? Just friends?'

She had to make herself keep breathing steadily, otherwise she was in danger of holding her breath and passing out.

'Umm, it wasn't something I was thinking too deeply about at the time.' He put down the menu. 'But I'm guessing you've been dwelling on that.'

She scratched the back of her neck. 'Nah, not really. Not thought about it until now, or not much anyway.' He was smiling at her. 'OK, I have been totally obsessing about it. Because I thought maybe we had something.

You know, like the thing everyone else has. And I think now that we threw it away. But maybe we shouldn't have done. I wonder whether if we hadn't broken up perhaps we'd still be together now. And maybe we'd be happy.' It wasn't at all how she'd rehearsed it in her head but at least it was said now.

'Ahh, the "what might have been" conundrum.' He gave a slow nod. 'We all do it. It's kind of fun to play out different endings in your head. I get it. Truth is that whether it would have worked out long-term is something we'll never know.' He picked up his menu again.

Nora pushed his menu back down on to the table. She looked him in the eye. 'I'm asking you if you want to try again, because I think I do.'

37

It was really hard for Nora to not hold her breath while she waited for Liam to respond. A couple of seconds felt like for ever. She was about to cave and say 'Only joking' in her best Alan Partridge when a firm hand on her shoulder made her freeze. If it was Gareth again, she was pretty sure there wasn't a jury in the country that would find her guilty if she chopped him into little pieces with a cake fork.

'Is it business or pleasure?' asked her dad, hovering at her shoulder.

This was possibly worse than Gareth.

'Dad, now's not a good—'

'Praise be. You are on a date at last,' said her mother, coming to stand at the edge of the table. 'I recognize you. Now don't tell me . . .' Una closed her eyes as if trying to contact the spirit world.

'Mum, it's Liam,' said Nora in her most embarrassed voice, one that was reserved exclusively for her parents.

'Liam. That's it. I would have remembered. I never forget a boyfriend. And there have been quite a few.' Una laughed. Nora died a little inside.

'Mum. It is lovely to see you but do you think we could catch up later?'

'It is lovely to see you too.' Una turned her attention to Liam. 'We rarely see her these days, Liam. She's either working or climbing or crafting. We don't even have a key for her house any more. Nora has such little time for us. Are you like that with your parents?'

'Why don't we see if there's a bigger table and you can join us,' said Liam. He seemed oblivious to Nora trying to vigorously shake her head without it actually moving, which probably gave her the look of someone being electrocuted. Why was he suggesting they join them? Did he think that was preferable to having dinner alone with Nora after what she'd just suggested?

Ali squeezed his daughter's shoulder. 'We don't want to bother them, Una.'

'But we've been invited,' said Una. 'It'd be rude to refuse.'

Nora looked up at her dad. A waiter hovered, awaiting a final decision.

'No, Una. Let's leave them to it.' Ali put a hand on his wife's waist to guide her away.

'There's a table here,' said the waiter, indicating one nearby.

Nora shook her head but her mother was already sliding into the seat the waiter had pulled out. 'The perfect compromise,' she said with glee.

Ali shrugged. Bless him; he'd done his best.

*

Nora tried to enjoy her meal but it was tricky because she knew her mother was eavesdropping. Although there was nothing interesting about her and Liam's conversation. All the fun shared memories had been covered when they'd met before. Perhaps it was because they were very aware of the proximity of her parents that topics were neutral and neither of them was addressing the question she had posed.

'Have you been on any nice holidays?' asked Nora, fearing she sounded like a bored hairdresser.

'Not had much time for holidays, plus they're not the same on your own.'

'I get you. I don't go away much. I have Oliver to think about.'

Liam's head shot up. And from the expression on his face she was worried he was putting two and two together and getting a much larger number – did he think she had asked him to join a thruple?

She almost choked on her tagliatelle in an attempt to explain who Oliver was.

Unfortunately her mother beat her to it.

Una leaned towards Liam. 'Nora has a lizard. His eyes are wonky.'

Nora hastily swallowed her mouthful. 'Oliver is a chameleon and his eyes are meant to do that.'

Thankfully Ali said something that pulled Una's attention away from Nora.

Liam was giving her an odd look.

'What?' she asked.

'I wouldn't have thought you'd be into reptiles. You always wanted a dog.'

'I have one of those too . . . kind of. I have a dog share with my friend Jay.' Pictures of Jay and Bruce on the beach flashed into her mind. Would she see more or less of Bruce now Jay's career was taking off? She couldn't bear to lose them both.

Liam started talking about the trials and tribulations of Leicester City football team and Nora concentrated on finishing her meal at record speed. Thankfully Liam didn't want a dessert. At least now they could escape. They paid the bill and Nora went to say goodbye to her parents.

'Night, Mum,' said Nora, giving her mother a hug.

'I like this one,' she said in a stage whisper. 'Love you. Stay safe. And remember to eat.'

'Night, Dad,' said Nora.

'Sorry,' said her father as he hugged her goodbye.

Nora and Liam left the restaurant. The relief was palpable. For a moment they stood outside in the light drizzle. Nora took a deep breath. 'Well, that was a nightmare and I am very sorry. I had no idea they were coming here. But now I say it out loud I have a niggle that in the middle of a conversation about onions my mother may have mentioned that someone recommended it. But I definitely didn't know they were coming tonight. If I had—'

'Yes,' said Liam, pulling her up short.

'Sorry?'

'Yes, I think we should try again,' he said.

They stayed staring at each other for a moment. Nora had no idea what the correct protocol was or if there even was one. She'd expected to feel something but perhaps that came later. And anyway she was still decompressing from the encounter with her parents. 'Great. OK. Then I guess we're dating,' she said.

'I guess we are,' he said, taking her hand.

After the most stilted meal out ever, they had walked to their cars, kissed each other on the cheek and gone back to their respective homes. It wasn't the romantic and passion-filled reunion she had envisaged, but she was still feeling good about things.

She'd messaged Jay as soon as she'd got to her car. She didn't need his approval but he'd been on the 37-per-cent-rule journey with her and she wanted him to know that her process had come good. It mattered what he thought.

He'd sent back a thumbs-up emoji, which had left her deflated. She had definitely shown more enthusiasm for his relationship with Tasha, so she was a little irked by his dismissive response. A thumbs-up was for 'Shall we have pizza for tea' or 'That thing you like is back on TV tonight', not 'I'm embarking on a relationship with my ex who might just be the one'. The latter was also bothering her. They had made the next move but at what point would she know it was the right thing to do and that Liam really was *the one*? She had filed that question under 'currently too difficult to answer' in the hope that it would resolve itself quite quickly. Going forward would anyone she dated have to measure up to Jay? Right now her feelings for Jay trounced how she felt about Liam. But Jay wasn't an option. It was all very confusing.

Back at home Nora updated her spreadsheet and called Dixie to check how she was and how things were going with getting Elsie towed. She'd been half expecting to see the campervan on her drive when she got home from work but then if she was coming from somewhere miles away like Northumberland it would likely take a while.

'Hey, Dixie, how's things? Are you on your way back to civilization yet?'

'Things are simply delightful. Renee couldn't get Elsie fixed but she fixed me and Ned so it's all fine,' said Dixie.

'Are you staying where you are? Exactly where are you?' asked Nora.

There was a pause. 'I'm in Belton. About eighteen miles away.'

'Dixie! Have you been there all this time?' asked Nora, flummoxed by the revelation her friend was so close by.

'Yeah. Sometimes things don't go to plan but they are exactly how they should be.'

'That's profound,' said Nora.

'I know, right? Ned says I'm full of insightful stuff. The things about me that I thought were just plain weird he sees as cool. How adorable is that?'

'Very. So what happens now?' asked Nora.

'I'm having a little gathering. I'll send you the details. It's sort of an announcement. You've probably seen my teasers on Insta.'

Nora hadn't but she didn't like to say. 'Do I get to know before everyone else?' she asked.

'I'm afraid not. I want to do a big reveal with you actually there. And Jay too.'

'Ooh, can Liam come?'

'Yeah, if he wants to . . . hang on a minute. Liam? Does this mean what I hope it does?' Dixie squealed down the phone.

Nora wasn't entirely sure it meant what *she* hoped it did but they were making moves in the right direction, or the first step at least.

38

A couple of days later Nora found herself traipsing through the woodland by Dixie's campervan with Liam. Since their stressful date with her parents earwigging from the next table she had received a number of nice messages from Liam, thanking her for her patience because he still felt it was a little soon after his split to be embarking on another relationship but, like her, believed they needed to give theirs another chance.

He'd been busy with work so they had not had an opportunity to meet up before now. Nora reasoned that this was different to a brand-new relationship because they had known each other before, in both the platonic and biblical sense, so it didn't hold quite the same initial thrill. Wandering through a woodland wasn't exactly the best second date they could have gone on but Dixie wanted to get everyone together. The alternative was to not bring Liam but as Nora wanted to show that she also had a *thing* she had decided he should be there.

Jay had brought Bruce, who was, as usual, excited to see everyone and especially the new person. Liam did not feel the same. He kept darting behind Nora, which Bruce thought was a very easy game of hide and seek. As the recall training had been going well, Jay had decided to let Bruce off the lead.

'Why won't he leave me alone?' asked Liam, dashing past with Bruce in hot pursuit.

'Because you're new and he wants to get to know you. Stay still. He won't hurt you, I promise,' said Nora.

'Dogs are unpredictable. Especially rescued ones. You have no idea what his background is.'

'We do. He was trained to rip people to shreds,' she said with a cheesy smile.

Liam looked terrified for a second before he realized she was joking. 'Not funny.'

'Watch this, he's a teddy bear.' She crouched down to give Bruce a fuss, but that just gave the dog easier access to the new person he wanted to get to know. Bruce leap-frogged Nora and lunged at Liam.

'Whoa!' The force of the big dog using her as a launch-pad sent Nora flying backwards.

'Argh!' Liam yelled as the dog catapulted towards him. Liam ran off with Bruce right behind him, leaving Nora in a heap on the ground.

'He likes dogs then,' said a smiling Jay, helping Nora to her feet. They watched Liam do a passable Jack Sparrow run around the trees. Jay sniggered. Nora wanted to do the same but needed to look supportive of her new boy-friend so instead she frowned at Jay, who looked suitably scolded.

'Maybe he's not used to big dogs.'

'Should we rescue him?' asked Jay.

'You OK?' called Nora.

'All under control,' said Liam, keeping a tree between him and the dog.

'My stalker got the airtime they were longing for,' said Jay.

'Why? What's happened?' asked Nora, feeling her stomach churn at the thought of the threats.

'Tasha did an interview and it all came out. The press are having a field day with it. Pictures of me next to a blacked-out silhouette with a big question mark on it. And lots of speculation about the type of person they are, which makes terrifying reading. Anastasia is thrilled because apparently all publicity is good publicity.'

'Bloody hell. Have there been any more messages?'

'Only one saying that they love me now. So that's nice.' They both pulled the same grimace at the same time, which made them laugh. Nora found she was staring at Jay. Was it what he was wearing or had he always looked that hot? She needed to pull herself together. He was with Tasha and she was with Liam. She looked around for him as Dixie caught up.

'We seem to have lost Liam,' she said.

'It's OK. We're going the same way as Bruce and Liam anyway,' said Dixie, almost skipping past them with Ned close behind.

'What exactly are we doing?' asked Nora, striding out to catch up with Dixie. 'It's just I . . . well, we . . . kind of have plans for later this evening.' By 'plans' Nora meant she was very much hoping that they could go back to hers and fast-forward their relationship to the part where they ended up in bed together.

'It's a surprise,' said Dixie. 'And then we're having a barbecue back at Elsie. Don't we sound all domesticated, hosting a barbecue as a couple?' She looked coyly at Ned.

Nora feared she wasn't going to be having the early night she'd planned.

Dixie and Ned went on ahead and Jay walked in step with Nora. 'How are you?'

'Good. I'm good. We're good.' She pointed at Liam, who was now running away from the dog with his arms flapping in the air as he called out Nora's name.

'That's um . . . good then,' said Jay.

'How are you and Tasha?' she asked, although she was hoping she would only receive the headlines. She was still coming to terms with it.

'Yeah. Work has been manic but we make a good double act. She was going to be here tonight but something came up last minute. It's OK, we have *Lorraine* tomorrow which she's dashing in and out for but I'll have more time with her when I see her at the premiere.'

'That'll be nice,' said Nora, the sentence not sounding like her at all.

Up ahead Bruce now had a terrified-looking Liam pinned to a tree while he tried to sniff him all over and lick his face.

'Brucey, come here please!' called Jay and the dog immediately complied. He'd come a long way – in fact, both Bruce and Jay had. He returned to Jay and relished the cuddle and praise he received. At least, now that Jay was giving him a proper fuss as a reward, a lot less chicken was needed. Liam was panting hard and leaning against the tree when they reached him.

'You OK?' asked Nora, trying to take his hand, but he was busy using it to stab the air in Bruce's direction.

'That brute!'

'Hey,' said Jay. 'There's no need for name-calling.'

Liam waved an arm. 'You could have called him off sooner.'

'By running off he thought you were playing with him,' said Jay.

'He won't hurt you,' added Nora, feeling that Liam was overreacting.

'I wasn't prepared to take the risk. Can you not tie him up somewhere? Or put him in the car?'

'No, but *you* could sit in the car if you like,' said Jay, searching for his car keys. The mood was getting more confrontational.

'Let's try and enjoy the walk to wherever Dixie is taking us,' said Nora, trying to distract the two men, who were now glaring at each other. Jay clipped the lead back on to Bruce's harness.

'I don't know why he's here anyway,' said Liam.

'I'm friends with Nora and Dixie and a regular member of the Crafting and Cocktails club. Why are *you* here?' snapped Jay. Nora hadn't seen him like this. The last thing she needed was for her friend and her boyfriend to not get on – that was always a recipe for disaster. She didn't want to ever be in a situation where she had to choose between them.

'I meant the dog,' said Liam. 'Nora invited me,' he added, looking about for her hand to hold as if belatedly remembering that was the sort of thing couples usually did.

'And I'd very much like it if we could all get on,' said Nora. 'This is important to Dixie, so let's try and have a nice time.' She sounded so much like her mother it was frightening.

When they reached a clearing Ned stood to one side and Dixie waved the others over as she got out her phone and began filming. 'This is what we wanted to show you.' She did a bit of a ta-dah.

Nora could see trees but other than that she wasn't sure what she was meant to be looking at. 'And what sort of trees are these?' she asked, keen to show interest.

'There's a mix,' said Ned. 'Hornbeam, hazel, oak, pine and birch.'

'But it's what's underneath that we're after.' Dixie held out a truffle.

Bruce was first there and had a good smell before Dixie passed the truffle to Nora for a closer look. Nora turned it over in her hand while Bruce continued to sniff it. 'Where did you find it?'

'Arnold found it and we've since discovered a couple

more so we think what we have here is a truffle orchard. Ned's gran seems to remember her husband planning one but she didn't know anything else about it. Apparently they take years to become established. Do you see that most of the trees are in neat rows apart from a few odd ones that look like they self-seeded?'

Bruce started pulling on the lead. Jay hung on but the dog was off with his nose to the ground. 'Heel, Bruce.'

But the dog wasn't listening. Instead, he was busy scratching at the earth trying to dig a hole.

'Can he damage the tree doing that?' asked Nora, going to join Jay to see if she could help distract Bruce.

'Tree roots are pretty tough,' said Ned.

Dixie didn't look as relaxed so Nora crouched down to try to flatten the ground that Bruce had dug over and there she discovered some recognizable lumps. 'There are more truffles,' she said, unearthing them.

'Good boy, Bruce,' said Dixie and the dog barked, his tail wagging.

'He smelt the one in my hand and then he found more. He's a sniffer dog,' said Nora.

'Truffle hound,' corrected Liam. 'Obviously he's not an actual truffle hound but that's how they find truffles.'

'The lady at the rescue said he would be good at scent work. I guess that's all this is,' said Jay.

'Probably a fluke,' said Liam with a dismissive shrug.

'Let's see,' said Jay, taking a mud-covered truffle from Nora and unclipping Bruce's lead. 'Bruce, sit, please.' The dog did as he was asked. Jay held the truffle under his nose. 'Find,' he said, unsure what the command for truffle-hunting might be. Bruce carried on sniffing the truffle. 'Fetch?' Bruce still didn't move. 'Get me more of these, please,' said Jay, sounding exasperated, and Bruce bounded off with his tail wagging and his nose down. He only went as far as the next tree before stopping and scratching frantically at the ground.

Dixie's mouth made a perfect O shape. 'See, he knows where they are.'

Nora went to where Bruce was digging and he was right, there were more truffles. As soon as she took over unearthing them, Bruce went back to searching.

'It means we definitely have a truffle orchard,' said Ned. 'We might need to borrow your dog,' he added, as Bruce began to scuff up the ground at the bottom of another tree.

'Whenever you like,' said Jay. 'He's having the best time.' He looked across at Nora and like proud parents they both watched Bruce dig up more truffles before smiling at each other. A shared moment that their adopted charge had come good. She wondered how many opportunities there would be in the future for moments like this.

Liam leaned into her ear and she wondered what he was going say. 'Any chance we can make a move now?'

Dixie had said they were doing a barbecue so it wouldn't be ideal to leave just yet but if Liam was thinking along the same lines as Nora had been – that an evening spent rolling around naked would be the ideal next step for their relationship – then she hoped Dixie would understand. 'It's a bit early but what did you have in mind?' She found she'd slipped into a slightly husky tone.

A small frown flickered across Liam's face. 'I've got a meeting in Bristol at eight thirty in the morning and I need to iron a shirt.' His eyebrow twitched. 'Maybe you could—'

'Nah-huh. You can think again on that score. I'm staying for the barbecue.' At least she'd be enjoying some sort of sausage tonight.

39

L iam left after giving Nora a perfunctory kiss on the
cheek, saying that he'd call her soon. They'd come
in his car, so she was now relying on Jay to give her a
lift home. Ned and Dixie were chatting but in that way
that new couples do: mesmerized by each other, oblivious to everyone and everything else. They were excitedly
discussing the truffle orchard. Jay had taken Bruce for a
walk so that the others could finish their food without
being stared down by a salivating German Shepherd.
When they returned, Bruce flopped down on Nora's feet,
pulling her attention away from Dixie and Ned. Jay got
himself a can of Coke from inside the van and sat on
the edge of the open doorway next to Nora. She sipped
her warmish glass of rosé.

'Liam seems a bit . . .' Jay twisted his lips.

'You've already decided you don't like him,' said Nora.
The frostiness between them didn't sit well with her.

'He was the one who was all *why are you here?* Not
exactly a great introduction.'

'You weren't particularly welcoming either.'

'Me? He called Bruce a brute. That was uncalled for.'
Jay squared his shoulders. Had he been working out? He certainly seemed to be filling his polo shirt better than he had before. She had a sneaky little look at his arms. There were muscles . . .

She shook herself. 'He didn't mean it,' she said, hoping that was the case.

'Tell that to Bruce.'

'I can't because he's a dog and he's only interested in sniffing things and eating sausages. Real relationships are between people.'

Jay pulled his head back. Nora had gone too far and she instantly regretted it but something made her feel she couldn't retract it without seeming disloyal to Liam. 'Fine,' snapped Jay and they fell silent. It broke her heart a little to quarrel with Jay.

After a few minutes Nora's phone pinged with a message from Liam.

Sorry I had to dash off. Maybe we need some time to ourselves. How about Saturday night here?

Nora clicked the attached link to a hotel in Nottingham. It looked nice. It was a bit close to home, but still. A night away was a positive step.

'Anything exciting?' asked Jay.

'Yes actually. Liam and I are going away on . . . oh shit. Saturday.'

'And when is oh-shit-Saturday?' asked Jay with a cheeky smile. 'Oh. You mean you've double-booked Bruce and Liam.'

'Liam's only just suggested it. I'll tell him I can't do it,' said Nora, feeling her shoulders sag.

'I did ask Renee if she could dog-sit.' Jay pulled a face. 'But she's at a food and wine festival all day.'

'Don't worry. I'll tell Liam we'll go another time.'

As she started to type, another message from Liam popped up.

> I'm golfing in the day so that's why I thought
> somewhere close would be best. Plus I get a
> discount ☺ Leave about 6.30?

She turned to Jay. 'Actually, could you see if Renee could have him overnight? And I can do the day shift?'

'OK. I'll check with Renee. And then Cinders shall go to the ball,' said Jay. When Nora didn't reply he added, 'Please yourself.'

Three days later and Nora was handing over Bruce to Renee at Jay's house.

Nora had made a Bruce handover list and went through it with Renee to be sure she'd not missed anything. She looked up and Renee was surveying her with narrowed eyes.

'Did that all make sense?'

'Dog has been walked. Food is exactly where it was

last time, blah blah blah. But what I want to know is this: what's up with you?' Renee's gaze didn't falter.

Nora self-consciously pushed a piece of hair behind her ear. 'Nothing. I'm fine.'

'No, you're not,' said Renee, sitting down on a kitchen stool and waving a hand for Nora to do the same.

Nora pointed towards the hall. 'I need to—'

'Sit,' said Renee forcefully. 'You can spare two minutes. Something is wrong.' Nora opened her mouth to repeat that she was fine, but Renee kept talking. 'Now, do you want to share what it is and unburden yourself? Or would you prefer to let it eat away at you?' Renee folded her arms.

'It's nothing major,' said Nora, deciding to share just enough to placate Renee. 'Me, Liam and Jay went to see Dixie and Ned.'

'Are they going steady?'

Nora pulled her chin into her chest. 'They're definitely into each other and they've hooked up.'

'It's a whole other language. What's wrong with courting, going steady and getting lucky?' Renee shook her head. 'Anyway. Carry on.'

'Liam and Jay didn't gel. That was all.'

'Jay said Liam is a bit of a dick. Is he?'

Nora was instantly cross. 'No, he's not! He's not a dog person and he didn't know anyone. Plus he needed to leave early.' Nora was smarting from what Renee had told her. 'Did Jay really say that?'

'No, that was what I gleaned. But he did say Liam seemed uninterested.'

Nora felt instant relief. 'At least that's better than calling him a dick.'

Renee pushed her bottom lip out in thought. 'Is it? It strikes me that Jay believes you deserve someone better.'

'That's what you get from him saying Liam was uninterested?' Nora laughed.

'Yes. Because a man who is uninterested isn't thinking about you. If they're not thinking about you and how you feel, then you're not a priority for them. And if that's the case, he'll be looking to jump ship as soon as someone else who does spark his interest bobs along.'

Nora blinked as she took it in. 'I think you're reading too much into that.'

'Maybe,' said Renee, nodding her head. 'But I know a man who *is* interested in you. Who hangs on your every word. Someone who checks that you're OK and knows instinctively when you're not. Who cares about you and would always put you first. And I reckon that's the sort of partner everyone needs. I had that with Theo and I lost it. Listen to me, Nora. Don't leave things for later. Because there's no guarantee that there will *be* a later.'

Nora's breathing had quickened. It was like Renee was unlocking a box of emotions Nora was too scared to open.

'Anyway, Brucey needs a cuddle and I need a G&T. Take care now,' said Renee, getting off the stool and leaving a bewildered Nora alone in the kitchen.

*

When Nora got home, she was feeling out of sorts. She'd heard nothing from Jay since the barbecue, apart from thumbs-up emojis to her updates on Bruce, but then he had been busy with the film. What Renee had said rumbled around her head. Did any of it indicate that Jay had feelings for her? If Renee was right, this was huge. But what, if anything, should Nora do about it?

She pulled her phone out of her pocket. First she needed to resolve their petty squabble. But if she sent Jay a text and he didn't reply, that would make things even worse. She could call him but then she'd miss the little subtleties of body language. Perhaps she could video-call him. That was the best solution.

She was about to hang up when Jay answered. 'Can you hold on a minute?' he asked.

What was this, a call centre?

'Sure,' she said with a tight jaw. Not a good start. She wasn't feeling very forgiving.

'You look amazing,' said Jay.

Nora instantly softened and self-consciously ran a hand through her newly blow-dried hair. 'Thanks, I—'

'Oh, I was talking to Tasha. She's had a professional makeover and her dress is on loan from Stella McCartney. Look,' said Jay, turning the camera on Tasha, who beamed into the camera phone.

What was she meant to say to that? 'Cool,' she muttered, willing Jay to flip the phone back to himself.

He did and held it at arm's length. 'I, on the other hand, look like I'm on display at Moss Bros,' he said with a chuckle.

Nora stared at the screen. Jay's hair had been trimmed and done, he was wearing a white tux and black bow tie. 'You look perfect,' she said without thinking.

'Aww thanks, mate.'

Mate? Why did that feel like a slight on her? 'You're welcome.'

'You OK?' asked Jay.

'Fine. You?'

'Had another weird stalker message, saying they're going to be at the premiere tonight, but the police are aware and there's loads of security plus the press are everywhere. I think they're keener to spot the stalker than anyone so . . .' He shrugged but she knew him well enough to know he was bothered by it.

'That's awful if they're getting bolder. Maybe you should give it a miss?'

'Come on, Schmoopy, the car will be here any minute,' said Tasha off camera.

'I don't mean to be rude, but we have some pre-red-carpet thing we need to go to. Drinks and food that'd not feed a budgie, followed by in-your-face interviews. Was there something you needed me for?' He paused.

'Er . . . I just wanted to check we were all good after . . . you know.'

'Yeah, of course. Gotta dash. Byee.' And with that he was gone.

'OK. Bye,' she said to a blank screen. Her shoulders sagged. That was that then. He said they were OK so she should be feeling relieved, but she wasn't.

Nora started putting things in her overnight bag. Renee had unhelpfully put all kinds of fanciful stuff in her head and she needed to refocus. This was her first time away with Liam in two years. There would definitely be sex. She should be as excited as Bruce when the tennis balls came out. But she wasn't.

Nora took a deep breath – she was being silly. She was just having a wobble, that was all. She put her best underwear in the bag followed by her comfy pyjamas and zipped it up.

Downstairs she had just put her bag by the door when there was a knock. Liam was standing on the doorstep with his hands in his pockets. 'Ready?' he asked, looking her up and down but making no comment about her freshly done hair and new shirt.

'I just need to give Oliver some crickets.'

Liam's face contorted. 'That's disgusting. They're not alive, are they?'

'Yes they are, because that's better for him. I won't be a minute. Come in.'

She fed Oliver and was telling him where she was going and when she'd be back when Liam snorted a laugh behind her. She spun around.

'Sorry.' He waved a hand. 'It's a lizard. It won't understand you. It probably has a brain smaller than a pea.'

Her phone beeped and she pulled it from her pocket. There was a message from Dixie.

This is sooooo cool. Jay's all over Insta!

Nora clicked the link. Up popped a video of Jay and Tasha being interviewed on the red carpet. Her heart squeezed at the sight of him. This was where he was meant to be.

Tasha was speaking to the interviewer while draping herself around Jay. 'It's a wonderful film and the perfect role for me. Well, for both of us, actually.' She giggled as she pulled Jay fully into shot.

Jay looked every inch the sexy film star. 'It's been an absolute honour to work with Tasha, and the director and the crew they're amaz—'

Another woman was trying to guide them away from the interviewer. 'Enough faffing about, Mr P, let's pick up the pace here,' she whispered, a little too close to the mic.

'Thanks for the interview,' said Jay with a beaming smile to the camera. The sight of him lit up something inside her.

Nora played it again and turned her phone so that Liam could see it too. 'It's Jay at his film premiere.'

He didn't look. 'We need to get going.'

Nora waited for herself to agree with Liam and follow him out, but she couldn't.

And in that moment, she realized the truth.

Liam might have seemed like the one on paper or according to her spreadsheet but in reality he simply wasn't.

'You're not the one,' she said flatly.

'What?'

'I thought I could trust statistics to deliver a sound solution, but I was wrong. You and I are not compatible. Not really. We'd probably be fine for a while just like we were before. But I know in my heart that this isn't forever.'

Liam frowned. 'Why? Because I think talking to animals is crazy?'

'Yes. That and lots of other little things. You don't think my weird bits are cool. And you're not interested in me. I don't have time to go into this because . . . I need to be somewhere else.'

'But I've booked us a non-refundable double room. Where are you going?'

'To a film premiere.'

'Why?'

'Because I need to tell Jay something really important.'

Shortly afterwards, Nora found herself on the fast train to London. She had no idea what she was doing. She had just thrown away the chance of a relationship with a perfectly decent person to go down to Leicester Square, where she'd likely be told that she'd have to get to the back of a very long line of fans. And even if she did get to see Jay, what was she going to do then? It wasn't like her to not consider all options and make plans. But sometimes it felt right to go with your gut, and something was telling her this was the right thing to do.

Jay had not been in her life that long but, without her realizing, he was the missing piece she had been searching for. It was him she laughed the most with. Around him she could be herself. Everything Renee had said was true, she'd just been too blind to see it.

Jay was the one.

Their friendship meant everything to her, but what if there was a chance of something more? She couldn't ignore that. There was also something else on the video clip that was bugging her.

Despite the train speeding through the countryside, each minute seemed to take an age. Every time she checked and rechecked the time it had barely advanced more than a couple of minutes. Eventually they pulled into St Pancras. Nora glanced down at her outfit. It wasn't the worst – she was wearing her new shirt and clean jeans – but it wasn't exactly film premiere level. Oh well. Too late to turn back now.

She raced from the train to the taxi rank and was quickly transported to Leicester Square. The red carpet had already been put away, only a few people were still milling around in the drizzle.

She checked the time. How long was the film? She had no idea. What if she'd missed him?

Nora looked around. The drizzle was turning into proper rain and she could feel her hair sticking to her face.

She pulled out her phone to message him. Perhaps she should have just texted Jay all along. But she had things she needed to explain that it would be easier to do face to face. If only her brain would make a decision. She looked at the glass doors of the cinema and the security guards in front of them. There was no way to sneak in. She sighed. This had all been a big mistake. Whatever she felt for Jay he was with Tasha now and she didn't want to mess that up for him.

Nora pulled back her shoulders. Now was the time to walk away. She took one last look at the cinema, and the great big digital poster above it, with Tasha and Jay's faces emblazoned in lights. She smiled to herself. He'd made it and she was ridiculously pleased for him. She hoped her heart wouldn't break every time she saw him on the big screen, but that was just something she'd have to deal with. She turned around.

40

Dixie was checking Instagram when she felt Ned kiss her neck. Shivers juddered through her body. When the van had broken down almost four weeks ago, the last thing she'd expected to find in the woods was a new relationship.

'What are you up to?' he asked.

'Jay's all over Insta. It's quite exciting. I've shared his post and it's getting lots of traction.'

'You're really good at social media,' said Ned. 'I think that'll definitely be your remit when we get the business off the ground.' They'd agreed they were going to make something of the abandoned truffle orchard.

'I would love that.' Dixie put down her phone and kissed him. 'I could sort out a logo too.' She clapped her hands together. 'My parents are back in the country in a few weeks. It would be so good to be able to tell them that we have an up-and-running, bona fide business.'

'Then that's our aim. Plus I spoke to Mike the truffle man. He's the go-to guy in the area, and he's going to help us avoid any pitfalls because he set his truffle business up from scratch.'

'That's so nice,' said Dixie, snuggling against Ned. 'I'm going to miss this when I move in with Nora.'

'But it's only temporary,' he said. 'And once Elsie is fixed, we can use her for travelling around to find potential buyers for our produce. She'll be the truffle van.'

'Oh, I love that for her,' said Dixie. She bit her lip as a worry niggled her. 'Once we have customers, we'll need to make sure we can meet demand.'

'That's where Mike can help. His truffle hound is expecting puppies, so—'

Dixie gasped. 'We're getting a puppy?' This was quite a serious commitment.

'Yeah, I think we're ready. We'll be an unstoppable team.'

Dixie kissed him hard on the mouth. 'You're brilliant and you think of everything.'

'I try,' said Ned.

Dixie's shoulders sagged. 'But if the puppy lives with you . . .'

'I figured that perhaps we could all live together. Only if you want to, of course.'

'I do!' said Dixie. With that there was a bang on the campervan roof and a scamper of paws. 'I think Arnold will be glad to get her woodland back too.'

*

Nora had taken a few strides away from the cinema when she heard someone shout.

'Nora!'

She spun around to see Jay standing outside the cinema, waving his arms like he was trying to direct aircraft. It made her smile. She waved and jogged back to the railings. Jay was speaking to one of the security guards who came forward and moved a barrier aside so that Nora could go through.

'It's so good to see you,' said Jay giving her a hug. 'What on earth are you doing here?'

Now that was a question. 'Well, I saw what you posted on Instagram.'

He was looking blank. 'The publicist does that. What was it?'

'It was you and Tasha being interviewed, and it was something a woman behind you said that made me—'

'Well, hello. Who's this?' said Tasha, sauntering out of the large doors and surveying the area. The few people still waiting started shouting her name. The other woman from the Instagram post was hovering behind Tasha. Nora figured she must be the publicist.

'This is Nora,' said Jay, and the pride in his tone gave Nora a warm feeling. 'Nora, this is Tasha.'

'Hi. Nice to meet you,' said Nora.

'I don't do selfies,' said Tasha.

Jay giggled. 'She's not after a selfie. Nora's a good friend of mine.'

'Oh.' Tasha pulled her chin as she surveyed Nora but seemed to relax after giving her the once-over. 'Fine.' Nora was mildly offended that Tasha obviously felt she was no threat whatsoever. 'Schmoopy, we need to go. There are no paps here. Anastasia says there will be plenty of photo ops at the party, so let's get there quickly. I heard Dizzee Rascal is coming.' She grabbed Jay's hand and went to pull him away.

This was it. Something clutched at Nora's gut. This was the moment she needed to tell Jay how she felt. It was now or never. 'It was her!' she blurted.

'What?' Jay was smiling at her.

'She's your stalker,' said Nora, because for some reason her brain thought this was a better thing to lead with than 'I love you'.

Tasha looked shocked as Anastasia tried to hurry them along.

'Not Tasha. The publicity woman.' Nora pointed.

'Anastasia?' Jay was looking confused.

'Can we please stop faffing and pick up the pace?' said Anastasia, trying to shoo them back inside.

'It's her who has been stalking you.' Nora's heart started to thump.

Jay let out a strangled laugh. 'That's a weird joke, Nora, even for you.'

'It's true. She uses the same words – faffing, and she referred to you as Mr P the same as the messages but—'

'I don't know what she's on, but we need to leave.' Anastasia waved at security to intervene.

'Hey. No need for that.' Jay turned to Nora. 'Nora, I think you're making wild accusations and that's quite dangerous.'

Nora didn't have to turn around to know that there were now two security guards standing close behind her. 'I know it, Jay. Trust your gut.'

'I can never trust my gut. I get IBS and—' he said.

'Well, trust mine then. My gut is never wrong.'

'Apart from that horse you thought was going to win the Grand National that unseated its rider on the first fence.'

Nora had to concede that one. 'OK, but aside from that. I know what I heard, and Anastasia called you Mr P. Does anyone else call you that, apart from your stalker? It's too much of a coincidence.'

'Jay, come on.' Tasha tugged on Jay's hand but he just turned to stare at her.

'Tasha, what's your take on it?' he asked.

She twisted her lips. 'Your friend's a kook,' she said in a poor attempt at a whisper.

Jay paused. Nora wanted to dig him in the ribs and nudge him into action.

'You need to come now or I'm going to go to the party alone, and that won't look good.' Tasha let go of his hand and began to walk away. Jay looked from one woman to the other.

He had a decision to make. He made one step towards Tasha and that was all Nora needed to see. She forced her way past the security guys and out of the barrier, ignoring Jay's yells behind her as she ran towards the main road.

By the time the black cab dropped her at St Pancras

station her face was wet with tears. She loved Jay – completely and unconditionally – but it was all pointless. She'd stuffed it up and he'd chosen Tasha and there was nothing she could do about it. The only positive, the tiniest of tiny positives, was that perhaps the 37 per cent rule had been right. She'd just given up too soon.

She paid the taxi driver, solemnly walked into the station and made her way through the masses of people to stare at the departures board and try to work out which was the next train back to Melton.

She had her neck craned to look up at the board when she heard her name.

'Nora! Wait!' She heard it but she didn't really believe it. She looked around her but couldn't see anyone. Then, there was the briefest glimpse of a white jacket as Jay leapt in the air. 'Nora!'

She tried to stay where she was, but the crowd was on the move towards a train and she was being carried with them. Maybe that was for the best. Just go with the flow.

'Nora! I love you!' That changed things. Nora spun around, as did a number of other people.

'Who's Nora?' yelled a large, leather-clad, tattooed man with a Mohican.

'Me,' she squeaked.

'Come on, love. Let her through!' yelled the man, waving folk to one side so that Nora could make her way against the flow. 'Oi! Move!' he snarled at a suited businessman, who slunk out of the way to let Nora past.

'Thank you,' said Nora, as she squeezed through the crowd. She could see Jay jumping up and down.

At last the group parted, and there he was. A youth started clicking his fingers and pointing at Jay. 'Aren't you the bloke from the indigestion commercial?'

The last thing this moment needed was a burping soundtrack. 'No,' snapped Jay and Nora together. The youth shrugged and moved on.

Jay and Nora stared at each other. He was a little more dishevelled than he had been earlier, but he still looked cute. They met and smiled at the same time. 'Hi,' she said, unsure of what else to say. 'I'm sorry about what I said about Anastasia. I was playing amateur detective and . . .'

Jay waved his palms in front of her. 'You were right. She admitted it. Thought it was an excellent publicity stunt because it had created a buzz around the film. She didn't seem bothered that it had scared the crap out of me for weeks.'

'I knew you were scared!' She jabbed a finger at him.

'Obviously I was crapping myself. I didn't want to end up as corned beef!'

They stood there with people shuffling past them, lost in a moment only they understood. All this time she'd been ignoring the obvious thing that was right in front of her. Her heart was thumping at the thought of him loving her. 'I liked what you said.'

'About corned beef?'

She shook her head.

'I mean it, Nora. I've known it from the start. You make my heart do this thing . . .'

'Flutter?' she suggested.

'More of a zing. Zing sounds better. Life is better with you in it. You're my very favourite person. I love you.'

'But what about Tasha?' Nora held her breath.

'I told her I was sorry but my heart wanted someone else.'

'Was she very upset?' asked Nora.

'She was on the phone to a magazine about doing an exclusive break-up interview as I left. So I think she'll be fine.'

Nora couldn't remember being this happy. And although she knew she risked getting hurt, she had a sneaking suspicion that the odds of Jay hurting her were incredibly low.

There was a pause. 'What do we do now?' she asked.

'Kiss her!' shouted the tattooed man, and there was a murmur of agreement from the slow-moving crowd.

Jay shrugged. 'Shall we? I mean, we don't have . . .'

Nora grabbed his face and kissed him. An instant energy surged through her. Endorphins flooded her blood-stream. She couldn't wait to rip his clothes off. It was actually nice that he was not much taller than her, no more craning her neck. Reluctantly they pulled apart. 'I love you too. It just took me a bit longer to work it out. You're the one.'

'Despite not being an alpha male?'

'That's the best bit,' she said, kissing him again. She didn't need someone to be dominant or assertive. What she wanted was someone who supported her, made her feel loved and safe, and with Jay she had that in spades. He was also hot as hell.

Jay pulled away and she instantly missed him. He held up a finger as if just realizing something important. 'By my calculations, using the 37 per cent rule, you are my best option.'

This made Nora so happy. 'Then we can't argue with the numbers.'

'Plus you're gorgeous,' he said.

'I know that's not true because the caught-in-the-rain look is never attractive.'

'Actually, I think you look great.' Gently he pushed a stray piece of damp hair off her face, sending a wave of sensations across her skin. 'Although I kinda meant you're gorgeous on the inside,' he said with a grin and she whacked him in the ribs. He barely reacted.

'Ooh, muscles.'

'I've been working out,' he said.

'I know,' said Nora. She went to kiss him again and he stopped her.

'There's something I need to confess.' His expression was serious. Nora felt her insides crumple. What was he going to tell her?

Jay took a deep breath. 'I'm not naturally sporty. I once sprained my wrist doing a crossword. So Crafting and Cocktails . . .'

'What about it?' asked Nora, tension making her neck ache.

'My leaflet wasn't missing the letter C. I never joined for the rafting,' he said.

The relief that it wasn't something serious was huge. 'I never imagined that you did,' said Nora, kissing him again as a ripple of applause broke out around them.

Epilogue

It was Tuesday so it was Crafting and Cocktails night but this week the tiny room was overflowing.

'I said we needed the *bigger* room, not the bloody broom cupboard,' said Renee, shaking the cocktail shaker and almost taking Nora out.

'It's fine,' said Dixie. 'Once we've served the Mojitos, we'll all sit down and then we can get on with crafting.'

Ned cleared his throat. 'We don't all have to do that part, do we?' He waggled his hands. 'I've got sausage fingers.'

'It's not compulsory,' said Jay, his knitting needles clicking away.

'We can get you started,' said Dixie. 'Don't worry. We were all beginners once.'

Nora kept sneaking a look at Jay. She still couldn't quite believe it. It felt like everything had slotted into place. Perhaps all she had needed was to realize what was really important. Jay looked at her and smiled. Something passed between them. They had a thing and it was extra special. She'd found her person and it was the best feeling ever.

There was a tap on the outside door and Jay jumped to his feet. 'Back in a minute.'

'It had better not be another bugger for Crafting and Cocktails,' said Renee, pouring out the last of the drinks. She re-counted the glasses. 'We've got one more glass than we need. Oh well, that's a spare for whoever finishes first,' she said, looking pleased.

Nora moved to stand in the doorway. 'Actually, we didn't miscount. We've an extra person tonight,' she said, stepping to one side.

Renee opened her mouth to say something but for once she was rendered speechless. She stared dumbstruck at the person Jay was helping into the room. A lady, a similar age to Renee, with a more conservative dress sense and a shock of neat grey hair and rimless glasses. 'Theo?' Tears brimmed in Renee's eyes. 'Is that really you?'

The lady looked at her and smiled. 'Nobody calls me that any more. It's usually Nanna, Mrs Benton or Theodora. But yes, Renee. It's me.' She opened her arms and she and Renee hugged.

Renee stepped back and wiped her eyes. 'Goodness! I can't believe it.'

'It's been too long,' said Theo. 'But it's good to see you again, Renee. You've not changed.'

Renee chortled. 'I'm no bloody better, that's for sure.'

'I think I'm missing something,' whispered Ned to Dixie.

'Theo was Renee's one who got away.' She drew a heart in the air.

'Oh cool,' said Ned, taking Dixie's hand and squeezing it.

Nora wiped away a tear. It was lovely to see Renee and Theo reunited. 'I'm so glad you're both pleased to see each other,' she said. 'I've been worrying that there was some old beef between you, and that was why you'd not tracked each other down before now.'

Theo sighed. 'It was all my fault. I married a man I didn't love because my parents expected me to.'

'It wasn't your fault.' Renee took her hand. 'It was a different time. That's all.'

'And now you've found each other again. Hurray!' said Dixie, handing a glass to Theo and raising hers. 'To Renee and Theo! Reunited at last.' Everyone clinked glasses.

Renee shook her head. 'But how did you find me?' Then, as the penny dropped, she pointed at Jay and Nora. 'You pair of buggers have some explaining to do!'

Acknowledgements

As always a big thank you to my agent, Kate Nash, for always going the extra mile and for securing my new publishing home at Transworld. Thank you to my editor Sally Williamson and the wonderful team at Transworld. Thanks to Irene Martinez for the fabulous cover.

A big thank you to my wonderful subject matter experts:

Thanks to Mike Collison and Oscar, the truffle hound, from Shropshire Truffles, for a tour of their truffle orchard and for answering all my questions (that part was mainly Mike).

Thanks to Charlotte and Ian Hancock for campervan ideas and for letting me use the name Elsie!

Thanks to Mark and Jenny Beaglehole for a tour of Melton Mowbray.

Any mistakes are my own.

Thanks to my family and writer friends for keeping me going when the ups and downs of life got in the way of writing.

Extra special thanks to all the brilliant book bloggers,

booksellers and library staff for their ongoing support and for championing the romance genre in general – every share, review and recommendation helps readers to find new books.

Lastly, my biggest thank you to each and every reader. I am so grateful to you, because without your support I wouldn't be able to do the job that I absolutely love. If you have enjoyed this story, a quick review would mean the world – thank you.

Bella has been jotting down stories for as long as she can remember and her first novel hit the shelves in 2015. Since then, she has written many bestselling and widely translated novels filled with heart, humour and characters who, like most of us, are just trying to cope with what life throws at them. In 2022, she was thrilled to win the RNA Romantic Comedy Novel of the Year Award. She secretly wants to keep her readers up late at night reading just one more chapter.

Bella lives in Warwickshire, UK with her husband, daughter and rescue cat and her garden is home to many rehabilitated hedgehogs and one particularly cheeky squirrel. She loves planning with sticky notes, researching biscuits and listening to music in a bath that's only slightly cooler than the sun.

For more about Bella, visit her website:
www.bellaosborne.com
or follow her on:

X @osborne_bella

BellaOsborneAuthor

bellaosborneauthor

On a station platform, with nothing to read,
and a four-hour train journey stretching ahead of him...

That's where the story began for Penguin founder Allen Lane.
With only 'shabby reprints of shoddy novels' on offer,
he resolved to make better books for readers everywhere.

By the time his train pulled into London, the idea was formed.
He would bring the best writing, in stylish and affordable
formats, to everyone. His books would be sold in bookstores,
stationers and tobacconists, for no more than the price
of a ten-pack of cigarettes.

And on every book would be a Penguin, a bird with a certain
'dignified flippancy', and a friendly invitation to anyone who
wished to spend their time reading.

In 1935, the first ten Penguin paperbacks were published.
Just a year later, three million Penguins had made their
way onto our shelves.

Reading was changed forever.

—

A lot has changed since 1935, including Penguin, but in the
most important ways we're still the same. We still believe that
books and reading are for everyone. And we still believe that
whether you're seeking an afternoon's escape, a vigorous debate
or a soothing bedtime story, all possibilities open with a book.

Whoever you are, whatever you're looking for,
you can find it with Penguin.